The Haunting of Tessa Pines

by

A. J. Maguire

The Haunting of Tessa Pines

Cover Art by *Abigail Owen*

The Wild Rose Press, Inc.
PO Box 708
Adams Basin, NY 14410-0708
Visit us at www.thewildrosepress.com

Publishing History
First Fantasy Rose Edition, 2019
Print ISBN 978-1-5092-2716-7
Digital ISBN 978-1-5092-2717-4

Published in the United States of America

"You shouldn't be here," she said, trying to work through the situation and praying Cordon would ignore the ten-minute rule and come for her. "Why are you here?" she murmured, squinting at his shadowed eyes. He looked hollow, empty, a mere echo of the man she'd known. "Did I bring you? Are you here for me?"

She glanced at the cement walls, sensing the unrest that had trailed her all night as it intensified around her. Gooseflesh pricked up her arms and neck. There was something in the walls here, something moving against the cement. She could make out the shape of a man there, like a profile had been drawn and come to life.

Tessa stared at them both, the man in the wall and Cabby, her mind blank. "My God, what is this place?"

As before, Cabby turned from her, moving to a door three spaces away. He stopped there, his back to her, and she recognized the shape of his ear in her light as he bent his head. A shiver slid up her spine and the shadows went darker, the cement walls colder, and she thought of Jackson roaming this place on his own.

If she'd brought Cabby, there was no telling what Jackson might have brought with him.

It was as though the foundations wanted to reach up and take her, drag her down and bury her under the Ashwood forever.

Dedication

For my husband

Chapter One

Tessa Pines stared out the window front at the sleeting storm, watching as great gusts of wind hammered rain onto the seat of her bike. The back-to-school display for Book Land hindered her view, textbooks and teacher supplies painted in cheery yellows and reds on the glass, but she could still see the damage being wrought. The cushion on her bike seat was glistening wet, winking at her from its stand outside the shop, and she glared at it.

Somewhere deeper in the bookstore someone was shifting books around, arranging them on shelves. Likely an employee. Most customers had fled for the night, not wanting to be caught in the storm.

Tessa sighed and rubbed at the ache in her forehead. She should have taken the Jeep.

Well, there was no helping it now, and if she waited a bit maybe the rain would stop. Or at least slow down. Shifting in the worn-down velvety chair she'd adopted for the day, she tried to put her mind to work. *An Introduction to Poetry* lay open in her lap, but the wind kept whistling past the window and the pounding of rain on cement seemed to get louder.

Drumming her pen on the textbook and eyeing her bike, she debated the merits of riding in the rain. She'd get soaked, of course. Probably catch a chill and come down with a mutated virus that would have her sniffling

1

and coughing through class, which was every student's dream come true for their first semester of higher education. But she had to get back to the barracks somehow.

Dorms! Barracks were dorms. D-Fac was the cafeteria, and the latrine was the restroom. She was not in the army anymore, damn it.

She snapped her book closed and sat up, reaching into her pocket for her phone. The pleasant black screen came to life, and she began scrolling, hunting for her roommate's number. Marisol was a sweet girl, young and flouncy and harboring a crush for some kid in her psychology class, but Tessa could never remember his name.

Bundy?

No. No woman in their right mind dated a Bundy; the name was synonymous with murder and date rape.

Chastising herself for being so elitist—there had to be some decent men named Bundy after all. Tessa found the number and hesitated. She glanced out at the blustering storm, her thumb hovering over the call button. Campus wasn't far, and this was just a little rain.

Or a lot of rain, but she could make it in ten minutes or less, barring any traffic. There was no reason to call for help, especially from a girl Tessa had only known for two weeks.

Shutting the phone off, she stuffed it in her pocket. She wasn't going to be able to concentrate until she was back on campus. Best to get it over with.

Standing, she leaned back, feeling the strain of two hours' worth of study in her muscles. The quiet bookstore was peaceful, and she remembered that the reason she'd come to Book Land was because her neighbors were enjoying their Friday night with too-loud music and a giggle-fest over the track team.

God, why had she chosen the dorms over her father's four-bedroom house on the other side of town? At least there it would have been quiet.

She scowled, remembering the superior smirk Todd Pines gave her at the airport. Three weeks in her old bedroom had been plenty. Sure, it was quiet, but it was a deadly quiet, like the kind of silence in a minefield where one is listening intently for that horrible click of an activated explosive.

Track team giggle-fests and riding home in the rain were much easier to live with.

Packing her poetry book at the very back of her bag, she began strategically arranging her things in the hopes it would stay dry. Unfortunately, everything she had consisted of paper; notebook, pocket calendar, course descriptions and assignments all bound into smaller packets from orientation, and all of it essential to maintaining a decent GPA.

Of all the times for it to rain, it had to be when she left anything waterproof behind.

"Always be prepared, Pines." Her first sergeant's voice pulled through her memory. "Best way to stay alive out there."

Yeah, well, this isn't war, it's school. And it isn't the army, it's civilian life. Nobody can ever be prepared for that.

The doorbell chimed, and a gust of wind whooshed in, stirring the pages of a paperback on the sales shelf and chilling through her leggings. Faint traces of rain slid through the open door before it closed, and she looked up at the newcomer.

Shock hit her hard, slapping memories to the fore as his face came into view. Clad in a worn jacket and jeans, his six-foot frame filled the doorway, and he looked just as startled to see her as she was to see him. His eyes went round for a second, recognition flashing there, and beneath the ginger beard his mouth tightened into a thin line.

Her mind conjured images of that mouth faster than she could stop it; the way it twitched in wicked humor, the dimples hiding at its corners, ready to flash whenever she made him laugh, which had been often. She remembered the feel of him against her, the rough scrape of his hands along her bare back, and the low timbre of his voice as he chuckled. Warm summer nights in the back of his pickup, snug in his arms as they talked about graduation and life after high school.

"Cordon…" An ache settled in her chest, coiling around her center as his expression hardened.

"Tessa, I heard you were out." His smile was strained. Then he shook his head and huffed a laugh. "I mean back. Sorry, I didn't mean to make it sound like you'd been in prison or something."

So, we're going to be civil. She tried for her own smile. "Well, according to my out-processing sergeant, there are a lot of similarities between prison and the army."

His eyebrows lifted and he smirked, which seemed a little more real than his smile, so she took that as a good sign. "Yeah? I suppose both require people guarding you." He scratched his cheek and glanced away. "Except one you choose to be in."

She flinched and bit her lip. *Maybe not so civil.* The ache in her chest squeezed, and she reached to zip her bag, then slung it over her shoulder. *Homecomings are a bitch.* Tessa searched for the quickest way out of this conversation.

"I'm sorry, that was a low blow," he said, quieter this time. He sighed and brushed his hair back with his free hand.

It was then that she noticed the green duffle on his arm, a jolt of recognition coursing through her; she'd bought him that bag years ago. An anniversary present, as she recalled.

"It's all right," she said, trying not to remember the way he'd kissed her after he'd opened the gift. All the heat and strength radiating through them, molding them together, and the scrape of his teeth across her lower lip. There was a familiar kick in her blood, a clenching sensation in the pit of her stomach, and it was all she could do not to reach for him.

She'd been such a fool. But then, there were other memories too. His phone always ringing or text messages dinging at them during any private moment they could find. The sense that he was only ever half with her, even if he was standing right there.

"No, it's not all right," he said. "You don't deserve that."

"Yeah, I kind of do."

Heaving a sigh, he glanced over his shoulder and frowned. "Where's your jeep?"

The change in subject startled her, and she checked the window. The storm was still going steady, water running in little rivers down the street and along the gutter. Spotting the gleam of her bike in the lamplight, she gave her own sigh.

"It's back at campus," she admitted.

Cordon's eyebrow hiked again. "You rode here?"

"Well, it wasn't raining when I made the decision."

He frowned at her backpack. Around them the bookstore was densely quiet, and her shoulders pinched like someone was watching. She glanced at the front counter.

A tawny-headed salesclerk stood there, his face full of freckles and inquisition, and a flush crept up her neck. The boy squeaked in alarm and snapped his attention back to the counter, only there was nothing there. Flustered, he escaped through the back office.

"You're leaving now?" Cordon asked.

He was either unconcerned by the audience they had or hadn't noticed.

Tessa shifted the bag on her shoulder and nodded, frowning at the window. "It's not letting up any time soon, and I do have to eat tonight," she said.

Cordon rubbed his face with one hand. He shook his head and, apparently having reached a decision, turned back to the door. "All right, I'll take you home."

"Wait. What? No." Tessa stepped back and shook her head. "You really don't have to do that."

She thought of the cab of his truck, the things they used to do there, and shook her head again. They'd been married in the cab of that truck, thanks to Ms. Corneal's Drive-Thru Weddings. Tessa still had her doubts as to the legality of a drive-thru specializing in marriages, but they'd been young and reckless, and too happy to care.

Cordon squinted at her, his frown twitching a little deeper, and her face heated even more. He still looked good, even if his beard did need a trim. He'd never been gangly or lanky, but the broad strength of him seemed to have settled into his bones, lending him a more imposing, confident stance than she remembered.

God, one look at him and she wanted to sink back into the way things were. What was wrong with her?

"Tessa, I am not watching you walk out this door," he said. "So, either you let me take you home, or I'm walking with you. And then we'll both be drenched. Your choice."

"Look, I don't need a rescue here. You should know better than to hit me with some macho attitude and expect me to give in. I can clean up my own messes, thanks." She went to move around him, and he sidestepped, blocking the path.

He smirked at her again, one dimple clearly visible, and there was laughter in his eyes. "First of all, you can't make it rain. So, the fact that there's a torrent hammering outside isn't a mess you created."

She scowled, wanting so badly to smack that dimple off his face that she adjusted her grip on her bag, shifting it so she could do just that if he made another comment.

"Secondly, it's not a macho attitude, it's common decency. I wouldn't knowingly let anyone walk through that storm, let alone someone I'm intimately familiar with." He hesitated, rocking back on his heels as though he'd surprised himself. Which he must have because he corrected his words. "Someone I'm familiar with."

Tessa checked the front counter again. Thankfully, the clerk hadn't returned. If there was a God, then the office door would be soundproof, and their little argument could remain private. She took a deep breath and prepared to decline, her gaze catching on the steady beat of rain outside the window.

Shouldn't it have stopped by now? Seriously, how long could a downpour last?

"Tess, it's just a ride. It's not a big deal."

She looked up at him, all that solid security watching her until finally she slumped her shoulders and glanced away. It was just a ride. And he was a good man. And she really didn't want to drench all her paperwork.

"All right," she said. "Thank you."

"See? That wasn't so hard." Cordon slanted a boyish wink down at her before opening the door again.

Wind swirled into the storefront, flecking her face with rain as she debated kicking him in the shin. It was the wink. The wink and that damn dimple flashing at her, telling her that he'd read her mind and knew precisely what she was thinking. "I'll be back in twenty minutes, Brian," Cordon called.

Tessa glanced back. The salesclerk had reappeared. He studiously wiped the counter with a rag and his cheeks turned red, but he nodded and waved them off. Frowning, she turned to Cordon, who held the door wide with one hand.

"Don't worry, they won't fire me. The kid has another hour before he's supposed to go off shift anyway," Cordon said and nodded at the door. "We're letting the heat out, Tess. Best we get moving."

Of course, he worked here. That was just her luck.

She stepped through the door, pinching her coat closed as the full brunt of the storm lashed against her. Cordon followed a step behind and led the way to a small four-door car that might have been green once, but time and weather had peeled much of the paint away. This was not the truck she remembered.

She frowned and tried not to acknowledge her disappointment. The truck had been a good vehicle. It had miles and history behind it. Why'd he let it go?

Still, it was better this way. At least now she could sit in his car and not be haunted by everything they'd been once.

He opened the passenger door and waited as she dove inside. Then he closed the storm out, leaving her to arrange her bag near her feet. He kept a clean car, which she appreciated. Most of the kids on campus left the seats littered with takeout and it took a minute before anyone could get in. But the cab smelled like him, warm spices and cognac, and for a heartbeat she couldn't move.

It's just a few blocks. Ten minutes max.

Nothing could possibly go wrong in ten minutes.

Chapter Two

Cordon put his rundown car in drive and pulled out of the parking lot, realizing a moment later that the steering wheel was creaking under pressure. He released it a little, turning onto Main Street. The storm beat into the windshield, giving his wipers a run for their money as they drove through town. Beside him, Tessa fidgeted with her bag, looking smaller and more uncertain than he had ever seen her.

That had been the first thing he'd noticed when he walked into Book Land. Not her face, familiar as it was, or the faded jacket two sizes too large that swallowed her whole, but the vulnerability. She seemed fragile, like cracked eggshells or porcelain, and as much as he wanted to demand some explanations, he couldn't summon the words.

Four years was a long time. Did he even have a right to be angry anymore?

Cordon shifted in his seat and hunted for a neutral topic. "So, are you adjusting to life as a civilian again? From what I understand, it can be difficult."

She hummed, a soft, almost sultry sound that jolted straight through him. He had to loosen his grip on the steering wheel again.

"It's different," she said. "I feel a little lost sometimes, to be honest."

"Well, you just had years where someone told you what to do and where to go every day. I imagine not having it can be…"

Freeing, liberating, a relief. But he didn't imagine she would appreciate that sentiment, so he hunted for something else.

"No, it's not really that," she said, and he breathed in relief. She flashed a smile that didn't quite reach her eyes. "School is a lot like it in ways, actually. There's a schedule you have to keep and being in the dorms is a lot like the barracks."

He'd been taking her to her father's house, assuming she'd be saving money by living at home, and switched lanes to alter their course. She hadn't left home on the best of terms, but Cordon assumed they would have mended that bridge by now. Unless she'd stopped writing to her father, too.

He ground his teeth and stared at the road. They were divorced, three and a half years divorced, and it was none of his business anymore. She'd made that clear enough when the letters stopped.

"It's the little things," she said.

Cordon blinked at her, then looked back to the road, trying to remember the threads of their conversation.

"Like the fact that I don't have to shine my boots anymore. Or starching my uniform. I actually miss my uniform. I feel…" She huffed a laugh and shook her head. "I feel exposed without it."

"You know how to use starch?" he asked, latching onto a neutral subject with relief. "I think my great-grandmother used starch once."

Tessa grinned and this time it looked real. "Well, the spray-on starch. I'm sure your grandmother used something else."

"Hey, I didn't even know it came in a spray, so I'm still impressed." He turned the car, leading it closer to the university. "I am curious, though, did you have to spit on your boots to shine them?"

She laughed, a full, bright sound that filled his car. "No, I did not spit on my boots."

"Damn," he said, fighting back the questions he truly wanted to ask. *How could you leave like that? Why did you stop writing? What happened to us?* Instead, he shook his head. "For years I've entertained myself with the idea of watching you spit. Thanks for crushing my dreams."

She laughed again, softer this time, and then hummed. She sat straighter in her seat, her shoulders less slumped, and for just a moment she seemed herself again—fierce and capable, hazel eyes alight with mischief. But then her smile changed, dissolving into something more sober, and the look she gave him was full of regret. The weight of years apart, of silence and anger and disappointment, settled between them and he took a deep breath.

How often had he dreamed of this moment? Of having her alone long enough to fix whatever had gone wrong?

To this day, it confused him. Everything had been fine. He'd been working, keeping them mostly afloat while helping his sister through her divorce, and Tessa had been prepping for school. There were financial questions about school, of course, but if she'd given him a little time, he would have worked it out.

He could still remember the look on her face when she'd come home from the recruiters, the sound of her voice as she announced she was shipping out for Basic in a few days. He couldn't go with her, of course he couldn't, not to training, but she'd promised they would work something out.

Only, there was nothing to work out. His family needed him here, there was no way he was going to pack up and leave.

God, how could she have made such a decision without even consulting him? They'd been married!

The main entrance for the dorms was well lit, making the rain on his windshield glisten and smear as the storm buffered against his car. He pulled up to the sidewalk and cut the engine, letting silence fill the cab. The wind whistled through the cracks and for a moment they stayed there, unable to look at each other.

"I..." she started and stopped, hissing something under her breath as she reached for the door handle. One hand on the handle, she turned back to him. "Cordon, I owe you the most profound apology."

He kept his gaze on the cracked surface of his dashboard. "I'd settle for an explanation."

She was silent for a moment, and when he looked up, she had her eyes closed. Her face held an expression of such pain that every instinct he had wanted to ease her, to fix it. But she'd left him, twice. Once to go to Basic and once in the form of divorce papers. He wasn't ready to be nice.

Holding tight to the steering wheel, he kept himself in check. When she opened her eyes, their gazes met and he could see the remorse in her, the conflict and pain and for an aching second, he couldn't breathe. Then, as though she couldn't stand it, she turned back to the door.

"I'm a big boy, Tessa. Whatever it is, I can take it."

he said. Her shoulders stiffened and he tried to prepare himself for the worst. "Was there somebody else?"

"God, no."

Some of the pressure in his chest eased and he nodded. "Then what happened? Did I do something wrong? I thought we were doing just fine and then you just left."

For the frigging army.

"No, it wasn't you," she said. She looked about to say something more, but then stopped and opened the door.

"See, this is the part where you say, 'It's me.' And we part ways and move on with our lives," he said, but she was already out the door.

She paused, rain whipping her coat open as she leaned back inside. "It's really good to see you, Cordon," she said. "Thank you for the ride."

"Yeah, of course," he said, shaking his head. God, she was infuriating.

The door rattled closed, and he flexed his fingers on the steering wheel. The irrational part of him wanted to chase after her and get some real answers, but it had been four goddamn years and he was supposed to be over this. He pulled away from the sidewalk and started back for Book Land.

It was his own damn fault for falling in love with a crazy woman. He should have walked away the minute she winked at him, told Old Man Joe that someone else should be her sparring partner, and saved his sanity. But then she'd laughed and her whole face lit up, and he swore it was the most beautiful thing he'd ever seen. There'd been no saving him after that, even with her father snarling that Cordon wasn't good enough.

Maybe he should swing by her father's place. Tessa had been so timid and uncertain when he walked into the store, vastly different from the girl he knew, and his gut was insisting something was wrong. Not that Todd Pines ever had anything polite to say to Cordon, but if something was wrong with Tessa then there was a chance the man might want to help.

Glancing down at the clock, he scowled.

Not enough time to swing by her father's place. Brian would complain if Cordon didn't show before his end of shift and then Sara would complain that Cordon was taking advantage of their brother-sister relationship and that was more of a headache than he wanted to deal with.

Well, Todd Pines was a headache of his own, and there was a good chance that when Cordon showed up, fists would fly.

He'd risk a black eye tomorrow. For tonight, he had to work.

Chapter Three

Tessa pushed her earbuds in and tried to concentrate around the cafeteria noise. The vast space amplified every conversation at once, melding voices together so that nothing coherent could be made out. Most of it was laughter, some of it was irate, and as much as she knew they had a right to eat their lunch the way they pleased, she still wanted to shove them out the second-floor window.

She glared at the half-empty page in front of her and flicked the volume up on whatever soundtrack her phone had chosen. Violins hummed into her awareness, underscored by cellos and clarinets in a sweeping sort of composition that barely covered the voices from the next table. Relaxing a bit, she re-read the page, trying to remember what point she was coming to. It was the first major paper for her Shakespeare class, a comparison of the use of ghosts in several plays, which should have been easy, but she'd been trying for two days now and couldn't quite get it finished.

Her mind kept conjuring images of a slumbering Richard III, with the ghosts of the man's victims cursing him through his dreams. There was something eerily accurate about the scene, something she wanted to convey in the paper that wasn't quite hitting the mark. She'd already compared Elizabethan culture with modern

American culture and the contrasts between belief in the supernatural and skepticism. But there was something more here, some deeper truth Shakespeare was alluding to, and as a fellow writer she felt particularly bound to reveal it.

Everyone has ghosts, she wrote in the margin. *Hopefully not cursing us in our sleep, but the souls leave an imprint, some mark that they were there.*

Her left earbud was yanked from her ear and she jumped as the cacophony of the room filtered back into her awareness. Marisol grinned cheekily and giggled, settling into the chair next to her. The smaller woman had managed to deposit her tray on the table and Tessa hadn't even noticed.

"You know, not all of college is work," Marisol said.

Tessa sighed and removed the other earbud, shutting down her phone and stuffing it into her pocket. "A good portion of college is supposed to be work. Otherwise the degree at the end doesn't mean much."

Marisol wrinkled her nose and squirted ketchup next to her pile of fries. Tessa eyed the pixie-like woman and throttled down her annoyance. She would probably burn those calories within the day and never gain a pound.

"Tell me about Bookstore Guy," Marisol said, then popped a fry in her mouth.

She had what Tessa could only describe as a bubble-gum voice that would, under normal circumstances, drive Tessa crazy. But Marisol was so incredibly good-natured it was hard to hate her for it.

Tessa groaned and closed her notebook. She'd gotten home just in time for Marisol to see the strange car pull up and the girl had been asking about Cordon ever since. It was like she was on a mission to uncover every secret

Tessa might have. Reaching for her own lunch—some kind of lentil soup that had been too hot to eat at first—she tried to think of the best way to end this conversation.

"Fess up, Tess," Marisol said. "You went to the bookstore, and some guy drove you home. Who was he?"

"Just a friend."

"Oh! Goodie! You're a local." Marisol grinned and wagged a fry at her. "There was a debate going on about you. Alyssa from 22B said she thought you might be local, and I have to admit, I'm relieved to hear it."

Tessa flinched, caught between the desire to fling herself out the window and wonderment that anyone still used the word *goodie* in everyday dialogue. "Relieved?"

"Well, yeah," Marisol said. "You're too closed off, you know? It's not healthy. But if you're local, then that just means all your friends are in town."

If only. Images of her unit floated through her memory. They should be back in Hawaii by now, safely out of the war zone and sleeping in their own beds.

She frowned, catching the other half of Marisol's statement a moment later. "I'm not closed off."

Marisol rolled her eyes. "No evasions. Tell me what happened with bookstore guy."

"I'm not evading…" Not much, anyway. "And nothing happened with bookstore guy. There is no bookstore guy. He's just a friend."

"Tessa," Marisol said in a voice that brooked no nonsense. Her face grew stern, perfect rosebud mouth pursing into a pink blossom on her face, and Tessa nearly wanted to throw the soup on her. Nobody should be that pretty. "*Just friends* do not make us want to take a long shower and watch reruns all night. You were still watching after midnight. I could see the light from your laptop. Now spill."

"Fine," Tessa said, taking the moment to crush her crackers and dump them over the soup. How in God's name had she ended up with such a roommate? "Bookstore guy is named Cordon Morant, and he was my high school sweetheart. We were married, briefly. But I left him to join the army, and he hates me now. The only reason he brought me home was because his sense of chivalry couldn't let a girl walk in the rain."

Marisol frowned, chewing on her fry. "You were married?"

"For about a year."

"And you left him to join the army? Why?" Marisol's eyes narrowed. "He's not one of those macho men who can't let a woman have her own career, is he?"

Tessa shook her head. "No, not at all. In any other circumstance, I think he would have supported me."

Heaven help her, why was she talking about this? She glanced around the cafeteria, struck again by how similar it was to the dining facilities on base. Chow line, standard tables, lots of noise. The only thing missing were the uniforms.

"What circumstances were those?" Marisol asked.

Groaning, Tessa rubbed her temple. "It doesn't matter. It went down ugly. Hence why he hates me. Which is fine because I am in school and have work to do. I don't have time for…that."

"There is always time for *that*." Marisol grinned at her and waggled her eyebrows. "*That* is what keeps the world turning. And *that* is what will keep you sane during midterms. Trust me. You need *that*."

Tessa laughed and shook her head. "Only you would think sex was a cure-all for midterms."

"Sex is nice, but I wouldn't call it a cure-all," Marisol said and sighed. "I'm talking about companionship. Which you are in desperate need of, my friend."

"No, I'm not." Tessa felt the buzz of her phone and pulled it out again, frowning down at the number. Why was her father calling her? She swiped to answer it and plugged one ear to hear better. "Dad?"

"Tess, I'm glad I caught you. I didn't pull you out of class, did I?"

Her father's rumbling voice was just loud enough for her to hear him.

"If I'd been in class, I wouldn't have answered," she said and made a face at Marisol, who crossed her eyes at her. "What's wrong?"

"Nothing's wrong, not really," he said. "I got a call from Dr. Freemont. She said you missed your appointment and was asking to reschedule."

Tessa held back a groan and closed her eyes, turning away from Marisol. Why had she put her father as her secondary contact? She had purposefully avoided meeting with the VA-appointed therapist and refused to learn where the cursed mental health building was located. The leading benefit to being out of the military was that she had no commanding officer to force her into things anymore and she had no intention of allowing the Veteran's Association to try dictating to her now.

Or her father, for that matter.

"Yeah, Dad, that's not really necessary…" she started but he cut her off with "So I took the liberty of rescheduling for you. Your appointment is on Tuesday at three."

"Dad…" She bunched her free hand into a fist and held tight, coaching herself into breathing. She would not see a shrink. She did not need a shrink. She was just fine.

"Tessa, I'm not kidding around here. You went through a trauma, and you need to talk about it."

The hell I do. But because it was her father and she knew this was coming from a place of love, she didn't say that. Instead, she took another breath and said, "I've got about ten minutes to finish my lunch and get across campus."

"Promise me you'll go."

"Fine," she said. There wasn't a chance in hell she would ever darken Dr. Freemont's door, but he didn't need to hear that right now. "Love you."

Lowering the phone, she hung up before he could say goodbye. One would think her stint in the military would have taught him not to shove his way into her business. Still, with Mom on the other side of the nation doing God knew what, he was her only family left. She would have to call him tonight, after homework and after she'd had several hours to prepare for the conversation.

"Everything all right?" Marisol asked.

Tessa tried for a smile and shrugged. "Yeah, just my dad being…Dad."

"They'll do that," Marisol said and smirked.

Tessa snorted a laugh and reached for her soup. She truly was running out of lunch hour and needed to get done here. Marisol seemed to read her mood because her roommate didn't return to the conversation about Cordon, which Tessa blessed her for. They ate in silence, Marisol munching on her fries and Tessa brooding over how to mend the fence with her father.

She missed the simplicity of the army. At least there she knew her job and how to function within the dynamic of her team. There was something about wearing a uniform unlike anything else in the world. She missed reveille in the morning and evening, everyone standing tall and saluting the direction of the flag no matter what they'd been doing prior to the trumpet's call. She missed having a purpose, even if that purpose was only to make sure the next soldier in line was safe.

And she missed the companionship.

Scowling at her nearly empty bowl, she realized that was what Marisol had been trying to tell her and put her spoon down. Well, it was mostly what Marisol had been saying. She might miss companionship and camaraderie, but that didn't mean she needed it.

A face flashed to mind, thin and pock-marked, with a geeky grin, and her whole body seemed to clench tight, trying to will the face away.

Cabby's face, she knew it like it was her own.

Specialist Robert Cabarton, aka Cabby, the radio man for her assigned vehicle, and the man who had saved her life. Her heart ached, remembering him just minutes before the explosion, before the world changed forever, and she abruptly stood. Reaching for her tray, she told Marisol she'd see her later and headed for the door. She counted her steps, trying to concentrate around Cabby's grin, but try as she might she couldn't dislodge him.

By the time she reached the stairwell, she swore she could even hear him laughing. Nothing evil, not cursing her like the ghosts from *Richard III*, just his normal laugh, and somehow that seemed worse.

Chapter Four

"No, Mom, I am not coming over for a reading," Cordon said into his phone as he turned into the strip mall. "Seriously, this has got to stop. I'm nearly thirty."

"Yes, you're nearly thirty and letting your life waste away," Amanda Morant said, sounding far more peevish than he'd expected. "I didn't go through seventeen hours of labor pains just to watch you twiddle your thumbs in your sister's bookstore."

He parked his car in the sparsely populated lot and pinched the bridge of his nose. If he'd known what was in store for him when he answered the call, he would have thrown his phone out the window.

"Mom, I am not wasting my life. I like my life. I don't need anything else."

"You're the biggest liar I've ever met," his mother said. "All you do is read books and play with Lyndon. That can't possibly sustain you. You need friends. A purpose. Sex."

Cordon cringed. "God, Mom. Boundaries."

"When was the last time you had a date?"

He thought of Tessa laughing from the passenger seat, her wide mouth curved and as inviting as the first day he'd seen her. And then he scowled, shoving her from his mind as he shut the car down.

"Mom, I'm at Book Land. I've got to go before Sara

fires me."

"Ugh, you're impossible," she said. And then, warmer this time, "You know your sister would never fire you."

"Of course, she would. She's spiteful like that," he said. "Trust me, she remembers the time I burnt her hair in the sixth grade. That girl knows how to carry a grudge."

His mother laughed, and he relaxed, pleased to be off the subject. "That was an accident," she said.

"I know. She knows. Her hair was still burnt." He glanced at the rack outside of Book Land, noticing at once that Tessa's bike was still there. "Listen, Mom. I've got to go."

"Remind Sara that she's supposed to bring Lyndon over tomorrow for lunch."

"Will do," he said and hung up before she could add anything else.

Sighing, he shoved the phone in his pocket and got out of the car. Cool air breezed over him, the bite of oncoming winter making him forget that summer had been just a week ago. The storm from yesterday had moved on, leaving behind a faded blue sky that almost matched the color of Tessa's jacket.

God, Tessa again. He was becoming obsessed.

Shaking his head, he grabbed the heavy duffle from the back seat and slung it over his shoulder. He'd tried to visit Todd Pines earlier, but the old lake house had been vacant. Or if it hadn't been, Mr. Pines was doing a masterful job of avoidance. To be fair, Cordon didn't want to talk to that man any more than Mr. Pines wanted to talk to him.

For whatever reason, Todd Pines had taken one look

at Cordon and hated him. Nothing Cordon could do seemed to fix the man's low opinion, especially after the elopement. He supposed he could understand a little of the man's dislike for him there. No man wants to see his daughter married a day after graduation at a drive-thru wedding lot.

To be fair, Todd hadn't left them much of a choice. He'd demanded they stop seeing each other and threatened to throw Tessa out. Which, of course, spurred Tessa into packing a bag that night. They'd always said they would have a proper wedding one day, after the dust had settled and they weren't dealing with one crisis after another.

Cordon shook his head and headed for Book Land. The cheery little store was full of warmth and light, and he breathed easier, heading for the front counter. Shelves lined the walls and made diagonal aisles through the center of the store, and interspersed were clusters of comfortable chairs with a side table or two for added convenience. The chair Tessa had been in last night was occupied by an older gentleman in a tweed coat, and Cordon smiled at him as he passed.

A small study group huddled in the southwest corner, quietly murmuring to each other and the two rentable rooms at the back both had their doors closed. Cordon took a deep breath and dropped his bag behind the counter, then glanced over the schedule. Sara had warned him a gaming tournament was coming up, but he thought that wasn't until closer to Halloween.

He relaxed when he saw the orange blocks on the schedule didn't start for another week. While he understood keeping the gaming rooms open and hosting events like this helped keep Book Land open, he preferred the store quiet. Flipping the page over, he discovered the room reservations continued through the rest of the year and frowned. The gaming tournament ended on Halloween night, what else was going on?

Pantsers Group 1 and Pantsers Group 2 were written in Sara's neat script for both rooms, three times a week.

What the hell was a Pantser?

"How's life as a librarian?" asked a familiar voice.

Tyler Brannings sauntered over to the counter, grinning like a ghoul with his too-long face and deep-set eyes. Nearly six years outside of high school and Tyler seemed permanently stuck in jock mode. He wasn't a bully or anything, not to Cordon, at least, but Cordon wasn't the sort of man who got bullied so that wasn't saying much. But Tyler was obnoxious and enjoyed his family's wealth. And ever since he'd gotten together with Alyssa, he seemed hell-bent to rub it in Cordon's face.

Not that it bothered Cordon in the least, he and Alyssa had been over for a year now. She was three years too young for him and equally stuck in the high school mentality. Hell, Cordon wished Tyler the best with her, they certainly seemed made for each other.

"I wouldn't know, Tyler, since this isn't a library."

"Yeah, yeah," Tyler said. "Listen, Alyssa wants some new book from some author she likes. You know the one."

"No, I really don't…"

"Oh, come on. You have to know. The one about those weird shape-shifty romances?"

Cordon squinted at him, wondering why he should know about shape-shifter romance novels. Was there an implied insult in that? He'd been about to tell Tyler he had no idea what he was talking about when the doorbell chimed. Grateful for the distraction, he looked up to welcome the newcomer.

Only the newcomer was his sister Sara, who wore an eye-catching red halter top, and tights tucked into knee-high boots. Cordon's day went from bad to worse.

He knew that outfit. That was a dating outfit.

His family was going to be the death of him.

"Who is it this time?" He didn't bother smiling anymore.

Tyler perked and whistled at Sara, and for half a second, Cordon considered throwing a book at them both.

"Hey there, Sara," Tyler said. "You're looking good."

Sara beamed at him and made her way to the front counter, almost bouncing on her toes in excitement. "Thank you, Tyler," she said and then wrinkled her nose at Cordon. "And I don't need my baby brother defending me, so back off, Cord."

An image of his six-year-old nephew flashed to mind.

"Where's Lyndon?" He placed as much meaning into the two words as possible.

She scowled, clearly understanding his implied insult. "He's with Uncle Phil," she said, coming around the counter and heading for the back. "And screw you too."

Tyler snickered, and Cordon ignored him, turning to lean one hip against the counter. Crossing his arms over his chest, he narrowed his eyes at his sister as she continued toward the office. Sara didn't date much, but when she did, she always dated wrong. She was like a homing beacon for deadbeats, and while Cordon was pleased none of them had been brought into Lyndon's life—save Lyndon's father—who revealed a desire to become a woman shortly after Lyndon had been born, Cordon felt justified in his worry.

He didn't have a problem with gender identities. People could do whatever they wanted with their own lives, but this was different. This was his sister left devastated to raise a son on her own. Promises had been made and broken, and that was where Cordon had a problem.

Come to think of it, that was part of his problem with Tessa too, but he could only deal with one fire at a time.

"Who?" Cordon asked again before Sara could disappear into the office.

She heaved a sigh and rolled her eyes at him before she slipped into the back.

"Relax," Tyler said when she was out of earshot. "It's Greg Parsons."

Cordon glanced at him and frowned. "How do you know?"

"Because Alyssa set them up," Tyler said with a shrug.

Searching his memory for this Parsons man, Cordon crouched behind the counter and started hunting for Alyssa's name. He didn't want to like Tyler, but if he was right about Greg then Cordon owed him. The least he could do was find a silly book. Sara had a system set up so frequent buyers could put books on hold and if the new book Alyssa was waiting for had come in, it would be there.

Parsons had been a scrawny, freckle-faced kid with goggle glasses that made his eyes look like a frog.

But that was ten years ago. Surely the boy would look different now.

At the very least, he must have gotten rid of the

glasses. Contacts or surgery or something could have taken care of that. What really mattered was, to Cordon's knowledge, Greg Parsons was a mild-mannered sort who had been in math club.

He relaxed. Nothing terrible could come from a math geek. And if anything did, he was certain he could break the man in half.

A little paperback sat on its side under the counter, surrounded by other unclaimed volumes. This one had a sticky note attached with Alyssa's name on it and he grabbed it. Rising to his feet, he put the paperback on the counter, eyeing its dark blue cover with a jean-clad, shirtless man. There was a wolf's head just behind the man, golden eyes glaring out at a full moon and it was all Cordon could do not to grimace.

As Sara would say, not all books are meant for all audiences and this one was clearly not made for him.

"How much?" Tyler asked, reaching for his back pocket.

Cordon shook his head. "On the house today."

"You sure?"

Eyeing the office door for a moment, Cordon nodded. "Absolutely."

Tyler grinned, showing off a mouthful of slightly crooked teeth. "Hey, man, you're all right."

Cordon smirked and made a note of the sale. He still didn't like the boy, probably never would, but things were even. As Tyler left the store, he caught sight of Tessa's bike again and frowned. She would need that. If she didn't show up before his shift ended, he would take it to her. And then maybe they could talk.

A real talk. With real answers.

Sara flounced out of the back office, looking far too

excited for her date with the mathematician, and moved to lean against the counter beside him.

"Sooooo," she said, grinning like the mad woman she was. "Brian says you played hero to a damsel in distress last night."

Cordon lifted the renters' schedule, hoping to distract her. "Brian has too much time on his hands. He's a terrible gossip and you should fire him." Then he pointed at the schedule. "What the hell is a Pantser?"

"Brian is a sweet boy and I will not be firing him," Sara said, squinting at the schedule for a moment. "Pantsers are writers. Mrs. Farris is challenging her students to collaborate on a novel this year and she asked to reserve the space."

"Huh," Cordon said, putting the schedule down.

"You should try it. I know how you like books." Sara glanced over the store, frowning at the back-to-school display. "Now tell me who this girl is?"

"Just because I like books doesn't mean I'd be a great writer. And I don't fancy sitting in with a group of eleventh graders," he said.

"Cordon, I'll find out about this woman one way or another. It's better if you tell me now."

Heaving a sigh, he leaned against the counter beside his sister and shook his head. She was right, of course. But he was hoping to avoid this confrontation.

"It was Tessa."

Sara's smile froze, her expression morphing from carefree-happy to rage in under a second. "Tessa?"

He nodded, opting to stay silent for the tirade he knew was coming.

"How dare she come into my shop! Well, we will just put a stop to this right now. She won't be allowed here.

I'll have her arrested for trespassing or something. I do have the right to refuse service to anyone. It's right there on the door." Sara pointed at the door in question. "She's got some nerve coming back here…"

"Sara," he said, crossing his arms and shaking his head. "She didn't know you own the place. And she certainly didn't know I worked here. If she had, I don't think she would have come in."

"Well, now she knows. Hopefully she stays away."

His heart pinched at the thought of his ex-wife avoiding Book Land, avoiding him, and he decided he would put her bike in his car. If she came back during his shift, she would be forced to come inside and talk to him. And then, because his sister still scowled and gave off a homicidal vibe, he reached out to touch her shoulder.

"I love you too, Sis. But I don't think you need to get so up in arms."

"She hurt you. That makes her the scum of the earth."

"No, that makes her a human being. And I don't think we have the whole story." Cordon shook his head, thinking of the way Tessa had huddled in his car. No, there was more going on, he'd bet his life on it. But he didn't think he'd get a straight answer from her father.

"What more could there be?" Sara crossed her arms and tapped her foot. "Mr. Pines told you she was fine. Said she was on a beach in Hawaii with someone named Billie. I remember your face when you told me. It was the worst look I've ever seen."

Cordon frowned, remembering that day far more acutely than he wanted to. Todd had been so smug, sneering from the lake house porch. He'd even offered to let Cordon read the letter Tessa had sent about it. But he had also refused to look him in the face.

"I'm not sure how truthful he was being," Cordon said.

"Why would he lie?"

"Look, I know you think I'm the most wonderful brother on earth, but that man hates me and always has. I wouldn't put it past him to lie."

Sara slumped against the counter and scrunched her nose. "Well, you did get married at Ms. Corneal's drive-thru."

"A crime which I will be paying for the rest of my life, apparently."

"Mom was so angry! I thought she was going to break every dish in the house that night." Sara gasped. "Oh! Have you told Mom you saw her?"

"No…"

"Good! Try not to tell her until I've taken the breakables out of the house."

Cordon rubbed his face. "It's been years, Sara. She won't freak out. I saw Tessa one time."

Sara gave him a knowing smirk. "You saw her bike outside already, right?"

He glared at his sister, knowing exactly what was coming next, but there was no getting around it. "Yes."

"And your bleeding heart already decided you were going to return it to her today, I'm sure."

He scowled. "Yes."

"Then do me a favor and wait to tell Mom. I bought her a tea set last year and I want it to survive the fight."

Chapter Five

Tessa frowned at the little hutch that served as her closet and eyed every boring shirt she'd packed for this semester. Would she ever grow a fashion sense? Squinting at the neatly sorted clothes, she realized her hutch looked quite a bit like her locker from the barracks. Everything was crisp and measured like she expected Sergeant Meehan to stalk through the door for an impromptu inspection. Scowling, she slid hangers one by one, reviewing what she had that wouldn't embarrass her during this night of living dangerously.

Well, night of letting Marisol dictate the schedule, which seemed dangerous on its own.

"Blue," Marisol said from her bed on the other side of the room. "Blue looks good on you."

"Are you sure?" Tessa asked, but she was already reaching for one of the blue V-neck shirts hanging in front of her.

"Positive." Marisol flashed a cherubic grin. "That and it's the only thing with actual color in there. I swear, you have more beige and brown in your wardrobe than should be legal."

"I like earthy colors," Tessa said and wondered why she had agreed to this. "How's this supposed to work again?"

"It's B-Movie Night and you are not chickening out

on me," Marisol said.

Tessa ducked into the shirt and buttoned its little pearlescent buttons. The material was light, and the sleeves cut off above her elbows, which she liked because she had a love-hate relationship with her biceps.

"I didn't say I was chickening out, I asked how it worked."

"We show up, buy some popcorn, and watch really bad movies in black and white."

"And this is entertaining because…?"

"Because the movies are so awful, they're funny and we get to make comments while it plays. I can't believe you've never done it before," Marisol said, sliding out of bed.

She was built like a pixie, a fraction over five feet tall with a spiral perm that made her brown hair bounce whenever she moved. Stretching her arms overhead, she leaned left and right, all elegance and sensual curves, like a ballerina.

Tessa had never moved like that in her life. She had a feeling her love life would have seen more action if she could.

Why had Tessa agreed to go to this thing again? She would look like a frumpy toad standing next to Marisol all night.

"So, how's Psychology Guy?" Tessa asked, desperate for a change of subject.

Marisol's rosebud mouth quirked up into a shy smile. "Good," she said. "He's really into this paranormal investigating stuff. He wants to prove it's all a trick in our heads or something so…"

Tessa finished lacing her boots, realizing as she did that they looked quite a bit like combat boots and frowned. Not exactly sexy, but her only alternative were her sneakers and those had a hole in the toe.

Unsexy, or poor and unsexy; the decisions she had to make.

"So, we're planning a paranormal investigation party out at the old Ashwood place and I really, really, really need you to come," Marisol said, clasping her hands in front and giving Tessa a wide-eyed, entreating look. "Please."

"A what?" Tessa blinked, wondering what alternate universe she'd stepped into where she was begged to attend a party. That hadn't even happened in the army and there'd been plenty of opportunity there.

"A paranormal investigation party," Marisol said, abandoning whatever she'd been doing with her hutch to bounce over to Tessa. "It's a party where we go through the institute after dark and try to find some kind of proof it's haunted, or it's just playing tricks with our minds. We'll record everything so Lundy and I can go over it all the next day."

Tessa stared at her, speechless. Since when did Marisol believe in ghosts?

"You know, like ghost hunters," Marisol said, beaming.

"And why do you need me?"

"Have you seen the Ashwood Institute? It's huge! We need all the help we can get."

Tessa's phone buzzed in her coat, which was hanging by the door.

Yes, I've seen the Ashwood. It's big and it's falling apart, and no one should go in there, especially after dark. It probably has football sized rats and bird-eating spiders lurking around.

"Don't you need permission to get in there?" Tessa swiped a finger over her phone to answer it.

"Not an issue."

A male voice purred into her ear; "Hello, Pines."

Pines? Tessa pulled the phone away to see the caller ID. It was a private number.

"Who is this?"

"It's David!"

"David who?" She crossed her eyes at Marisol's curious look. The girl was still on the hunt for any and all personal information she could gain, and Tessa had no intentions of helping her out. There were moments when she swore Marisol watched her like some experiment for her psychology major.

Shrinks everywhere. Tessa decided it was a good thing she was going out tonight. Her father would forgive her for not calling if it looked like she had some kind of social life.

"David Jackson," the man on the phone said, sounding a little peeved now. "Jesus. You're out six months and forgotten everyone?"

"Seven months," she corrected him and then froze, memories hitting home fast.

Sergeant Jackson from her unit, giving nearly every female soldier a lecherous sort of wink followed by an almost-but-not-quite good-natured chuckle. The kind of man who insisted he was only joking even when all your instincts told you different. Why was he calling her?

"Jackson?" She ruthlessly willed thoughts of Cabby away.

"Yeah, baby. In the flesh, sort of."

No. Not tonight. She would not remember this tonight.

There was a light rapping on the door and Tessa turned. Torn between the desire to hang up on Jackson and confusion as Alyssa's buxom frame filled the doorway, Tessa frowned.

The blonde wiggled her fingers at Marisol before announcing; "Tessa? Someone's downstairs looking for you."

She pressed the phone to her chest and concentrated on Alyssa. "Who?"

"Well," Alyssa glanced at Marisol before lowering her voice a fraction. "It's Cordon."

If lowering her voice had been meant to keep Marisol from hearing, it failed miserably because Marisol perked. "Oooo! He's downstairs right now?"

Alyssa nodded and Tessa's heart lurched in her chest. Why was Cordon here?

Marisol scuttled for the door, giggling with delight. Alyssa stepped aside so the girl could pass, giving Tessa an apologetic smile as Marisol disappeared from sight. Tessa closed her eyes and counted to ten, concentrating on breathing. The last thing she needed was Marisol talking to Cordon, needling the poor man for information and psychoanalyzing him for class. She opened her eyes again, but Alyssa still stood there, watching her with keen interest.

Disconcerted, Tessa said, "Uh, thanks. I'll be right there."

Alyssa smiled again, shyer this time, which weird because Alyssa wasn't the shy sort. But before Tessa could ask her anything, she slid out of the room, leaving the door slightly ajar.

"What the hell?" Tessa asked the empty room. Then, remembering Jackson was still waiting, she pressed the phone to her ear again. "Jackson, are you calling me from—"

"Nope. I'm state-side, babe. Enjoying civilian life for thirty days." He sounded as smug as ever.

"How'd you get this number?"

She grabbed her jacket by the door. There was no way she was leaving Cordon to Marisol's interrogation.

"Ouch. That hurts," Jackson said. "And here I thought you and me was friends."

"You and *I* were friends," she corrected him, shrugging on her coat and zipping it closed. "And that doesn't really answer my question."

"Your dad. I dropped by to return some of the stuff you left, and he gave it to me."

"What stuff?" Tessa opened the door. She checked her pockets for keys and wallet and then headed out, hurrying for the stairwell. "I already got my stuff…"

"Relax, it's just a box of books and some letters from the squad."

She paused, remembering one leather-bound copy of Shakespeare she'd been reading out there. But that brought memories of desert heat and dusty tents, lounging in her bunk and trying to ignore Murphy's complaints. The girl hated everything about being deployed and constantly talked about the things she missed, dates with a myriad of men being at the top of the list.

"Everyone misses you, you know? You weren't gone a week before Lincoln was complaining about his computer constantly breaking. He said you were the only one who could keep that thing running." Jackson said.

Her shoulder began to ache, and she tried to tell herself it was a phantom pain. Just a memory, nothing more. But it was a vivid memory and for a breathless moment there was the tilt of the vehicle, the hard edges of the doorframe against her side. Fire roared its way through metal and oil and skin, the heat of it searing up her leg.

Cabby shouting her name, flinging himself at her as the world swung upside down.

"Pines? Hey, Pines, you all right over there?"

Maybe Dad was right. Maybe she did need to talk to someone about this.

"I'm fine," she said, forcing herself to think of Cordon and his perilous conversation with her too-nosy roommate. Even if her dad was right, she certainly wouldn't be opening up to David-goddamn-Jackson. She wasn't desperate. "I'm sure my replacement does just fine fixing those computers."

"Eh, he's all right," Jackson said. "Nothing like you…"

Reaching the stairwell doors, she peered out the little rectangular window and spotted Cordon on the sidewalk, hands in his pockets. He warily nodded at Marisol, who bounced on her toes with excitement beside him.

"Listen, Jackson, I've got to go. Thanks for dropping my books off."

"No problem. You think maybe we can get together for lunch or something? Catch up? I've got all month."

"Yeah, maybe. We'll see," she said, her hand on the door. "I've really got to go. Take care of yourself."

She hung up and hesitated, staring at the screen of her phone while the lights died down. Her hand shook, and she smelled the desert again. Closing her eyes, she took another breath, concentrating on the scent of whatever pine cleaner the school used. She was not in the desert. She was not in the vehicle.

God, Cabby. I am so sorry.

After another steadying breath, she shoved the man from her mind, praying wherever his soul might be, he'd found some peace there. Then she pushed the door open and went to save Cordon.

Chapter Six

Tessa forced a smile as she approached Cordon and Marisol, noticing Cordon didn't seem enamored with the petite brunette beside him. In fact, he looked increasingly worried as Marisol continued to talk. When he spotted Tessa's approach he straightened, relief in his eyes. His shoulders relaxed and he smiled, though she could see it was strained, and she did her best not to laugh as she stepped into the conversation.

"Tessa," he said, stopping Marisol midsentence. "I brought back your bike."

Marisol beamed at them, not the least bit disconcerted at having been cut off. "You didn't tell me what a hero he was," Marisol said. "Rescuing you from the storm and now delivering your bike? It's hard to find chivalry like that these days."

Cordon rubbed the back of his neck and glanced at his car, looking so uncomfortable he might run. "It was nothing, really."

Still not great at being appreciated. For a second, she was tempted to tease him. But that wouldn't help matters and it would all come out botched anyway. So, she went for a friendly smile and nodded to the bike.

"You didn't have to do that. I planned on coming up tomorrow to grab it."

"It was on my way," he said with a shrug.

"But the school isn't anywhere near Auburn street."

His eyebrow quirked and she realized an instant later her mistake.

"I moved a couple years ago, Tess," he said.

"Right." A flush inched up her neck and she wished she could melt into the sidewalk. Of course, he wouldn't stay in their old apartment. He'd only chosen it because she loved the walk-in closet. And the oven. It had a great oven. God, why did she miss a damn oven?

Her stomach pitched as a thought hit her. Had he remarried?

She glanced down but his hands were still in his pockets and she tried to remember if she'd seen a ring on him last night. It had been dark and there'd been all the rain. And honestly, she'd been so distraught sitting in his car, all the unsaid things suffocating them both, that she hadn't looked.

"I think heroics like this deserve a treat, don't you, Tessa?" Marisol said.

Recognizing the wicked glint in her roommate's eyes, Tessa stiffened, "A treat?"

"Yeah," Marisol said, batting her eyelashes. "I think he should come with us to B-Movie night. I'm sure he's heard of it and would love it."

Tessa fought the urge to smack her upside the head. There was something distinctly flirtatious in the way Marisol watched Cordon, and Tessa eyed her. Wasn't it an unwritten code amongst women that friends do not date their roommate's ex-husbands? That seemed like common decency.

"Actually, I was hoping to steal Tessa tonight," Cordon said. "That is, if you don't mind?"

"Not at all," Tessa said, far more quickly than she'd

intended.

Cordon's mouth twitched into the briefest grin and she flushed.

"I mean, I think we have some things to talk about."

"I can think of one or two things."

An awkward silence enveloped them, everyone glancing at each other as Tessa tried to think of how to escape Marisol. The invitation had clearly been made for Tessa, but Marisol still stood there watching them. In fact, she had a studious look on her face, which was even more alarming than any social faux pas they might have stumbled into.

"Rain check?" Tessa suggested.

Marisol wrinkled her nose at them and smiled at the same time. She looked like a little kid who'd been promised ice cream another time. But then her expression morphed from mild disappointment to delight as she reached out to touch Tessa's arm.

Tessa wondered how many prescriptions Marisol was on. Nobody was this cheerful all the time. It was physically impossible.

"It's fine," Marisol said. "You can totally ditch me for a hot date. I'm good with that. But you owe me one favor."

"It's coffee…" *With my ex-husband.*

Why had she said yes again? It was like someone else had control of her mouth sometimes. Her cheeks warmed and she did her utmost not to look at Cordon. "But all right, one favor."

"It's coffee with the bearded god standing next to you that makes it a hot date. As for the favor you owe… You'll be coming to the Ashwood with us for our investigation."

Tessa flinched, remembering the institute and all its dirty floors and ramshackle buildings. B-Movie Night would be far more pleasant to get through. But Cordon stood beside her, waiting for explanations he more than deserved. So, reluctantly, Tessa agreed to the bargain. Marisol beamed and clapped her hands.

"Oh, it'll be so much fun!" Marisol said, turning her attention on Cordon. "You can come too."

Cordon blinked at her, then glanced at Tessa. "Me?"

"Yes, you," Marisol said. "We need all the people we can get. Besides, you wouldn't want Tessa wandering through that place alone, would you?"

"Uh—"

"It's settled then," Marisol said. "Now take this beautiful woman out to coffee and work through whatever drama you guys need to." She wiggled her fingers at them, pivoted on her toes, and practically skipped toward the doors.

Tessa was too flabbergasted to formulate words. If she didn't know better, she'd think Marisol had planned the whole conversation to get what she wanted. That or she'd just anticipated Tessa's every move and boxed her in.

"She's…interesting," Cordon said.

He sounded so diplomatic Tessa snorted a laugh.

"Marisol Williams. Bright and bubbly on the outside, sneaky and manipulative on the inside."

"Well, she's got your number at least," Cordon said, turning toward the car. "I've never seen anyone handle you like that."

"Hey, I wasn't handled."

"So, you want to go to the Ashwood?"

He'd managed to park by the sidewalk again, which

was amazing since the space was almost always full. She started for the passenger side, scowling at him because he was right, damn his hide. By the smug smirk on his face, he seemed to know it too. Still, Marisol had recruited him as well and Tessa wasn't about to forget it.

"She's a psychology major," Tessa said. "She was probably psychoanalyzing you, too."

Cordon stopped with his hand on the passenger door. Frowning, he glanced back at the dorms. "Well, that's unsettling."

"Try living with her," Tessa said.

"She doesn't really expect me to come to this thing, does she?"

"All signs point to yes."

"She just met me."

"And over the course of that three-minute conversation she managed to call you a bearded god and a hot date," Tessa said. "Trust me, she expects you there."

Cordon's face resembled a man choking on a lemon as he opened the car door for her. Laughing, Tessa ducked inside and settled against the seat. This car seemed so different for him, not at all like the truck he'd driven in high school. It was on the smaller side, low to the ground, and it had a back seat occupied by several books and a car seat.

Her good humor died, and she stared at the car seat, questions bombarding her. Did he have a kid? Why hadn't he told her already? That seemed like something he should have led with.

Hey, Tessa, it's good to see you again. Me? I'm good. Got a healthy, happy baby girl at home whose mother is wondering why I'm sitting here talking to my ex-wife.

For a heartbeat she considered letting herself out, but Cordon was already sliding into the driver's seat, looking amused and confident and everything she remembered. The Cordon she knew would never hide something as important as a kid. Granted, there hadn't been much time for him to mention it last night. It was entirely possible he would work that in over coffee.

She bit her lower lip and tried not to look at the car seat. Her heart hammered against her ribs and it was difficult to breathe. She focused on the window and coached herself into a calm tone, "Interesting back seat."

Out of the corner of her eye she saw him swivel in the driver's seat to look back.

"I work in a bookstore. It's hard not to build up a collection." He sounded amused.

Tessa eyed him. He knew exactly what she was talking about, she could see it in his face, but he would make her ask. Well, to hell with that. Two could play that game.

"It's a relief to see you read more than the *Iliad* these days. I thought for sure we'd have to bury you with a copy."

"Oh, that's still my favorite," he said. "But I did have to buy a new one. Lyndon got a hold of my first book and decided it needed an upgrade. He took crayons to it."

"Not the hardback you pilfered from one of those estate sales!" Tessa gasped.

Cordon nodded solemnly. "The same."

She flinched, imagining old paper drawn over with green and yellow crayons, and shook her head. "That's sacrilegious."

"It is, but since I left the book where he could find it, I can admit to being at fault. I take him to school sometimes when Sara can't get away from the store."

Tessa flushed. Of course, he would be taking care of his nephew, Cordon was good like that. And bad like that.

She swallowed the thought down, determined not to bring up more painful memories for them both. Why was she doing this? Wasn't it better to leave the past in the past and move on? Maybe she should ask him to turn the car around and forget about Book Land and the Morants. She'd certainly done enough to them, leaving Cordon in the lurch like she did couldn't have gone over well with his mother or his sister.

But Cordon was already pulling out of the University lot and she owed him an explanation. Her gut clenched, remembering how he'd looked in South Carolina. He'd come to see her graduation from basic training, and they'd been allowed a scant few hours to try patching their broken marriage. Nine weeks apart, dealing in letters, had allowed her the chance to really tell him how she felt, but nothing could prepare her for seeing him again.

The reality of what she'd done was written on his face. He'd been terrified and angry, and her eyes burned just thinking about it.

She should have tried harder. Maybe they could have made it work. It would have been difficult, but they could have figured something out.

"Lyndon will be seven in April. He's constantly asking questions and talking at the speed of light. It's exhausting."

Tessa tried to smile, imagining Cordon with a six-year-old bouncing around him, chattering up a storm. "Do you take him to Joe's?"

"Every Tuesday and Thursday. I don't teach

anymore, not since Joe Junior took over, but I try to make sure Lyndon practices. It isn't easy, given his age, but he seems to enjoy it."

She sighed, remembering the smell of heavy cleaners in the dojo and the shuffle of little feet across the mats. Joe Senior kept them all laughing despite the seriousness of what they were learning, and she had a flash of his familiar, aged face crinkled in mirth. Her heart squeezed, fond memories swirling to the surface; Joe helping her through the basics of self-defense, empowering her to face the sparring ring even when her opponent was twice her size.

"Dad said Joe was in a retirement home now?"

Cordon nodded, his face sober. "I visit him whenever I can. He's still alert, but it hurts like hell to see him so weak."

Tessa hummed as Cordon pulled into the lot of an unfamiliar coffee shop. She didn't want to think of her capable, good-natured mentor as weak and felt a twinge of guilt at avoiding the retirement home. Her father had given her the address, hoping she would go visit, but with school and recovery keeping her busy she hadn't found the time.

No, you just haven't had the guts to go there. God, she was such a coward.

The coffee shop was a small establishment boasting a sign with a large frog in mid-hop that said; "Put the Leap Into Your Day." Cordon led the way to the doors, which had large, wavy handles in wrought iron. The fragrance of coffee beans breezed over her and she inhaled, savoring it as she took in the cream-colored walls and dark brown counters. There were frog figures everywhere in vivid greens and absurd polka-dot pinks, perched on any flat surface.

She must have looked surprised because Cordon chuckled beside her. "I know, but the coffee really is good. Hazelnut with sweet cream, right?"

"Right," Tessa said, startled and pleased he would remember how she liked her coffee.

She followed him to the counter, still taking in the frogs and the colors. For a moment she worried about letting him pay because this wasn't a date and he shouldn't have to, but he glared when she reached for her pocket.

The barista, a pleasant-faced boy with spiky brown hair and the barest patch of a goatee, snickered at the silent argument. Tessa's hackles rose, but Cordon slid his card over the counter, shoving his shoulder in her path so she couldn't get her own through.

Exasperated, she picked a table at random and flopped into a seat. Cordon joined her a few moments later, depositing a steaming cup in front of her before sitting. The fragrance stole her attention and she held the cup in both hands, letting the heated drink warm her palms and inhaling sugary hazelnut.

"I love coffee."

Cordon chuckled. "I remember."

Sipping, she savored the burst of cream and nuts and coffee, letting it coat her tongue before swallowing. She sighed, relaxing further into her chair. She hadn't had coffee this good in years. Army coffee, as strong as it was, didn't count. It was too grainy, too black, and had none of the finesse of a civilian shop.

"So," Cordon said.

He let the word hover between them, and she looked up, grateful for the patience she could see there. It was just like Cordon to ask for explanations but never demand them. The man never *demanded* anything, which had been half the problem.

Swallowing another sip of coffee, she dropped her gaze to the table.

That was the past. The very distant past. They'd moved beyond it, damn it.

"Tess," he said, and she blinked at him.

There was an expression on his face she couldn't recognize, hurt and conflict and not a little fear. It was there for a moment, and then he seemed to realize she was staring because he glanced away. Her heart ached just looking at him.

Falling in love was so easy, why was living in love so hard?

"You know, the day you graduated from basic training I stood in the parking lot, in the rain, and just sort of stared at the barracks until one of those drill sergeants walked by. He asked me if the girl I was waiting for was worth it and I told him she was worth the world," Cordon said. "And that's when I promised myself, we would find a way to make it work."

Tessa looked at her coffee because watching him was too painful. She wanted to tell him she'd felt the same way, that she'd had every intention of fighting for their marriage, but she knew what was coming next.

"And then, not even a month later, I was given those divorce papers."

Maybe he was trying to hide the anger in his voice, but if he was, he couldn't hide it from her. She knew his tones and inflections too well for that.

"I am so sorry I hurt you," she said.

"Just tell me what happened. What made you leave?"

Her hackles rose, images of him slouched against their kitchen counter coming to mind. At first, that had been their fighting place, small enough for them to talk and large enough they had space to move if needed. He couldn't really need her to clarify this, they'd been over it hundreds of times.

"You know what made me leave."

"No, I don't. You said you needed more out of life, but I could have given you more. I would have given you anything you asked for." Cordon's brow furrowed and he leaned forward in his seat, shaking his head as if clueless.

"I asked for you!" Tessa snapped, earning a few wayward glances from other coffee shop customers. She lowered her voice; "Look, it doesn't really matter. What matters is I got shipped out to Hawaii and I knew there was no way you were leaving your family behind."

"First of all, it does matter. Of course, it matters. One day we were fine, the next you were enlisted and packing your bags," he said. "It happened so fast it could give a man whiplash."

"Fast?" It was her turn to shake her head. "I went months trying to get you to talk to me. It was only fast because you weren't paying attention. You were too busy with your family."

"They were in crisis."

"I know." *But there should have been some healthy boundaries.*

"If you'd just waited…"

She barked a laugh; she couldn't help it. He frowned at her, his face a combination of annoyance and frustrated patience.

"How long?" Tessa asked. "Tell me, how long was I supposed to wait to start my life with my husband?"

Cordon leaned back in his chair, looking like he'd been struck in the solar plexus. He opened his mouth to speak and closed it again, his gaze fixed on the frog-patterned napkin dispenser. Tessa closed her eyes and let go of a breath, all the anger and pain from those last few months settling around them. None of this mattered, not anymore. She'd moved on, hadn't she? Why were they doing this? All it did was hurt.

"Cordon, I know you feel responsible for your family. You couldn't leave them because they needed you. I understood that. Hell, it's one of the reasons I fell in love with you in the first place," she said. "So, I did the only thing that made sense. I let you go."

"Without even talking to me?"

He sounded so angry she kept her eyes closed, unable to look at him. "There was nothing more to say."

****

Cordon tried to get himself to relax. His shoulders and back were aching with the strain of sitting still, of not crushing his coffee and shouting at her the way he wanted to. He thought back over their brief marriage, trying to pinpoint the moment he'd lost her. But she hadn't said anything, not like that. Nothing that indicated she was ready to leave. There were arguments about how much time his family demanded of him, requests for him to stay home, and in retrospect he probably could have said no to the simpler tasks, but he didn't think any of that was divorce worthy.

Trying to get a handle on his temper, he moved on to what happened after she'd graduated Basic Training. "We'd been corresponding pretty regularly. I thought we were working things out, but then you sent divorce papers without even calling me."

She shrugged and stared at her coffee. "Two weeks after I sent the divorce papers I was on a transport to Afghanistan. I knew my duty station wouldn't be anywhere near home, and that you couldn't leave your family. It seemed better to cut things clean."

"Better for who?" he asked, not bothering to hide his bitterness. "Don't make this sound like some kind of sacrifice for my benefit. You have no idea what it was like watching you leave."

Tessa sat up in her chair and scowled at him. "And you have no idea what it was like to walk away. Do you know the day I realized I had to get out?"

"Get out? I didn't realize it was so horrible for you."

She went on as though she hadn't heard him. "I asked you to go one night without your phone. Just one night where you were really with me instead of running out the door for hours on end. Do you remember what you said?"

Cordon froze, that night coming back to him with acute clarity. He'd been at Sara's new apartment helping her unpack. Lyndon wasn't walking yet, and Sara had spent two weeks with boxes cluttering the place because school and work and Lyndon had overwhelmed her. His mother had been in a bad place, addicted to painkillers from her knee surgery, so she was no help. Which left Cordon to pick up the slack.

"You told me to stop being ridiculous, that I was overreacting because you were right there," Tessa said. "And twenty minutes later your sister called."

He stared at his coffee lid. Sara had needed diapers, he recalled that much. She couldn't go herself because Mom had taken off with the car seat and God only knew when she'd be back. Maybe if he'd explained what was going on, Tessa would have understood, but they'd already been fighting about this exact thing and he hadn't wanted to throw fuel on the fire.

He'd known when he left that something had changed. When he'd returned, Tessa was asleep, something she'd never done before. They always tucked in together, reading for a bit before turning off the lights. He should have roused her then, apologized for not listening, but he'd been so damn tired.

"Do you know the worst part?" Tessa said and gave a sad laugh. "It would have been all right if you'd just talked to me. If you'd involved me, let me help too, I wouldn't have felt so abandoned."

"I didn't want you involved," he said. "I didn't want you to see my mother like that. And Sara was such a mess, she wouldn't have appreciated having you there."

Tessa shook her head, looking so furious he leaned back in his chair. She turned, prepared to stand, but appeared to think better of it. Instead, she faced him and said; "It wasn't about them for me. It was about you. I was your wife and I wanted to help you."

"So, you left?"

Her eyes narrowed into angry slits. "I was as much use to you in the army as I was right beside you."

Too stunned to respond, he stared at her. Was that really what she thought? She'd been the best part of his day, the only thing he looked forward to. How could she not have known that? He opened his mouth to tell her just that, but she shook her head and stood.

"You know what, forget it. If you don't see how awful that was, there's no way for me to make you understand."

She scooted her chair into place and Cordon stayed where he was. He wanted to demand she stay and finish this but knew her well enough not to. Like always, when Tessa made up her mind there was no changing it. So, he sat there scowling, wondering why in God's name he'd ever gotten involved with the woman.

And why it still hurt to watch her walk away.

Chapter Seven

Cordon spent his week dodging calls from his mother. He enjoyed Lyndon in the afternoons and worked at Book Land in the evenings, which was busier than normal thanks to the gaming tournament. By Wednesday he swore he would soundproof those rooms so he wouldn't have to hear dice rolling and by Thursday he'd already taken measurements with the intent to visit the hardware store over the weekend.

On Friday afternoon Cordon parked outside Book Land. He felt good, mostly. He'd cut his time short at the forge so his uncle could get out of there early. Uncle Phil was head of the art department at the university and that came with some benefits, such as allowing his favorite students and family free use of the forge during off hours.

Cordon still wasn't sure if he would stick with blacksmithing, but for the time being it gave him something to hit.

As he walked into Book Land, he checked the corner armchair Tessa had used, but it was occupied by an elderly gentleman with a newspaper. That was probably best. He hadn't seen her since the coffee shop and, God willing, never would.

The nerve of that woman, saying he'd abandoned her.

Cordon strode to the front counter, glancing over the rest of the seating areas to make sure she hadn't just relocated, but there was no sign of her. In retrospect, there hadn't been any sign of her since that first night.

"She hasn't been in today." Sara said as she came out of the back storeroom.

He smirked at his sister. "I'm that obvious, huh?"

"It's a good thing too, I'm not sure I'd be good at kicking someone out. Don't forget I promised Lyndon someone would take him to the Corn Maze tonight."

"You're taking Lyndon to the Corn Maze?" He dropped his bag under the counter, choosing to avoid any further conversation about Tessa. "I thought you had a date tonight with Archimedes."

"No, you're taking him to the Corn Maze tonight. I'll be meeting you there." Sara grabbed her purse and keys from under the counter. "Which one was Archimedes, and should I be worried that you're calling him that?"

Cordon sighed. "I don't understand how you can own a bookstore and never read."

"I read, just not the ancient crap you like," she said. "Never mind, I'll look it up."

"Relax, it's mostly good." Cordon laughed and held up his hands in surrender. "I swear. I have no problems with this guy."

After a moment, Sara relaxed. A genuine smile lit up her face and Cordon chuckled a little more. It seemed that Greg the Mathematician wasn't doing so bad for himself if he could illicit that kind of smile.

"Well, all right." Her smile slipped. "Listen, about Tessa…"

Cordon groaned and lifted his gaze to the ceiling. "There is no 'about Tessa' anymore. We had our conversation and that's all there is."

"Yeah, you told me," Sara said, crossing her arms.

"She's still the scum of the earth for hurting you, but I understand why she did it. And there's more here than you know."

"You understand? Maybe you can explain it to me!"

"If Matt had left me alone for days on end without really talking to me about it, I would have been pissed too," Sara said.

"Matt did leave you alone for days on end, he was just out at the bar."

"You know what I mean. Just because you weren't at a bar doesn't mean Tessa would have felt less abandoned."

God, there was that word again; abandoned. He needed to get a dictionary out and paste the definition somewhere for everyone to see.

"I did not abandon my wife," Cordon said through his teeth. "I came home every night. I never even looked at another woman."

"Just because you were home, doesn't mean you were there."

Cordon glared at his sister. "Are you done?"

"No, there's more," Sara said, sounding exasperated. "One of Tessa's army buddies was in earlier. He was here for hours waiting to see if Tessa would show up, but she never did."

"Army friends?" Cordon leaned against the counter and crossed his arms. Tessa hadn't mentioned any friends coming to visit. Then again, they hadn't gotten around to that.

"Yeah, he seems pretty intent on catching up to her," Sara said. "Alyssa wheedled the story out of him while he was here waiting. It was awful. I can't even imagine what that must have been like for her."

Cordon frowned. Whoever this idiot was, he obviously didn't know Tessa. There wasn't a chance in hell Tessa would want her story repeated, whatever it was.

"What exactly happened?" Cordon asked.

"Let's just say, whatever Todd Pines told you was bullshit."

Wariness churned in his gut and he peered at Sara. He'd gone to see Todd several months ago because Tessa's letters had stopped coming to Joe. While he understood why she hadn't written to him after the divorce, she'd kept contact with their mentor. But Todd had given him a sneer and insisted Tessa was lounging on a beach in Hawaii with someone named Billie.

"What do you mean?" Cordon asked.

Sara flinched and glanced at the storefront, then lowered her voice. "From what I understand, she got hurt out there. Like, almost died. But I can't tell if this buddy of hers was exaggerating or not. You'd have to ask her."

"Now you want me to talk to her?" Cordon asked, trying for a joke and missing. The knot in his stomach tightened, images of Tessa injured bombarding him.

Why hadn't she said anything?

"Hey, I've said my piece." Sara lifted her hands in defense. "I'll bar her from the store as long as you're uncomfortable, but I think there's more going on here. And honestly, she was good for you. I might have had my head up my ass, but I remember how happy you were together."

Cordon sighed and rubbed his temple. "You don't need to bar her from the store, Sara."

"Good," she said and then gasped at her phone. "I'm late! Don't forget, Lyndon will be here at six. I'll meet you at the Corn Maze around eight. Mom's going to come in and close the shop."

Sara grinned and winked as she hurried to the front door. "Good luck figuring out a way to avoid her this time. She'll be bringing Lyndon in."

"Sara!"

But she was already gone, waving at him through the window.

"God damn it," Cordon muttered, which was perfect because Tyler and Alyssa walked into the store.

"Oh, you kiss your mother with that mouth?" Tyler asked, earning a giggle from Alyssa, who was looking slender and venomous in tight jeans and a halter top that showed a lot more skin than was appropriate for October.

Cordon glanced between the two as they sauntered their way to the front counter and mentally counted to ten. This day was going from bad to worse. The last thing he wanted to do was deal with these two. Which was par for the course because he never wanted to deal with them, but he couldn't see Brian anywhere so there was no helping it.

"I'm not sure he kisses anyone with that mouth anymore," Alyssa said. Her red-tinted lips twitched with a sly smile.

For the life of him, Cordon could not remember what he'd found attractive in this woman. Then she leaned forward, letting her low-cut top slip open a bit more and he caught sight of her red frilly bra and a pair of fantastic breasts. *I was shallow once.*

He eyed her face, not her décolletage, and she flushed a little.

"Something I can help you with?"

"Actually," Tyler said, "I hear old Cordy-Coo went

on a date Saturday."

Cordon stiffened and bent to shove his bag under the counter better while he counted to twenty and tried to breathe.

Why the hell did this matter to them? Alyssa broke up with him a year ago and Tyler... Well, there was no explaining Tyler Brannings to anyone with a testosterone level lower than 1500.

Dubbing them both bored assholes, he tried for a professional attitude. "Are you looking for something in particular today?"

"Oh, come on, Cordy. Give us the scoop. Are you and Tessa really back together?" Tyler asked, smacking him in the shoulder like they were friends or something.

Call me 'Cordy' one more time and I'm going to slam your face into this counter until you lose teeth. But that wouldn't be civilized. "It's really none of your business."

"Back together?" Alyssa asked.

"Oh, yeah. Tess and Cord were married right out of high school." Tyler said, turning to review the shop. "It was a huge scandal in town."

The doorbell dinged and Cordon stiffened, glancing over to make sure it wasn't Tessa. The last thing he needed was for her to see this spectacular display of idiocy. But it was a group of middle school kids with emo attire and dyed black hair. "Look, unless you need help finding a book, I have work to do," he said.

"Is she as pretty as me?" Alyssa asked, leaning on the counter so that her bra was on full display.

Cordon frowned at her. "You know, you're the only woman I've ever met who has the gall to refer to herself that way."

"I'm unconventional," Alyssa said, and her mouth curved into a wicked, red smile.

"No, you're just vain. Now I really do have work to do." He turned from the counter.

Alyssa gasped, "Hey!"

Tyler's sneer morphed into a scowl. "What the hell, man?"

He passed Brian on the way to the back storeroom, who rolled his eyes and headed for the counter. Cordon felt a little bad leaving Brian to handle that, but he was done being nice and professional. There was only so much abuse he could take, even for his sister. And at least he hadn't laid the man out. Sara would thank him for that much.

"Yeah, well, at least I'm going somewhere with my life!" Alyssa shouted. "I'm not just working at my sister's store until I die or something!"

Cordon shoved the storeroom door open and stalked inside. The little stockroom had several boxes on labeled shelves that ran from floor to ceiling, caging him in and adding to his growing temper. Alyssa wasn't "going somewhere" with her life, she was banking on Tyler sliding into his family's used car business. If the poor sap married her, she'd be sitting pretty in a house uptown, complaining about which hairdresser had mucked up her latest style.

And so what if he did work in a bookshop all his life? There were worse fates.

He frowned, glaring at the storeroom door, and tried to imagine Tessa working the counter. But no, Tessa had plans. Tessa always had plans. That was half the problem back in high school. She tackled life, not just daydreaming about what she wanted but going for it.

That's why she'd left. Because sitting on the wayside, watching him take care of everything, would have killed her.

Damn it, why hadn't he seen that at the time?

And where exactly did that leave him? He'd always floated along doing odd jobs that helped keep his family fed and kept him close for Sara and Lyndon. He'd never had big dreams for anything other than keeping food on the table and a warm house.

Tessa's voice echoed back to him. *You're allowed to have something for yourself, Cordon.*

She'd said that the night before she shipped out, frustrated to tears and unwilling to back down from her decision. Not that he'd imagined there was much she could do at that point; she'd already been sworn into the military. Still, their last fight hadn't been about her leaving so much as it was about his staying and he knew it.

You can't live your life just for them. You need something more.

But he'd had something more. He'd had her. And in his youth, he'd thought that would always be enough.

Clenching his fists, he refrained from kicking the nearest table.

Chapter Eight

Tessa wandered through the pumpkin patch with Marisol and wordlessly thanked her boots as they saved her from twisting an ankle. The ground was uneven, and several vines snaked across its surface, linking to some of the more stubborn pumpkins. The sun was still high in a sky full of thin clouds and on the distant horizon there was the promise of rain, but the wind seemed to be in their favor. The storm wouldn't reach them for a few hours at least, if at all.

"Even if you find the perfect pumpkin, where will you put it?" Tessa asked, thinking of their tiny dorm.

"You're such a nay-sayer, Tess." Marisol bent to inspect a large, bulbous pumpkin, tilting it this way and that until she sighed and shook her head. "It's got pimples near the butt."

"Pumpkins don't get pimples," Tessa said with a laugh.

Marisol eyed her for a moment, then bent to tilt the pumpkin again, turning it so that Tessa could get a better view. Near the base of the orange fruit were several small protrusions that looked quite a bit like acne. Tessa laughed again.

"I stand corrected, that pumpkin definitely has pimples," she said.

Marisol snickered and straightened. "I mean, it's

nearly perfect but…"

"Well, who likes perfect anyway? I say you take that one and call it your middle-school boy pumpkin. Use the pimples to your advantage."

Marisol turned the nearly perfect pumpkin and hummed. "Highlight its flaws and make a wholly unique jack-o-lantern experience," she said. "You think the judges would go for it?"

"If you do it right, I'm sure they would."

"Yeah but the pimples are too close to its base. If I'm going to do that, I should find a pumpkin that's covered in whatever that stuff is."

Being just as clueless about agriculture as Marisol, Tessa chuckled. "I'm sure that will be easier than hunting for the so-called perfect pumpkin. I think I saw at least a dozen acne-riddled souls over the last hour."

Tessa tried not to stress the fact that they'd been out there hunting for an hour and a half. She didn't mind hunting for pumpkins, but she did want to make it through the corn maze tonight and her knee was already starting to ache. Without thinking, she rubbed at it, remembering all too well how long it had taken the break to heal.

"I like it," Marisol announced with a decisive nod. "Let's find the most pimply pumpkin we can and call it good."

Grinning, Tessa began a new hunt, splitting off to cover more of the area. Keeping her eyes to the ground, she had to make a wide step over a pit in the dirt and knelt to inspect another pumpkin. This one had large warty-like protrusions that would be more suitable for a witch than a middle-school boy. She put it back and stood, feeling the creak in her knee again.

Ugh, she would have to live with that for the rest of

her life.

And then she thought of Cabby, who didn't have to live with anything anymore, and kicked herself for whining.

Or at least thinking about whining.

"There she is," said a familiar voice.

Tessa stiffened. Looking up, she found her father making a quick progression over the patch to reach her. Trailing close behind was David Jackson, sporting a week's worth of beard and two extra inches of hair.

She frowned at them, torn between annoyance—blasted Jackson still hunting her down, and outright fury—damn her father for not taking a hint. Her father was angry too, it was written in the tight lines of his mouth and pinch between his brows, and she clenched her fists.

"What are you doing here?"

"I called the dorms looking for you and someone said you were here," Jackson said.

"Someone," Tessa said, narrowing her eyes at him. She was ninety-percent certain it was illegal to give out information regarding a student's whereabouts to anyone other than the police. He must have wheedled the information out of Macy at the front desk, playing the wounded parent card or something.

That was classic Todd Pines for you, unwilling to take no for an answer.

"You missed your appointment again," Todd said and then nodded back at David, who was looking uncertain and lost. "And your friend has been looking for you. The least you could do is pick up your phone, Tess."

"I had my phone off all day for classes, thank you very much. And as for Jackson," Tessa met David's wide-eyed stare, "I'm not ready to talk to him. I figured those boundaries had been made clear."

"Maybe you would be ready if you'd stop missing your appointments," Todd said through his teeth.

She took a calming breath. "I don't need a shrink, Dad. I never did. I'm fine."

"You're not fine if you're not willing to talk to your friend…"

"Hey, maybe tonight's not the best…" David said but Todd cut him off.

"No, she can't keep dodging this. She has to face it."

"Last I checked," Tessa said, her voice rising, "I was the one who got blown up. Not you. So, I get to decide when and where I face it, not you. You're done making decisions for me, Dad. Period. I managed just fine on my own in the army without you hovering over my every action and I can damn well take care of myself now."

Todd rocked back on his heels, his face taking on an expression somewhere between stunned and furious. David had the grace to understand what he'd walked into because he raised his hands in what looked like surrender. Heat blossomed in her face and Tessa glanced away, trying to coach herself into breathing steadier.

God, had she just said that out loud? She wished suddenly that she could be in the maze, lost from sight and far away from her father. He wouldn't have been able to find her there.

"I don't make your decisions for you," Todd said. "If I did, you would never have been in the army to begin with."

Tessa took a deep breath and glanced at David, seeing not the civilian attire he wore but the desert uniform he'd been in when she'd last seen him. Her ears had been ringing from the explosion and there'd been a confusing mix of pain and numbness in her body, but she remembered the sound of his voice telling her that she would be all right, that he had her. That a medivac was inbound.

She blinked and the memory was gone, leaving her with a fuming father and clueless comrade. Shaking her head, she concentrated on the part of her life that needed a firm boundary.

"I don't need your help, Dad," she said.

"You think Cordon Morant can help you—"

"My relationship with Cordon is none of your business, Dad," Tessa said. "Like I said, you do not get to make my decisions for me."

"I knew it! Charles Holden said he saw the two of you having coffee the other day, but I said that was impossible. I said my daughter was too smart to make the same mistake twice."

Fury welled in her chest and she clenched her fists. She didn't know why her father hated Cordon, he'd taken a dislike to their relationship early on and never given Cordon a chance. And even though she knew the relationship was over, long since over, something about the vehemence in Todd's voice made her hackles rise.

"Look at him now, working in a bookstore of all places. Mark my words, Tessa, that man is going nowhere fast. And if you stay with him, you'll be stuck in a nothing job too."

"Well that's funny, Dad, because I'm pretty sure I already went places and I can't say I much enjoyed the way it ended." Tessa nodded once to David, turned on her heel, and walked away. Then she thought better of it and faced him again. "Cordon Morant was never a mistake.

Leaving him was."

Turning once more, she clenched her fists and stormed away. Todd shouted for her to come back, that they weren't finished with this, but she kept going, heading for the maze. She spotted Marisol several feet away, giving a doe-eyed look and hugging a pimple-infested pumpkin to her chest. Marisol took a step forward as though to meet her, but Tessa shook her head and she stopped. The last thing Tessa wanted was company.

The entrance to the corn maze had a large sign stretched over the top and she strode under it, letting rage fuel her as she took several corners at random. Memories hounded her, surfacing faster than she could stop them; the vehicle, the fire, and the feel of cooler air as she'd been pulled from the wreck.

****

Jackson's voice again, telling her over and over that it was all right, that he had her, that a medivac was inbound. Blood made a rusty smear over his uniform and it took several seconds before she realized it was her blood, that he was holding firm to a wound in her leg that she could neither see nor feel.

What coherency she'd had zeroed in on Cabby and she asked for him, choking on his name because something thick was in her throat and her tongue didn't want to cooperate. Someone else, she couldn't move to see who, told her not to worry about Cabby and that she needed to focus on breathing and staying awake. But there'd been a look on Jackson's face, a flicker in his eyes that Tessa managed to see, and she'd known her friend was dead.

"You've got to keep her talking."

That had to be Dresmond, their medic.

Tessa stopped walking and closed her eyes. "One," she said and took a deep breath.

Jackson gave her a wobbly smile, the only real smile she could remember him giving, and asked about home. Was there someone she was looking forward to seeing when she got back? But she hadn't wanted to think about home and Cordon and all the bridges she'd burned when she got sworn into the army.

She'd imagined Cordon would have moved on by then and that thought hurt more than she wanted to admit.

"Two," she said and exhaled slowly.

There'd been a pinch somewhere and a strange rushing sensation and then she was floating, bobbing weightless through the air because the ground seemed to have disappeared. Jackson asked her something else, but she couldn't hear it.

"Tessa?"

"Three…" she said and inhaled again.

The steady whomp-whomp of helicopter motors pounded in her ears and she resumed counting, breathing out slow.

****

"Tessa?"

That voice did not belong in her memory, that was Cordon. She became aware of warm fingers on her elbow. The helicopter faded, replaced by the rustle of corn stalks and shuffling feet nearby and she opened her eyes. Cordon was at her side, his brow pinched in concern. Under his beard his mouth tugged downward into a frown and she realized a heartbeat later that they were being watched.

A small boy holding a green plastic sword gazed at

them, wide-eyed and curious. He had his mother's sandy hair and pert nose, and a mouth that almost resembled Cordon's. Except Cordon had a scar near the left corner at the bottom lip from when he'd tripped and bitten through it as a child.

"Tess?" Cordon asked again. "Are you all right?"

She gazed at him for a long moment. *No, I'm not all right. I'm the furthest thing from all right.*

But the boy was still staring at them and she realized he must be Lyndon, so she cleared her throat and focused on the corn stalks behind Cordon's shoulder. "Yeah, I'm fine," she said.

Cordon eyed her. "Uh-huh," he said.

Meeting his gaze, she tried for a smile and prayed he would have the sense not to push. This wasn't the time or the place to discuss it, especially if her father was still anywhere in a two-mile radius.

Thinking of her father made her angry all over again and she straightened. Cordon's hand left her elbow and she nearly reached for him. But she imagined that would be hard to explain to Lyndon, so she shoved her hands into her pockets instead.

"Are you lost?" Lyndon asked.

Kid, you have no idea.

"As a matter of fact, I am," she said, smiling a little better this time. "I came barreling in here without a map, so I have no idea where I'm going."

Lyndon frowned at her, his little face scrunching up with so much animated confusion that she nearly laughed. He looked over at Cordon, who held their copy of the maze map, and then heaved a dramatic sigh before shaking his head.

"Well, we only have one," Lyndon said. "But we can

share. Right, Uncle Cord?"

"Absolutely," Cordon said, doing a terrible job at hiding his own amusement. "It wouldn't be right to leave her here on her own."

Lyndon nodded his approval and he began walking, swishing his sword back and forth with so much enthusiasm that Tessa grinned. Beside her, Cordon chuckled and then gestured forward. They fell into step together and trailed the boy, who continued to vanquish phantom enemies with every corner they turned. Tessa took another deep breath and the muscles in her back unclenched, relaxing as they continued to negotiate the maze.

Chapter Nine

Tessa kept pace with Cordon, listening to the steady crunch of fallen corn stalks underfoot and the pleasant chatter of other groups trying their luck with the maze. An earthy smell mixed with the cold air, stirring through raspy stalks and she imagined they must be nearing the back of the maze. They'd lost the smells of popcorn and corndogs ages ago and there was no more music to guide them.

"Are you doing all right?" Cordon asked.

It took her a minute to realize he was talking to her, not Lyndon.

"Yes. Just wishing I'd brought my heavier coat." She smiled even though she knew that wasn't what he meant. But she didn't want to talk about what he must have seen when he stumbled on her; pale, sweaty-faced, and dazed, half her mind in Afghanistan.

Even if she was ready to discuss it, Tessa didn't think there were enough words to describe how she felt. Or maybe she was just a coward and didn't want to try.

Cordon, bless him, didn't comment. He eyed her thin blue jacket and began shrugging off his own, shaking his head in wry amusement.

"And here I thought the military would have taught you to be better prepared," he said.

"Har, har," Tessa said, taking his jacket.

It was thick and warm, at least two sizes too big for her so she had to bunch the sleeves up, and it carried the scent of his beard balm around the collar. It had been a long time, but she remembered that he had two brands he preferred.

Sniffing the collar twice, she gazed at him; "Cigar Blend?"

Cordon grinned. "Bay Rum," he said. "Should I be embarrassed you remember that?"

Heat crawled up her neck and into her cheeks and she looked away, scanning the juncture Lyndon had led them to. Cordon chuckled, a low, soft sound that made her belly clench and stirred distant memories to the surface.

Their first kiss had been in a corn maze. They'd just sent off the last of the dojo kids and, because she'd talked about wanting to do the maze the entire night, Cordon had taken her by the hand and led her straight to the entrance.

There'd been a little bubble of happiness in her chest as they made their way through the first few corners, she could feel it even now. They got lost near the seventh trail marker. Cordon had to use a little flashlight to read the map, but Tessa had taken the light and stepped in close. She remembered the feel of his arm around her waist and the heat of his breath on her mouth and huddled into his coat more.

God help her, she was impossible.

"I'm going to have a beard just like Uncle Cordon when I grow up," Lyndon said.

Cordon grinned down at the boy. "I support this."

"Yeah? What does your mother think of that?" Tessa asked, grateful to be thinking of something else.

"She supports it, of course," Cordon said.

"She says it's my face and I can do what I want with

it," Lyndon said. "But that girls might not like it."

"Nonsense," Cordon said and sent her a boyish wink. "The right girl will love it."

Laughing, Tessa shook her head. "Or the right girl will just deal with it because she knows you love it."

Cordon stopped walking and slanted a knowing look at her. "You did not just 'deal' with my beard. I remember quite clearly that you said you enjoyed..."

Terrified of where that sentence was going, Tessa reached out and covered his mouth with her hand. The beard in question tickled her palm, and his eyes danced with mirth and for a heartbeat they were themselves again. No uniforms, no war, no divorce between them. He chuckled, his breath warm on her skin, and a tingling sensation shot down her spine. Doing her utmost to glare at him without smiling, she withdrew her hand.

Blushing, Tessa turned her attention to the map in Cordon's hand. It was difficult to meet his eyes and there was a familiar flutter in her belly, an unsettled and happy sensation that pooled through her. As disconnected as she felt from everything in life, the thread that bound her to Cordon seemed more vibrant and alive than ever.

Which was odd because things hadn't been happy at the coffee shop. In fact, she hadn't meant to see him ever again. She'd just forgotten how small the town was.

"You guys are weird," Lyndon said.

"You're one to talk, mister," Cordon said to his nephew as he steered them around the next corner. "I happen to know you're wearing one red sock and one blue sock."

Lyndon lifted his chin and, affecting a voice that no doubt mimicked his mother, said; "Life is too short for matching socks."

Tessa choked on a laugh.

"Says who?" Cordon asked.

"Says Mom." Lyndon nodded once, as though this put an end to the discussion.

"Not everyone would agree with that," Tessa said. She thought of her drill sergeant and all the stringently matched socks in her drawer.

"But it's Mom," Lyndon said.

"Yes, I know. There's no going against Mom," Cordon said. "But it's still weird that you're wearing two different socks."

Rolling his eyes, Lyndon said; "It's OK, Uncle Cordon. You're too old to understand."

Tessa laughed, unable to contain herself as Cordon gave his nephew an offended look. A heartbeat later, he scooped the boy up and over his shoulder. Lyndon squealed and squirmed, giggling as Cordon tickled his sides and demanded he take it back. Warmth spread through her at the familiar sight of Cordon at play.

She'd almost forgotten how good he was at the everyday stuff. Her mind was constantly at work and she often missed the here and now. Cordon was opposite, grounded and capable, resigned to whatever needed doing right in front of him.

History seemed to pool around them. She remembered the way he kept the kids laughing at the dojo and all the times he brought fried rice by the library just to make sure she ate something that day. There was laughter, lots of laughter, and late nights in the back of his truck gazing at the stars.

"I take it back! I take it back!" Lyndon wheezed out the words between gales of laughter.

"That's what I thought," Cordon said and lowered the

boy to his feet again. Giving her another grin, he winked and nodded to the next corner. "I think we want to go that way."

God, I've missed you. She shoved back all those memories as they resumed the trek through the maze.

His hand found the small of her back, guiding her around the next few corners while Lyndon began suggesting that the maze would be more fun with dinosaurs in it. Biting her lip, Tessa concentrated on the familiar presence of Cordon's palm through the jacket. Everything about Cordon was solid and sure, from his walk to the smirk he gave whenever he was teasing her, and for one aching minute the years apart gulfed wide between them.

Maybe Marisol was right, maybe she did need companionship.

But no, this was something more and she knew it. She didn't want just any companionship, she wanted Cordon. The way she'd always wanted Cordon, from the moment she'd laid eyes on him at the dojo to the day she'd come home on leave and spotted him at the grocery store. All his stubbornness and resilience, all his wit and humor, and even that part that put his family above his own needs, she wanted it all.

She thought of her father shouting that Cordon would never amount to anything, with that obstinate look on his face and frowned. Todd was wrong. Cordon Morant was every inch a man, and a good one at that.

And she'd lost him forever.

****

At first Cordon worried there would be some awkwardness between Lyndon and Tessa, but as they made their way through the corn maze his worries lessened. Lyndon insisted there were dinosaurs hiding in the maze and if they weren't careful, they would all be eaten and Tessa, being Tessa, slid into the game with ease.

They crept up to each corner, each taking a turn at the lead, and peered around, checking for any carnivorous creatures lying in wait. It was slow going but fun and by the time they reached the end of the maze they were all winded and laughing.

They took the last corner at a dead sprint, Lyndon shouting that a T-Rex was almost on them. Cordon hoisted Lyndon over his shoulder and carried him through the exit, concentrating on his feet because the ground was so uneven, he was afraid he might break an ankle or something. As they burst into the open pumpkin patch Lyndon slumped against Cordon's shoulder, all his limbs going limp at once.

"It…got me…" Lyndon said in his most theatrical voice.

Tessa laughed.

Lyndon straightened for a moment. "You do not laugh at a dying man. It's rude."

"Oops," Tessa said with another giggle. "I mean… Oh, no! Not Lyndon! But he was the bravest!"

Lyndon slumped again and gurgled.

"Well that's not a good sound," Cordon said. "He's really done for."

There was more gurgling, and Cordon glanced at Tessa, who was biting her lip in the effort not to laugh again. She looked better than when they'd stumbled over her in the maze, her face alight with mischief and smiles, and he nearly bent down to kiss her. But Lyndon still dangled over his shoulder and there'd been that haunted expression on her face earlier, and hadn't they said goodbye?

There was no opening that door again.

Lyndon's noises were growing more pronounced, hitting a pitch that sounded more like a strangled chicken than a dying boy.

"I think I know a cure," Tessa said, stepping closer.

Cordon half-turned, giving her better access to his nephew.

"…blaaahhhgggg…" Lyndon said.

Tessa tickled Lyndon's sides until he squealed and squirmed with laughter.

"I'm OK! I'm OK!" Lyndon shouted, laughing more.

Chuckling, Cordon lowered the boy to his feet. "Yep," he said, "He looks completely healed to me."

Lyndon pressed his hands to hips and huffed, "That wasn't fair. Tickles cannot heal a dinosaur bite."

"They can if they're the right tickles," Tessa said.

"I'm with her," Cordon said. "The right tickles can cure just about anything."

Lyndon rolled his eyes at them, clearly exasperated, and they walked toward the front gate. Tessa fell into step beside Cordon, tucking her hands in her pockets as she made that happy little hum he knew her for. Smiling, Cordon glanced at her, wondering if she was aware of the sound. Whether she was or not, she looked content walking with them and something deep in his belly clenched at the sight.

Alyssa's voice taunted him, telling him he wasn't going anywhere in his life, and he looked away from Tessa.

So what if he didn't have any grand plans for his future? So what if he wanted to work in a bookstore for the rest of his life? What was so bad about that?

Work wasn't what defined a man. Being there for the ones who need him, taking care of the people in his life, that's what made a man. He didn't need to aim for the Presidency or try to work for NASA to live a full life.

No, but I might need her.

"Thank you," Tessa said, drawing him back into the present.

"Hmm? For what?"

She gave a tentative smile; "Just thank you. I was a little lost back there."

"More than a little, I would say," Cordon said and kicked himself when she flinched. He thought of his sister insisting that something had happened overseas, and now that he thought about it, she did have a slight limp. "You forgot to mention you had an army buddy in town."

Tessa's scowl was instantaneous, evaporating any traces of jealousy he might have had. Not that he had any right to be jealous.

"I heard he was making a nuisance of himself," she said.

When they reached the front gate, dusk had given way to full night, only the thinnest trace of sunlight at the horizon, and the flood lights had been turned on throughout the lot. He spotted Marisol talking with Alyssa and Tyler and nearly cringed. But Marisol detached from their group, toting a sickly looking pumpkin as she made her way to Tessa's side.

"You all right?" Marisol asked, glancing over Cordon and Lyndon though it was obvious she was speaking to Tessa.

"Yeah, I'm fine," Tessa said.

"That was your dad, right?" Marisol asked.

Cordon straightened.

"Todd is here?" he asked, trying to keep the growl out of his voice.

He started scanning the crowd, but Tessa's voice stopped him.

"Not anymore, not if he knows what's good for him," she said, sounding grim.

"What happened?" Cordon asked.

Frowning, he spotted the silhouette of a man roughly Todd's height and build but Tessa's hand on his arm distracted him. He glanced at her, startled by the shy smile on her face and his heart thumped in his chest. He smiled back, leaning closer to her as she told him not to worry, that she'd made her feelings about Todd's behavior clear, but he scarcely heard a word she said. For a moment he was lost in her smile and her voice, his skin warm where she was still touching him, until Marisol piped in, her higher, girlish tone yanking him back into reality.

"If it wasn't for that other guy, I think he would have followed you into the maze," Marisol said.

Cordon frowned some more; "What other guy?"

At this Tessa's face went stony, the smile evaporating as she looked to the front gate.

"Sergeant Jackson," she said, her voice clipped. "The army buddy we were just discussing."

"Todd Pines and Sergeant Jackson," Marisol said. "That's quite a pair."

"Yeah, well, after tonight I think the sergeant will be staying away from my father," Tessa said. "He didn't seem happy to be caught in our family drama."

"And wow, all the drama," Marisol said, her smiling turning mischievous. "Cordon was never a mistake, huh?"

"What?" Cordon asked, glancing between the two women.

Tessa glowered at Marisol. "Don't worry about it, Cord."

Not sure how to interpret that sentence, he glanced at Lyndon, who was fidgeting on his feet and looking impatient to move on. Experience told him that he had all of two minutes before Lyndon started doing something obnoxious out of boredom, so he decided to leave the conversation for another time.

"What are you doing tomorrow night?" Cordon asked.

"Studying," Tessa said.

Marisol rolled her eyes. "She's always studying."

Tessa shook her head. "I'm paying for this education. I intend to get my money's worth."

"Trust me, you've already squeezed every penny out of this semester," Marisol said.

Lyndon started tugging on his hand and Cordon glanced at the boy.

"I see Mom," Lyndon said.

Scanning the crowd, he hunted for his sister's head, spotting her a second later. She walked hand-in-hand with a tall, sandy-haired man wearing wire-rimmed glasses. Greg the mathematician had apparently stayed with the specs but toned them down quite a bit.

Deciding it was safe to let the boy go, he nodded. Lyndon sprinted toward his mother, who spotted him only a few seconds before he reached her. "You know you can come back to Book Land to study," he said before he could stop himself.

It was crazy, more than crazy, but the words were out, and he couldn't take them back.

No, he didn't want to take them back. Maybe they'd had their issues in the past, but that didn't mean they couldn't be friends. And after what he'd seen tonight, he knew that Tessa needed a friend. She'd looked so lost in the maze, her face pale and glistening with sweat, and it had taken three times calling her name before she'd heard him.

That wasn't like her.

Tessa blinked at him. "I was afraid you wouldn't like it."

"But I would," Cordon said. "Like it, I mean."

"And your sister?" Tessa asked, glancing over at where Lyndon and Sara were chatting.

"She's over it," Cordon said, earning a grin from Marisol and a suspicious squint from Tessa. Raising his hands in defense; "I didn't tell her anything. Apparently, that army buddy of yours was regaling them with tales of your exploits and she overheard."

Tessa exhaled sharply. "Of course."

"What sort of exploits?" Marisol asked. "I haven't heard any exploits…"

"Forget about it," Tessa said. "God, why can't that man take a hint?"

Cordon frowned and eyed her. "He needs a louder message? I can make that happen."

"No." Tessa sighed. "He's just trying to be nice. I'm being difficult. I'll fix it."

"You're sure?" Cordon asked.

She smiled at him and nodded. "I promise, he's not a problem. But I think your family wants you now."

He glanced back at where Sara and Greg were listening to Lyndon. Sara's gaze kept flicking their way and he knew that Tessa was right.

"It looks like it," he said and sighed.

"We need to get back to the barracks anyway."

"Dorms," Marisol corrected.

Tessa flinched. "Right. Dorms."

Chuckling, Cordon shook his head at her. "You'll acclimate to civilian life soon, don't worry."

When she scrunched her nose at him, he grinned and headed off to deal with Sara and her date. By the time he reached Lyndon's side, Tessa and Marisol had disappeared into the parking lot. A part of him wanted to follow, to make sure they made it back to the car safely, but with the eye his sister was giving him he knew he wouldn't be able to, so he turned his attention to interrogating Greg the mathematician.

Chapter Ten

By the time Tessa arrived at Book Land it was nearing eight, almost closing time, and she took a deep breath as she locked her bike up. The bite of oncoming winter was in the air, breezing through her jacket and she remembered half the reason for her visit tonight. She shrugged her backpack off then unzipped it and pulled out Cordon's coat. It was old and thick and barely fit in her pack, but she couldn't justify wearing it on the ride over. The weather wasn't cold enough, not yet, and the sight of her in it would illicit more questions than she had time to answer.

Or at least, it would illicit more questions from Marisol, who had done nothing but question Tessa since the moment they'd left the corn maze the night before. Questions about what prompted her to join the military and what happened between her and Cordon before she'd left, and as good as Tessa was at evading the girl most of the time, it seemed that Marisol was becoming more determined.

Satisfied her bike was safe, Tessa made her way to the door, pausing outside the window. Cordon stocked the Halloween display. His back was to her, the happy Book Land emblem stretched across the pale blue of his shirt as he shifted books around the shelf. From this distance his beard looked dark, with only a rim of red, but up close she knew how many different shades were there. Auburn and blonde and brown, just like his hair; a fun mix of light and dark all tangled together.

The scent of his balm caught her again, carrying the memory of his kiss with it. Hot nights pressed together in the cab of his truck—always in that truck, as if they'd never kissed outside of it—with the soft brush of his beard against her face and the sharp contrast of his teeth on her lower lip. For a second, she couldn't breathe, transported to her father's driveway where they'd lingered for twenty minutes, neither of them wanting to end the night.

God, what she wouldn't give to go back there. Maybe things hadn't been perfect, but they'd been happy.

Looking down at the coat in her hands, she flexed her fingers into the soft leather. It bent and curved under her palms and she took a breath. It wasn't worth dwelling over. She'd made her choices and now she had to live with them. Cordon was a good man, he deserved better than her latching onto him again. She was a mess, and if she let herself, she would grab onto him and drag him down into all the awfulness that haunted her.

With another deep breath, Tessa opened the door and went inside. Cordon glanced back at her, his smile strained, or maybe just tired, she couldn't quite read him like she used to. She checked the rest of the store as she made her way toward the display shelf and got the sense that they were alone, which was good because she didn't want an audience tonight.

"It's a little late to start studying, isn't it?" he asked, straightening as she approached.

"I'm sorry to come so late. My roommate does not understand Shakespeare, so I just spent three hours doing a line by line of *Henry V*."

"'That's a decent play at least," he said, but his smile did not reach his eyes. "Stiffen the sinews, summon up the blood, disguise fair nature with hard-favored rage."

"Somehow it does not surprise me that you can quote a play about war as opposed to something like *The Taming of the Shrew*," she said, trying for a joke.

"The *Shrew* is all right." He shrugged and turned back to stocking. "Not as overdone as *Romeo and Juliet*."

"On that point I would have to agree with you. I think every high school requires it these days."

His shoulders bunched, making a rigid line under his shirt, and she could sense that something was wrong. She just wasn't sure if that something had anything to do with her. Maybe he regretted inviting her back. Maybe he hadn't meant to extend the olive branch and let her into his life again. Kicking herself for being vain—his whole life did not revolve around her, damn it—she bit her lower lip and tried to think of something to say.

Maybe she should head back to the dorms, wait it out. They could try this again tomorrow.

Or never. Never was good, too.

"Are you all right?' She asked at last. "You seem…" *Distant. Upset. Angry.* "…different."

He faced her, leaning one shoulder against the shelf and crossing his arms. He didn't look inviting, but he didn't look outright angry either. In fact, he looked more uncertain and vulnerable than anything else and she flinched.

"I'm fine. I just had some trouble customers earlier."

"Oh, all right," Tessa said, not fully believing him. How much trouble could a customer be in a bookstore, after all? "I can go if you want."

"God, no. Please." He touched her elbow. "Trust me, you're the highlight of my day."

She met his gaze, enjoying the strength of his fingers through her jacket. "How can I make it better?"

His gaze dropped to her mouth and her heart kicked a little faster, breathing a little unsteadily for the long moment it took him to reply.

"You already are," he murmured. "Promise."

"Yeah?" she whispered, moving in closer, so much closer his body heat warmed her skin.

His hand left her elbow, circling her waist instead, and pulling her in until she was pressed against him. *Oh, god yes.*

His breath was warm on her cheek, his face tilted down just so, not quite committed to the kiss and for an aching moment she wondered what he was waiting for. But there was four years between them, and she'd come here to put boundaries up, not tear them down. Still, she gazed at his mouth, at the thin shape of it under his beard and nearly forgot to breathe.

His other hand cupped her face, long fingers splaying out into her hair as his thumb tilted her chin up and he leaned in. His lips were gentle on hers, a light brushing across her mouth and there was the soft tickle of his beard on her face.

She found his sides, curling her fingers into his shirt to steady herself, to keep him there as long as she could because the kiss was so soft, so tender she never wanted it to end. It washed through her, a sweet, soothing caress that promised the utmost care and Tessa fell into it, letting him take her weight as she molded into his body.

She made a sound then, a little hiccup of a gasp and the kiss changed, all that care and gentleness morphing into something deeper as his tongue swept over hers. Heat spread through her, welling up from someplace deep inside and she clutched at his shirt, wanting more and groaning with it. His teeth scraped over her lower lip, tugging lightly, and something deep in her belly tightened. She shivered, dizzy with the taste of him.

His fingers curled into her hair, angling her for a still deeper, more demanding exploration of her mouth and she clung to him, lost in a flood of heat and want until her back hit the bookshelf.

Oh, God.

That was good too; the smell of new books mingling with his rum scented beard balm and the hard press of the shelf unyielding at her back.

The hand on her lower back shifted to her hip. His thumb grazed inside the waist of her pants and she breathed out a soft; "Oh," against his mouth that was mingled pleasure and desire.

He hummed back, a low, questioning sound that washed her body in heat. Some distant part of her brain said this was crazy. This was Cordon and she'd broken this relationship to hell and back, it was ludicrous that they should rebuild it.

But his mouth brushed hers again, light and tender, and all her thoughts scattered. She kissed him back. His hands anchored her, one at her nape, the other sliding under her shirt and up her side, making her whimper and curve into him. His breath caught on a groan and she slid her arms around the broad strength of him as his mouth trailed from her lips to her neck.

He dallied there, his beard tickling against sensitive skin before the heat of his breath and the light scrape of his teeth could take it.

"Oh, *God*," she murmured, and he chuckled against her throat, sending her into another delightful spasm of pleasure.

"Right here, hmm?" he whispered and nipped her again.

She lost her voice. His hand left her nape, moving down to cup her butt and boost her onto the shelf. Silently praising the sturdy craftsmanship of the bookshelf, she wrapped her legs around his waist, drawing him closer still as he kissed her again. She could feel the tension in his arms as he held her, raking hot, demanding kisses over her mouth, and Tessa lost herself there, letting the world melt away.

****

Some part of Cordon told him they should stop, but her teeth caught on his lower lip, denting soft flesh enough that his stomach clenched. It was all he could do not to unsnap her jeans and fall to his knees. But somehow through the fog of want and need and full-blown lust he remembered the door was unlocked and the window wide open. He didn't think he'd heard any customers come in, which was good because they were two seconds away from indecent exposure and God help him if his sister heard of this.

"I've wanted to do this for ages," Tessa said.

"Is that so?" he murmured, trying to coach himself into slowing down.

But her mouth teased his and her fingers were digging into his back. Her legs were hooked around him and, lower, he could feel the warmth of her flush against his lap, soft and yielding where he'd gone hard. For a blind second he imagined what would happen if they were rid of these damn clothes.

God, he'd missed her.

Some distant part of him was reminded that she'd left, that she would probably leave again, but for the moment he didn't care. She was here now, that would have to be enough.

"Yes," she said, running her hands down his back.

He thought about carrying her to the storeroom where there was a lock. And no windows. He could make the trip without bumping into anything on the way.

"God, you kiss well."

"You're not so bad yourself," he said, moving to do it again.

She smiled against his mouth, letting out a soft, sultry moan that undid all his better intentions. He lifted her from the bookshelf and turned toward the back storeroom, prepared to make the trip when there was a trilling beep followed by the low buzz of her cell phone. He froze, still holding her aloft, and gazed into her glossy hazel eyes.

She didn't seem to hear the phone yet, even though it rang again, which was fine because all he could think was how to keep that look on her face; dazed, pleased, unguarded, everything she'd been with him before and more.

But then her expression cleared, and she shook her head, finally realizing what was happening. He carefully put her down, holding her elbow while she fished in her pocket with one hand. She pulled out the still jingling phone and frowned at the screen.

Please don't be important.

"It's Marisol," she said with a resigned sigh and answered it.

It still might not be important. Her lips were swollen from his kisses and a blush seeped into her cheeks. God, she was pretty. He wanted to lay her out on the back table and nibble his way down her throat, spread her thighs with his hands and explore all those soft places with his tongue while she squirmed and whimpered in pleasure.

He imagined it all quite clearly and became annoyed with Marisol. What could the girl possibly need at this hour?

"Marisol, I can't understand you when you screech like that," Tessa said and mouthed an apology to him. "Well, I mean, are you sure Lundy is even worth…"

Cordon frowned. Who the hell was Lundy?

"All right. I'm on my way. We'll get it figured out. Just stop panicking. Panicking never helps," Tessa said and hung up. Sighing, she met his gaze, her cheeks deepening into a brighter red. "I really have no idea what is going on but apparently Marisol is in crisis and needs me."

"Right now?" he asked, visions of the storeroom diminishing, which was depressing but probably for the best.

As hot as it would be to have sex in the storeroom with Tessa—and good God, it would be so damn hot—he was afraid his sister might have a security camera back there. It would be supremely awkward explaining that to Sara tomorrow.

"Yeah, right now," Tessa said and glanced away from him.

He checked the clock over the counter. 8:15.

"Well, we're past closing time. If you hang on a moment, I can drive you back."

Tessa smiled, her whole face lighting up. "You don't mind?" Grinning, he leaned forward and kissed her cheek before whispering in her ear. "I'm hoping to get another kiss like that before the night is out."

She bit her lower lip. "And here I thought you only liked me for my mind."

"Oh, I adore you for your mind." He winked at her as he shut the cash register down. "But I swear to God, your mouth is going to be the death of me."

She laughed, another bright, happy sound that filled the room and Cordon chuckled with her as he counted out the till. She looked like he remembered her, vibrant and full of life, the old Tessa back in the flesh instead of the ghost that had haunted the bookstore for so long.

His phone rang. "Hello?"

"Cordon," his mother's voice practically shouted into his ear. "Tell me you haven't been seeing Tessa again."

He glanced over at where Tessa reviewed titles on a shelf, and he prayed she hadn't heard. "Nice to hear from you too," he said, trying to keep a light tone.

"Cordon Morant, I am not kidding. That woman tore you to pieces last time and I will not watch her do it again."

"Actually, Mom, you and Sara tore me to pieces last time," he said, counting through pennies. "So, I would suggest you back off and give me some space."

"A wife is supposed to stay with her husband during the bad times," his mother said, still shouting. "She couldn't do that for you. She doesn't deserve an ounce of your pity."

He lost count on the dimes and had to start over. Fighting for a neutral tone he said; "Mom, I understand your concern, but there are more things involved here than you know."

"I don't need to know anything more. I don't care if she was blown up over there, as far as I'm concerned, she had it coming."

Blown up?

Sara said she'd been hurt, but blown up?

"Are you listening to me?" His mother was still talking, and he suppressed a groan. "There's danger coming, Cord. Real danger. She's going to break your heart."

"Mom, what have I told you about reading my cards?" He finished with the register and stuffed the profits of the night into the deposit bag. "I swear, I'm going to burn those things if you don't knock it off."

"Stop evading. Now I am telling you to stop seeing Tessa right now."

"Or what, Mom? You'll disinherit me from your nonexistent will? I'm telling you for the final time, this is none of your business."

"Oh, my God, it's going to happen all over again," his mother said. "You'll elope because God forbid you invite your own mother to your wedding. And then she'll leave you when things get rough and you'll be left picking up the pieces."

He closed his eyes and counted to five. Well, he'd known it was going to be a battle inviting Tessa back into his life.

When he opened his eyes, Tessa had found a book and was seated in the chair by the window. She had her legs tucked under her and was already several pages in. He smiled; his mother's voice barely audible.

Maybe it was destined to fail again, but he was willing to risk that. He hadn't realized it before, not even last night in the maze, but he knew it now.

"Goodnight, Mom," he said and hung up the phone.

Chapter Eleven

Tessa helped Cordon load her bike in his trunk, anchoring it down with bungee cords as best they could. She knew she could ride back but was willing to undergo just about anything to keep near him at this point. Her body was still tingling where his hands had blazed a competent, familiar trail and for one aching second, she'd been home again. Home in their apartment, experimenting with recipes because Cordon believed good food could be learned and shouldn't cost half a paycheck to eat. Home at the dojo, with Joe reminding them that they had a class to teach and could flirt later.

Home, like she'd never left.

Cordon opened the passenger door for her, and she moved to get in, pausing as he leaned down to kiss her once, soft and lingering on the mouth. She hesitated there, poised with one foot in the car. The chill of night air blanketed the street but where his mouth held hers was warmth and she didn't want to move.

"Never stop doing that," she murmured against his mouth and he chuckled low in his throat, a purely sensual sound that brought all the heat back to her in a wave.

God, she wanted him.

All the good intentions to distance herself from him, to try fixing what had been broken overseas had fled with that first taste of his mouth. They could talk later, after she calmed Marisol down.

He gave a lazy, boyish grin and she couldn't help smiling back because he looked so happy. Then she slipped into the passenger seat and let him close the door, watching as he came around to the driver's side.

She wasn't that broken. The event had been bad, and Cabby still haunted her sometimes, but she could learn to live with that. And really, after all the bad, didn't she deserve a little good?

If there was any chance at all to repair this relationship, she had to take it.

"For the record," Cordon said as he buckled his seatbelt, "I sort of hate Marisol today."

Tessa laughed. "I can't decide if I hate her or love her. I'm pretty sure I was ready to do criminal things back there."

His hands tightened on the steering wheel; "I can turn the car around…"

"No, no," she said. *Yes, please*. But better sense won out and she tried for honesty. "As much as I want to, I think my father would disown me if he saw how far we went back there."

Thankfully, he took the change of subject. "Given Todd's track record, I'd say he would disown you just for talking to me."

She wrinkled her nose and crossed her arms. "I never understood his attitude toward you."

"Daddies and their daughters," Cordon said. "I'm sure he just meant to protect you or something. But it would have been nice if he hadn't rubbed things in my face."

Something in the tone of his voice worried her and she squinted over at him. "What do you mean?"

"Nothing, forget I said anything."

His fingers were tight on the wheel and his jaw flexed the way it always did when he was repressing something.

"Cordon, when did you talk to my dad?"

After several seconds, Cordon sighed, releasing his grip on the wheel. "After you stopped writing Joe. I understood why you didn't write to me, but you were consistent with Joe so when the letters stopped coming, I got concerned."

Tessa leaned back in her seat and rubbed her forehead. She should have known Joe would keep Cordon in the loop. Part of her had even hoped he would. A wave of guilt hit. She needed to visit Joe soon.

"What did my father say?"

There was a tic in his jaw before he answered; "He said you were on a beach in Hawaii with someone named Billy."

Her stomach clenched and she closed her eyes.

Good old Todd Pines did it again. Would the man ever learn?

"It's all right," Cordon said. "I understand we're divorced and it's none of my business."

"Billie was my nurse," Tessa said, opening her eyes. Cordon glanced away from the road long enough to meet her gaze. "Our vehicle caught an IED on the side of the road. Cabby saw it first and shouted a warning, but it was too late."

Her throat closed on the words. Because she couldn't bear to look at him, she faced the window. Streets and houses passed by, tall Victorians and smaller, modern homes that looked nothing like Afghanistan huts. That was enough to keep her grounded and she was able to find the words to continue.

"Murphy took the worst of it. The explosion tore right through her and the lieutenant. But Cabby flung himself over me. He just…" Tessa shifted in the seat and clenched her jaw so tight her teeth hurt. "He just slid over and covered me. I got shrapnel in three places on my left leg and a piece of the vehicle tried to tear my right arm off, but the brunt of the explosion hit Cabby."

The burns were the worst, but she imagined saying that out loud wouldn't help anyone. Especially Cordon, who had gone still and quiet in the driver's seat.

"I was unconscious for a long time. When I woke up, I was in Hawaii. The doctors said I was lucky. Shrapnel had just missed the major arteries in my leg, or I would have died before the medivac could reach me."

For a heartbeat she thought she could hear a helicopter and had to take several seconds to breathe. The words were so simple they sounded absurd. They couldn't convey the terror of those moments, couldn't show him how long it had taken before she could walk again. How could they? Some things could only be lived through.

"Billie was the nurse who kept hounding me to write home. She said people deserved to know I was still alive, even if I didn't feel like myself anymore. I gave her dad's address and name and told her she could do it herself because I wasn't interested."

"God, Tessa," Cordon said.

He sounded pained, like someone had reached into his guts and torn the words out, and she took a deep breath. "I am so sorry he lied to you," she said.

"You're not the one who needs to apologize."

There was a clipped note to Cordon's voice, and she suspected any apology her father tried to give would fall on deaf ears. And really, Todd deserved it at this point. What kind of a man could do that?

She didn't know what Billie had written, but she was for damn sure it wasn't about lounging on a beach.

"He either apologizes or gets a broken nose," Tessa said. "Because that was lower than low."

"Just curious but do I get to break his nose or were you planning on doing the honors? He is your dad, so I thought you might want to."

"I think it's safer if I do it," Tessa said, surprised into a laugh. "He's less likely to have me arrested."

"I don't mind doing time for assault."

Tessa eyed him, sensing that the conversation had turned but uncertain which way. "The sad thing is, I can't tell if you're joking or not."

He grinned at her, a dimple forming at the corner of his mouth and she laughed again, settling more into the seat. Oddly enough, it was comforting that he wasn't totally joking.

Outside the road curved in his headlights, with spindly trees rising up against a shadowy background. It was so different from Hawaii's tall, sometimes lonely palm trees that for a moment she felt homesick for Oahu. She'd spent years going back and forth between the island and various deployments, but enough of her time had been spent on North Shore or Sunset Beach, or the little shaved ice shack in Kawela Bay, that it had become home. But Massachusetts was home too.

She seemed to belong to both and neither at the same time. There'd been a moment when she debated staying in Oahu and going to school there, but with her unit still at war and Cabby's voice urging her to repair the relationships she'd left behind—he was always doing that—Tessa had felt it wiser to move back to the mainland.

And Cabby had been right. She wouldn't be whole again until the threads of her past were confronted. She'd felt that tonight as Cordon kissed her, the subtle righting of her soul that seemed to deepen and spread with every laugh they shared. There was something about Cordon Morant that made her want to be the best version of herself.

"You're far away from me right now," Cordon said.

She looked at him, seeing the solid profile of his body, the blunt curve of his nose, and the bushy shadow of his beard all set against the streetlights. Who he'd been and who he was now meshed in her vision, Cordon the man and Cordon the youth coming together for one heartbeat.

My God, he hasn't changed.

The physical had altered a bit, time settling into his bones and new scars peppering his features, but who he was remained the same. He was still the strong provider, the concrete foundation family and friends could build on, and for an aching moment she wanted to take him by the beard and kiss him until he was breathless.

Smiling, she thought about telling him that but didn't. Instead, she fell back on a habit she'd taken to in high school and said; "I'm writing about you in my head."

"Oh? Please tell me we're naked in this," he said as he pulled the car into the university lot.

"Well, now we are," she said, leaning forward to kiss his mouth just as he put the car into park.

He kissed her back, slow and gentle and Tessa slid closer, her hip bumping into the gear shift but neither of them seemed to care. His fingers brushed against her jaw, drifting over the soft places of her neck as he pulled her closer until she was pressed into his side. Balanced on the arm rest, she inhaled his rum scent, and enjoyed the soft touch of his beard on her chin and lips.

Her cell phone rang, and they broke apart, panting. Tessa fished it from her pocket again, swearing when she saw it was Marisol, but she recognized that they were in the parking lot now so at least she could reassure the girl that they were on the way.

"We're here," she said as she answered the phone. "And I'm bringing Cordon up so make sure you're decent."

"Oh, good. He can help." Marisol said.

Tessa glanced at Cordon, who quirked an eyebrow at her in amusement. "I'm sure he'd love to help."

The amusement vanished quickly from his face, replaced by clear wariness and Tessa sent him a bratty grin. "He likes to be the hero."

"OK. Quit flirting with him and come up. I'm decent," Marisol said and hung up.

"I like to be the hero?" Cordon feigned offended. "Have you met me? I'm clearly the antagonist."

"The anti-hero," Tessa suggested with a wink and got out of the car.

****

Cordon followed Tessa through the dorms feeling completely out of place and outnumbered. The clean, narrow hallway reminded him of a hotel except that many of the doors were open and girls kept drifting between them. One or two eyed him like an intruder and he made certain to keep close on Tessa's heels. Someone liked country music because a twangy woman's voice crooned through one of the open doorways. Several feet later and a heavy bass drowned out the country song.

It was no wonder Tessa frequented Book Land. How did anyone get any work done here?

Tessa stopped in front of a door that was almost precisely in the middle of the hallway and unlocked it. She cast him an apologetic smile and pushed the door open, admitting them into a tiny room cramped with two beds, two small desks, and two hutch-like closets flush against the walls. Marisol's petite, bird-like frame sat cross-legged on the bed, surrounded by odd electrical equipment and a yellow legal pad.

"Shut the door," Marisol said.

Against his better judgment, Cordon reached back and closed it, feeling the solid click as they were sealed inside. He leaned against the door and crossed his arms, asking himself for the dozenth time what the hell he was doing here. But then Tessa moved to stand beside him, looking more frail and vulnerable than she had in the corn maze.

No doubt telling the story of the IED had dredged memories up she was fighting hard to forget.

Cordon did his best not to scowl and concentrated on the room because if he didn't, he might hightail it to Todd Pines' house. The man was in desperate need of a broken nose and some cracked teeth.

"All right," Tessa said. "Why are we here?"

"Three of my investigators cancelled and nobody has any recording equipment of any kind and all I have is this stuff…" Marisol swept a hand over the expanse of her bed, her voice rising as the list grew, "Which I have no idea how to use and Lundy needs at least four people to do his study. And if I don't get this done, he will never notice me, which means he'll never ask me out and we'll never move in together with a dog and two cats and have a mountain lake view."

Cordon stared at Marisol. *What drugs was this girl on?*

He glanced at Tessa, who seemed to think this was normal behavior because she didn't look overly concerned by the outburst.

"Why isn't Lundy helping you?" Tessa asked.

"Lundy is setting up the test parameters or something like that. It's all very technical. He's super smart," Marisol said, turning defensive.

Lundy was probably getting high somewhere and didn't give a damn about any of this. Which made Cordon feel bad for Marisol.

It sounded like Lundy needed a good punch in the mouth. After Todd.

"Uh-huh," Tessa said, her face clearly readable.

She thought Lundy needed a punch in the mouth too. But she didn't say that, much to his disappointment. Instead she asked, "So what do you need?"

Marisol perked up, eyes wide and pleading. "I need you both to commit to bring investigators that night and I need three camcorders. I already have three on hand, but Lundy and I will both need one. That leaves only one for actual investigators. There are four of you. I need at least one extra laptop and several backup batteries for everything. And a dozen flashlights."

Cordon frowned, not quite sure where this was going.

"Investigators?" he murmured to Tessa.

"Paranormal investigators," Tessa whispered back. "It's some weird experiment she's trying to set up at the Ashwood place."

"I thought that was a joke," he said, remembering the

day he'd met Marisol outside. She'd mentioned this, hadn't she?

"No, it isn't a joke," Marisol said.

His mind conjured images of the old, abandoned institute with its dilapidated buildings sprawled over several acres of land. The place was falling apart, far from safe and, according to local legend, haunted. Not that Cordon put any stock in ghost stories, but he'd stayed clear of the place anyway, preferring not to contract tetanus or get his leg stuck in the crumbling floors. Some kid had done that a few years back and there'd been a debate about tearing the place down, but nothing had ever come of it.

He imagined Tessa out there in the dark, picking her way through dirty hallways and rooms and his first instinct was to tell her no, to strongly insist that she not take part in any of this. But he knew her well enough to know that was a bad idea. It wouldn't matter that he was thinking of her safety, it would look controlling and a little weird of him.

"All right," Tessa said again. "Three camcorders. A dozen flashlights. One laptop and as many batteries as we can get. I'll promise to go but you have to promise to keep looking for more people, so I can man the computers or something. I'll do some investigating if I absolutely have to but I'd rather not."

Marisol nodded once. "Done!" she said.

Then her gaze shifted to Cordon and he took a deep breath of his own, resigning himself to the situation even before she asked.

"And you?"

Cordon nodded slowly, hating the idea but recognizing they were trapped. "I'll be right next to

Tessa, wherever she ends up."

And please, God, let us man the computers.

Chapter Twelve

Cordon spent the next week-and-a-half in high spirits. Tessa remained in constant contact, texting him reactions to her classes or calling him over her lunches, and every night they met at Book Land to review their growing list of supplies. As always, when Tessa Pines committed to something, she gave it her best effort, even if she didn't happen to believe in it.

In addition to flashlights and camcorders she added voice recorders for electronic voice phenomenon, thermometers for cold spots, a couple of night vision video optics—a loan from someone on base, she'd said, and two electromagnetic field readers that Cordon recognized from the reality shows he'd seen. All of which Tessa had researched thoroughly even though they'd both expressed their unwillingness to believe the Ashwood was haunted. Or to believe in hauntings in general, for that matter.

Given the cost of several items, and that most of it was on loan from various friends and family, they'd agreed to keep it all stored at Cordon's apartment. He lived alone so there was no fear of anyone pilfering through it and gave him an excuse to have Tessa there; which was the only good thing to come of the whole situation.

He was back to dodging calls from his mother, which

caused some flack at work with Sara, but thus far he'd managed to keep his family at bay. Sara at least seemed to understand his need to work through the Tessa issue on his own, even if she didn't like that he was avoiding Mom. And really, he needed to face his mother at some point, he just wanted to know where things were headed with Tessa before he did.

Peering at the glowing red tip of the spike he was forming, he pulled it from the forge and turned to the anvil. Cordon laid it flat and raised his hammer, striking firm and even, the sparks flying as the metal connected again and again. He worked, pushing all thoughts of the upcoming weekend and Tessa aside to concentrate on the shape of steel.

Sweat stuck his shirt to his back and his arms began to strain from exertion, but he kept at it, flattening the spike down to a thin length of metal. Still being new to blacksmithing, he kept his work contained to knives, trying to get the right balance.

"It's coming along," Uncle Phil said.

Cordon glanced up from the anvil.

There was something about his scrawny, wild-haired uncle that made him look permanently startled and not for the first time Cordon wondered how they could be related. He was thin, but not so thin as to be considered sickly, and his bristly, graying hair was in a constant state of disorder, sticking out in all directions. He exuded a sort of nervous energy, like he wasn't quite sure what he should be doing in any given moment.

It was contagious, too. Just standing with the man for a few minutes and Cordon worried he'd forgotten something somewhere.

"Sort of," Cordon said and grinned, then turned the

blade toward his water bucket.

Steam hissed up as the hot metal connected with water, adding to the sweltering heat of the forge. Steam filled his lungs, a muggy, unpleasant pressure that made him want to cough. The whole place was full of gas and heated metal and soot, but for that moment all he could smell was hot moisture.

"No, really. You're getting the shape of things down. I imagine you'll have a real product here soon." Phil nodded at the submerged metal.

"Well, I hope so anyway," Cordon said. "Were you needing me out of here? I can clear my stuff in a second."

"No, no. You're fine," Phil said, looking suspiciously uncomfortable.

He couldn't be sure if that was Phil's normal anxious energy coming out or if there was something else the man needed. When Phil continued to watch Cordon work, his bushy eyebrows pinched into a furrow, Cordon suspected there was more going on.

"What is it?"

Phil smirked, giving him a resigned shrug before glancing to the forge. "Your mother asked me to talk to you."

"What?" He didn't have to ask why, but it was still startling to find that she'd resorted to extended family for contact.

"Well, apparently you haven't been around much the last couple of weeks…"

Cordon stared at him for a moment, wondering how much his mother had relayed to the man. He liked Phil; he just wasn't sure he was ready to have his romantic life a matter of public speculation.

Which was probably already the case. Grimacing,

Cordon shook his head. "I've been busy."

"That's what I told her. But you know your mother. She got it in her head that you were up to no good or something, which I told her was ridiculous. You've got enough shit occupying your time."

Cordon lifted his gaze to the ceiling and sighed. "I haven't been in a fight in ages. I haven't been to a bar in years now. What sort of trouble could I possibly be in?"

Phil shrugged. "I have no idea. She said she read your cards last night and something is coming."

"Damn it, I told her to stop that," Cordon said, pulling the would-be knife from the water.

"Apparently it didn't take."

"Well, you tell her to stop," he moved to put his tongs and his hammer in his bag again. "Nothing is coming."

"I heard you're with Tessa again?" Phil asked.

"Yeah," Cordon said. *Why does this matter to you?*

His phone rang and he snagged it from his jacket, which he'd laid over his bag in the corner of the large room. Cordon straightened, amused to see Tessa's name on the caller ID.

"Hey," he said into the phone, giving his uncle a brief grin. "I was just talking about you."

"So that's why my ears are burning." Tessa sounded amused.

"What's up?"

"Marisol says there's a big sale on batteries over at the pharmacy."

She seemed to be moving. He could hear a lot of background noise; wind and people talking, and it smothered her voice. "I figured maybe we could go pick some up tonight?"

"Sure," he said. "As soon as Book Land closes, we can go."

"Good," Tessa said. "Now go talk about me some more. Tell whoever it is how fantastic I am and that you can't live without me."

He chuckled. "What if I already did that part?"

"Did you?"

He could tell she was smiling, which made him grin too.

"No, not yet. But I was getting around to it."

"Well, if it's another girl you'd best tell her fast."

The sounds around her changed and her voice dropped. He imagined she'd stepped into one of the campus buildings and wondered which one. Maybe he could catch her before her next class.

"I've decided I'm the jealous type and I might have to get territorial if you don't warn her off."

He glanced at his uncle and laughed. "Trust me, you have nothing to worry about," he said. "It's Rusty Phil."

"Find out why everyone calls him that for me. Marisol is dying to know."

"Everyone is dying to know," Cordon said. "It's the mystery of campus."

"I'm sure," she said. "All right, I'm at class now. I've got to go. I'll see you at Book Land."

"Absolutely," he said and hung up.

Phil eyed him, clearly amused, his long face crinkled up like he was about to laugh but instead he just said; "You really like this one."

"I've always liked this one, Phil. She's the one who's been on the fence," Cordon said, grabbing his coat.

"Oh, this is the one that joined the navy?"

"Army. And yes."

"Well that explains why your mother is going a little crazy." Phil shook his head. "I'll try to warn her off but you're sure this is the one for you?"

"Hell yes, I'm sure. So much so that I've agreed to go on this crazy paranormal party thing Saturday. Which reminds me, have you got any spare SD cards laying around? You know, for a camera?"

Phil's brow furrowed. "I might," he said slowly. "This girl of yours believes in ghosts?"

"Nah, not at all. But her roommate is doing some experiment out at the Ashwood place and we got roped in."

His uncle froze, real concern lighting through his features.

What the hell?

"You OK?" he asked.

Phil shook his head. "Ashwood is dangerous. Not to mention illegal. You'll all get busted for trespassing…"

"Marisol got a permit for the night. We'll be legal." Cordon said. "It's no big deal, really."

"It's still dangerous. Don't go."

"What? No. Why?" Cordon had never seen his uncle so distressed. His face was flushed, and he looked like he'd just bitten into a lemon. "I know the place is falling apart. Certain buildings on the property are closed off to us because they're condemned, but with any luck we'll just be manning the computers all night. Tessa and I will be perfectly safe."

Phil frowned even deeper, if that were possible, and averted his gaze. Cordon sensed there was something the man was holding back, something he didn't want to say out loud, and stopped with his coat half fastened. God, his family was so weird.

"You're not telling me you believe in ghosts, are you?" Cordon asked, earning himself a glare from his uncle. "Shit. You really do."

"Find something else to do that night," Phil said gruffly. "Anything else."

"Trust me, I'd rather be doing anything else that night. But that's where Tessa will be so that's where I'm going."

"Then take Tessa out!" Phil snapped. "Hell, I'll pay for it. Whatever you want. A hotel room for the whole God damn weekend. Just stay out of that place."

Cordon opened his mouth to respond, a little shocked by the vehemence in Phil's voice, but his uncle stalked toward the doorway. Cordon stared after him, wondering what the hell had just happened and if his entire family might need to be committed.

He'd call his mother later to talk her down from Tarot reading, and he'd call Sara just to make sure there was still at least one sane person left in his bloodline.

Chapter Thirteen

Tessa pulled her much-neglected jeep into the lot outside of Ashwood on Saturday afternoon. A heavy layer of clouds hung low in the sky, casting the whole place in gray light. Unrest seemed permanently etched into the brick buildings, age and weather having taken their toll over the years. Something like eight hundred acres housed many crumbling buildings and Tessa was grateful that Marisol had only been given permission to explore six of them.

An IED couldn't kill her, but this place might. Maybe she didn't believe in ghosts, but she certainly believed in entropy and wood decay. And possibly natural selection.

"I'm so glad we brought the tarp." Marisol frowned at the overcast sky. "I think it might actually rain on us."

"It *is* going to rain. The weatherman said the chances were eighty-five percent. That means rain."

"That means there's a fifteen percent chance that it won't," Marisol said, determinedly cheerful. "Come on. Where's your sense of adventure?"

"I buried it in Afghanistan," Tessa said. "Please tell me you got more investigators."

Marisol opened the door and jumped out; "Come on, let's go set up."

Tessa gripped the steering wheel harder. Chances were that Marisol hadn't bothered hunting for more people, which meant that Tessa would end up knee-deep in rodent central with a camcorder and a lot of rusty metal. And probably asbestos.

God damn it all to hell.

The area was too open for a good echo but slamming her door had the desired effect. Marisol flinched, which only confirmed Tessa's suspicions. But she asked anyway.

"Did you even look for more investigators?"

Marisol avoided her gaze and grabbed the first tarp from the back of the little jeep.

"Not exactly, no," she confessed.

Tessa battled her temper down.

"I got one other person and Lundy says he needs skeptical people like you and Cordon so anyone I asked who really wanted to come weren't the sort of people we needed anyway."

"Why couldn't Lundy have found some of the investigators?" *Or supplies, computers, batteries, anything.*

"I told you, he's been working on the test parameters and things."

Uh-huh. For a smart girl, Marisol sure had her stupid moments.

Then again, Tessa had agreed to this, too. She supposed that said more about her own intelligence than she wanted.

"Hey, stranger," said a familiar male voice from behind her.

Tessa stiffened. Her stomach knotted like a pretzel as she faced David Jackson, recognizing his jackal-like features even in civilian attire. She'd done such a good job avoiding him the last week that she'd imagined he would have given up by now. But there he was, stubbornly present in a situation Tessa hadn't wanted to be part of in the first place.

Perfect.

"Jackson," she said, slanting a look at Marisol. "What are you doing here?"

Marisol's wide-eyed, nervous expression closely resembled recruits on grenade training day, as though she feared she'd pulled the pin too early and was waiting for the explosion.

He smiled faintly at her. "Well, a little bird told me where you'd be tonight, so I signed up."

"What?"

"You weren't returning my calls, so I came by the dorms." He nodded toward Marisol, who had gone paper-white and shifted back and forth on her feet.

"Yeah, he's the other investigator," Marisol said and quickly grabbed the other tarp. "Did I forget to mention that? So sorry."

She headed for the main building, fairly tromping her way over uneven ground in her escape. Tessa stared after her and seriously considered strangling the girl.

"Look, I know what your dad did was wrong, but why have you been avoiding my calls?" Jackson asked. "It's not like I did it."

Tessa took a deep breath and reached for the compact folding table they'd managed to fit in the back of the jeep.

"I've been busy," she said, knowing how lame that sounded and that he was about to call her out on it.

"Too busy for the man who saved your life?"

Damn, damn, double damn. Why was it so hard for people to respect boundaries anymore? She was going to buy a cabin in Alaska, miles from the nearest town, and live off fish and read novels. Then maybe she could get some peace.

She'd invite Cordon. They could adopt dogs and a cat and fend off any bears together.

"Hey," Jackson said when she started to turn away.

She paused and glanced at him, then over his shoulder at the empty street beyond. "What am I supposed to say to that, Jackson?"

"I don't know," he said, running a hand over his shaved hair. "Thanks, might work."

"Thanks?" Tessa asked, incredulous. "Can *thanks* even cover it?"

"Well it's a hell of a lot better than nothing," he said, getting that mulish look to his face.

That told her things were about to get ugly.

Tessa shook her head and lifted the table, heading for the main building without bothering to look at him again. Behind her, he cursed and then there was the sound of his feet in pursuit. He was being impossible, and she knew she wasn't helping the situation by remaining closed off but, damn it, this was how she'd survived the last year. And if she was going to open up to anyone it would be to Cordon, not that jackass.

The jackass who saved your life, Cabby's voice said, and she flinched.

Jackson deserved better from her, there was no escaping it.

"Look, I just need to know that you're all right," Jackson said as they climbed the steps to the old administration building.

"Why?" She stepped through the only open door and into a dark, barren foyer where she paused.

The only light in the place came from the open door behind them, casting her shadow across a debris-riddled floor that she really, really didn't want to speculate about. Paint-chipped walls that might have been white once were cracked in various places, revealing the red brick beneath and there was a heavy smell of dead things on the air.

How many rodents were dead in the walls here?

"What do you mean, why?" Jackson asked, stopping just beside her.

She had to shake her head to concentrate on him again, focusing past the awful room and on his face.

"Why does it matter if I'm all right or not? We barely tolerated each other in the unit. You can't possibly want to extend that relationship."

"I didn't tolerate you," he said, sounding offended.

Done with being polite, Tessa glared at him. "Yes, you did. I was that bitch who kept catching you trying to work around the firewall so you could watch porn."

His cheeks flushed a little and he glanced away from her. "Well, you were a little uptight, yeah," he said. "But I figured that was the uniform talking."

She blinked. "Unbelievable."

"I'm a guy," he said, spreading his hands wide as though he couldn't help himself.

"And absolutely responsible for your actions," she said. "Now do us both a favor and go away, would you?"

"No," he said, his jaw set.

"Fine."

Tessa picked her way through the room. Marisol's flashlight shone through the office closest to them and she headed for it, noting that the windows were all missing glass. Or at least the internal ones were. Some of the outside windows were still intact, though most sported several cracks and the ones higher up seemed occupied by nests.

Jackson's boots crunched through the debris, close on her heels again, but she didn't address him as they entered the smaller office-like room. It had a long, splintered table flush against one wall and one old, rusted wheelchair in the corner. Marisol had already pinned up one tarp with bungee cords, covering the cracked window in the far wall. It cast the room in an eerie bluish light and lengthened the shadows in the corners.

Tessa couldn't decide if that was better or worse than the grungy once-white everywhere else, but she imagined when it was dark it wasn't going to matter. Marisol shone her flashlight up at a gaping hole in the ceiling and frowned. "I can't see the sky but that doesn't mean it won't leak."

"All the spare batteries and equipment will be in here," Tessa said. "Best put it up anyway."

"Yeah." Marisol was still not willing to look at Tessa.

Which was a good thing because Tessa still wanted to strangle her.

After toting the table inside, she unfolded it and set it in the center of the room, far from the dark corners and littered perimeter. She did not want to think about how many rats she would be sharing her night with.

Jackson moved to help Marisol with the tarp, thank God, so Tessa left them to it, stalking back out and heading for the front doors. Brisk autumn air hit her full on, made all the colder by the oncoming storm, and Tessa zipped her jacket a little higher. Standing on the building's steps, she tried to remember if they'd packed gloves for this trip and wished for Cordon. He had a few things he needed to take care of at the store today, but he would be arriving before it got dark.

Just a few more hours and then she'd have backup.

Another car pulled into the lot, sleek and red and far too sporty. Tessa frowned at it as she stepped down the stairs, recognizing the butch-haired man who got out of the driver's seat. It took a moment for her to place him and when she did, she muttered a curse under her breath. Tyler. And the slender, well-breasted woman in the tight jeans and neon pink jacket could be none other than Alyssa.

God help me, can this night get any worse?

Thunder growled overhead, and she glared up at the sky. "Yeah, fuck you. Right on cue, too."

Chapter Fourteen

"No, Mom, seriously, quit it with the Tarot," Cordon said into his phone.

He turned the car onto Institute Drive and kept going, listening to his mother as she tried to get him out of this party. Her concern was sweet in an unhinged sort of way, and he didn't want to be running around inside half-rotted buildings any more than she seemed to want him there, so he tried to keep the exasperation out of his voice.

"Cordon! This is not about Tarot. Your uncle really needs your help tonight. Just go down to the University. I promise, he's waiting."

"He does not need my help tonight. It's Saturday. There are no art classes on Saturday," Cordon said. "No more Tarot, Mom. I mean it. Or if you're going to do it, read someone else."

"Oh, Cordon, but I did! I read Tessa's. She really loves you, just so you know. But she's in great danger. You both are. Please, stay out of that place tonight."

"Mom, you cannot tell that a person is in love with you by reading some old cards," he said, though he did hope that part was true.

"Ugh, your Leo is showing in bright colors today," she said.

And now they were into astrology. Some days Amanda Morant was such a nut.

An irritatingly loving nut, but a nut just the same.

"I love you, Mom. I'll talk to you tomorrow. I've got to go." He hung up before she could protest further and sighed, tossing the phone onto the passenger seat.

Turning the car into the lot outside Ashwood, he parked beside Tessa's little white jeep and smiled. One of these days he would convince her to buy a new one, but for now it was nice to see the familiar vehicle, even if they were parked outside a mostly condemned institute.

Another car pulled up beside his. It was dark blue and clunky and the boy who got out of it was on the gangly side. Long hair that looked somewhere between brown and red cut to his chin, and a lazy grin with sleepy brown eyes and Cordon knew without a doubt this kid was high.

His uncle's offer for a weekend in a hotel looked more enticing by the second.

The kid gave him two thumbs up and nodded, vacantly cheerful, and Cordon returned the gesture. Maybe he could convince Tessa they didn't have to do this.

But they'd come too far for that and he knew it. He sighed and opened his door, climbing out just as the kid came around to his side.

"Hey, man, I'm Lundy. Thanks for coming."

The infamous Lundy. Well, that made sense.

He shook his hand, trying for polite. "Cordon Morant. I've got most of the supplies in the back."

"Oh! Bookstore Guy!" Lundy laughed, looking like even more of a goon.

What did Marisol see in this guy?

"Yep, that's me," Cordon said and jerked his head toward the trunk. "Help me tote some of this in."

"Oh! Right, right!" Lundy moved to the trunk with

him.

The hinges squeaked as Cordon lifted the trunk open. He'd need to fix that soon, the sound grated on his nerves. Lundy took one small bag and stepped aside, and Cordon thought about leaving the kid to bring it in on his own. But no, that would prolong things, and the last thing he wanted was to prolong anything tonight.

Shaking his head, he reached in and grabbed the two remaining bags, both hefty thanks to numerous batteries and cords, and dragged them out.

"Hey, man, it means a lot that you're here. I really need this for my class," Lundy said and closed the trunk for him.

Cordon clamped down on his temper. *Yeah? Then why do I feel like Tessa did most of your work for you?* Instead he said, "No problem."

And they started for the administration building.

They made their way up the steps, Lundy practically having to jog to keep up with Cordon's longer strides. He slowed down as they reached the doors, not because he cared if he was rude to Lundy, but because he had to turn to make sure neither of the bags bashed into the doorframe on the way in.

Stepping into the deteriorated foyer, Cordon automatically scanned the room for Tessa. But, lo and behold, there was Tyler and Alyssa cozied up in a corner looking amused about everything.

Oh, God damn it. He ground his teeth to keep from saying it out loud.

"Oh! Yay!" Marisol said. "You're here."

Cordon focused on the girl as she waved them over, though he imagined most of her cheer was meant for Lundy. He followed her around the corner and into a smaller office room decorated in blue tarp. Tessa leaned over a folding table with a laptop open in front of her, obviously working on something and by the frown on her face he imagined it wasn't going well. But there was another man in the room; a tall, fit man whose haircut screamed the military and who smirked down at her like he knew her.

"What's the matter, Pines?" the man said. "Finally found a computer program you can't figure out?"

"Go away, Jackson," Tessa said flatly.

Cordon headed for the table, setting the bags down. She looked up from the computer and smiled at him, but it was strained, and he could sense a tension in the room that he didn't like.

"Hey," he said, deliberately glancing at Jackson. "Everything all right?"

Tessa straightened, closing the laptop to move closer to his side; "Just fine," she said and tiptoed to kiss his cheek.

Cordon slid his arm around her waist, keeping an eye on this Jackson fellow, who looked a little surprised. She fit against Cordon's side and as curious as he was about the undercurrent in the room, she felt so good there he decided not to ask questions yet.

"Marisol will give all the rules and whatnot at seven," Tessa said.

Cordon checked the clock on his phone. Six-fifty.

"I think we can leave them to set this up," he said. *God knows they made us do enough of their work for them.* "Let's get out of here for a bit."

"Yes, please," Tessa said, smiling a real smile this time.

He nodded to Jackson, who looked less sure of

himself. Not bothering to wait for Jackson to return the gesture, Cordon pulled Tessa out of the room and they left the building. She fell into step beside him, her familiar warmth a comfort as they passed Tyler and Alyssa.

"This will be a long night," Tessa said as they came out onto the stairs.

They paused on the old steps, chill air sinking in through layers of clothes. A reddish-gold hue rimmed the horizon, tapering off into soft blue and then darker shades of twilight the higher one looked. Long shadows were forming, stretching out from buildings and trees, swallowing the ground until gravel and grass disappeared beneath the dark.

"So that's Jackson, huh?" Cordon asked.

"Yes," she said with a heavy sigh. "Sergeant David Jackson. Not my favorite person in the world on the best of days and he's here on leave because apparently he's gone crazy."

"Crazy?"

"He seems to think it is his job to watch out for me."

The hell it is, that's my job.

Or at least he wanted it to be his job. Tessa was pretty good at watching out for herself most days, IED's aside. Still, Cordon could back her up against this twerp. A broken nose was always a good deterrent.

"Jackson was one of the men who got me out of the wreck," Tessa said, scowling at the darkening sky.

Well, damn. I'll thank him and then I'll punch him.

"I've tried to get him to leave but he seems hell-bent on staying," she said, finally turning to him.

Cordon didn't like the idea of Jackson being hell-bent to stick with Tessa and he nearly said so. But then she closed the gap between them, going up on her tiptoes to reach him and all her warmth seemed to short-circuit his brain. He slid his arms around her waist again, drawing her even closer.

She brushed a kiss against his cheek and murmured; "It's going to suck, but we should try to be nicer to him."

Cordon wrinkled his nose. "How about I be nice to him and you not talk to him anymore. Would that work at all?"

Tessa smiled, the blue of her eyes catching what light was left, and he relaxed.

"It's selfish and immature, but I like that you're jealous."

"You won't like it so much when I break his face," he grumbled.

Her giggle released all the tension in him, and he smiled. "I'm not bluffing."

"I know," she said. "But you have nothing to worry about. I think I've made my affections very clear."

He hummed a noncommittal response and, because she was close and felt so good pressed against him, he leaned down to kiss her. She met him, her warm mouth firm instead of pliant, challenging a response that he was more than willing to give. Her hands slid around his neck and he held her waist tighter as the heat spread between them.

"Geez, guys," Marisol said. "Could you maybe wait for after we've done the party?"

Cordon broke the kiss but didn't bother looking at Marisol, choosing instead to watch the dazed and lustful expression as it faded from Tessa's face.

"We were discussing leaving," he said to Marisol. And then, lower, almost a whisper; "No, really. My uncle offered us a hotel room for the weekend. Interested?"

"God, yes," Tessa said just as Marisol's voice rose into a squeaky, panicked; "No! I need you!"

Tessa slumped and pressed her forehead into Cordon's chest, groaning in a frustration that he completely shared.

"You can't leave! You promised. Both of you promised!"

"Yeah," Cordon said, unable to restrain himself further. "And then we did ninety percent of your job for you. Believe it or not, I have no problem walking away now."

Marisol's expression crumpled, and she looked like she was about to cry.

Dick move.

He expected Tessa to spurn him for it but, much to his surprise, she turned to her friend with a frown of her own.

"You promised to at least look for other investigators and you didn't," Tessa said, and Marisol flinched again. "Cordon is right. We put a lot of goddamn work into *your* project and I have half a mind to just go."

"Tessa—"

"But I did give you my word. So, I will give you one hour. After that hour, Cordon and I are leaving. You can handle the cleanup on your own. You and Lundy owe us that much."

"Ok," Marisol said, apparently recognizing a firm boundary when it was laid down. "No problem. That's fine, seriously. Thank you so much."

"Mm," Tessa said in response and, taking Cordon's hand, headed for the door again.

He followed, unable to hide his grin. The vulnerable, timid woman he'd met in Book Land was giving way to the woman he'd known in high school and he could see it. He wasn't sure she did yet, and he knew she would never be the same, but at least there was progress.

There was an odd pressure in his chest, and he rubbed at it as they made their way to the tarp room again. It was faint, a minor irritation, and in the next moment he forgot about it because Jackson came into view. The man looked like he was chewing on coffee grounds and his gaze followed Tessa through the room.

It was an effort, but Cordon kept in mind that this was the man who had saved Tessa's life and tried for a polite smile.

****

Tessa walked back into the office, dubbing it the command center and praying she could get through this hour without being bitten by a rodent. Or stabbed in the foot by anything rusty. Cordon was close behind her, a sturdy and comforting presence that she refused to let go of. When she grabbed up a camcorder and passed it to him, he smiled and leaned in close to whisper in her ear.

"God that was hot."

"The kiss? I know. I want to go do it again right now."

"Well that can be arranged," he teased. "But I meant the way you took charge just now. Very hot."

She blinked at him, amused and caught off guard, then reached for her own camcorder. "That wasn't taking charge, that was being pissed off."

He chuckled. "Still hot."

Blushing, she led him to a corner and then decided against it. The debris littering the floor was more evident in the corners and she preferred not to be near it. Or near the walls, for that matter. Cordon trailed her, still chuckling as the others filed in; Tyler and Alyssa, Lundy and Jackson, and finally Marisol, who gave them all a bright smile.

"All right!" Marisol said, sounding irritatingly excited. "Now, we only have permission to explore four of the buildings. There are maps on the table that tell you which ones are off limits. Please don't go in them. They are condemned for health reasons and we don't want anyone getting hurt."

"This whole place is a health hazard," Alyssa said, earning a few snickers from the room.

"Yes, I know." Marisol continued seamlessly, sounding almost professional, bubble-gum voice and all. "Each building has a sign out front, so you shouldn't run into one of the bad ones on accident."

Good, because if this building wasn't condemned then she hated to imagine what the others might look like.

"We have three teams," Marisol said. "Alyssa and Tyler are Team One. Cordon and Tessa are Team Two. David and I are Team Three. Lundy will be here manning the computers and the phone. I didn't think about getting radios because I knew everyone had a cell phone they could use."

"So!" Lundy interrupted, opening a bag Tessa didn't recognize. "In order for this whole thing to work, we're going to have the regular camcorders that everyone will use and a mini camera. You can turn the regular camera's on and off at will, for when you're doing your investigating, but the mini camera's must be on the whole time. They're already set up for night vision, so you won't have to worry about adjusting anything."

Tessa frowned as Lundy handed her a small box-like camera mounted to an elastic headband. She was simultaneously impressed that Lundy had put any work into this and annoyed at the idea of wearing such an obnoxious thing.

She heard Tyler across the room say; "Cool." And spotted Jackson's conflicted expression. Cordon eyed his mini camera with so much loathing she almost giggled.

"Remember," Lundy said. "mini camera's stay *on*."

"All right, everyone," Marisol said, taking over again. "Let's get our equipment and head out there. We've got a lot of ground to cover."

The room surged to life, everyone heading for the table to collect flashlights and camcorders. Tessa shared a look with Cordon, who mouthed "Hotel" at her with a pleading expression. For a heartbeat she considered it, imagining soft blankets and Chinese takeout and some easily ignored movie playing in the background.

But then Marisol stepped into view, dousing her imaginary cozy night with a sleek, black camcorder and a package of batteries. Tessa took the camcorder, trying to smother a scowl.

"One hour," Marisol said. "Thank you so much!"

"Don't mention it," Tessa said as Marisol handed a voice recorder to Cordon.

He pocketed the item and a handful of triple A's with a sigh.

"Follow me," Marisol said, packing the words with so much exuberance that Tessa nearly cringed. "I'll be taking you to the first building."

After another hesitation, Tessa stepped behind Marisol, who waved for everyone to come along.

Behind her, Cordon heaved a sigh and muttered; "Once more unto the breach…"

Chapter Fifteen

Cordon kept pace with Tessa as they crossed the pitted yard. Buildings loomed above them in odd, shadowy shapes, cutting across the gray horizon and adding to the growing dark. For a moment they looked like enormous headstones, their widths hidden by dusk so that only the front facing walls were visible. Some of the more deteriorated buildings had jagged edges where age or fire crumbled the brick, leaving a snaggle-toothed imprint against the sky.

There was history here. Old, deep history steeped into the very ground they were walking on and Cordon marveled at his own audacity for coming. What he knew of the Ashwood painted a dire picture of neglect and abuse, inmates ranging from the autistic to the outright insane all grouped together because family or the state didn't have time to care for them. It was a place where humanity was at its worst and he had the overwhelming sense that he was trespassing.

"So why do these paranormal investigations have to be done at night?" Tyler asked. "I mean, if there is such a thing as ghosts, I don't think they'd care about the time of day, you know?"

Cordon grudgingly appreciated the man for saying that and he appreciated Tessa more for her response.

"There are no such things as ghosts," she said.

"There's just some primal instinct that tells us the night is dangerous. It stems from before we had fun technology like flashlights."

"There are thousands of reports supporting paranormal phenomena," Alyssa said. "I swear, why are you guys even here?"

"Why indeed," Tessa mumbled beside him and Cordon snorted a laugh.

"Hey, don't look at me," he said, trying to keep his voice low. "I'm still game for a hotel room and some inventive hands-on flirting."

"Inventive, hm? Sounds fun," Tessa said.

Jackson shot them a look that Cordon ignored as they made their way up a new flight of stairs. Marisol stopped them outside the building's doors and beckoned everyone close. Flecks of rain peppered Cordon's face as he squashed up next to Tessa, who leaned into his side while Marisol gave the last of her instructions. He only partially paid attention, choosing instead to snake his arm around Tessa's waist.

"Cordon and Tessa will be on the second-floor critical wing," Marisol said. "Alyssa and Tyler have second floor B-Wing, where exam rooms and offices were. And David and I will be C-Wing, first floor, where solitary confinement was."

"Solitary confinement?" Tyler asked. "I thought this was a mental hospital."

"Padded rooms," Alyssa said. "You know, straightjackets for the really dangerous ones."

Tyler made a disgusted sound and Cordon smirked. They'd learned about this stuff in high school but apparently Tyler had missed that week.

"Remember, you all have cell phones so if you need

something, don't hesitate to call," Marisol said.

"Unless you're Tessa," Jackson said. "She's forgotten how to use a phone."

Cordon tensed, eyeing the man as he debated how offended he should be. But Tessa's voice stopped him.

"Shut up, Jackson. It's your own fault for not getting the hint in the first place," she said.

Tyler snickered, Alyssa made a nervous titter, and Jackson turned as though to say something else, but Marisol cut him off, which was good because the mulish expression on his face had Cordon ready to make a move.

"All right," Marisol said. "The clock is ticking. You all have your maps and assignments. Meet back here in thirty minutes."

In an impressive display of backbone, Marisol took Jackson by the arm and turned him back to the door. Cordon tried reminding himself that this was the man who'd saved Tessa's life, but every withering glare he sent their way was scouring at Cordon's resolve to be nice.

Or at least to pretend to be nice.

Tyler and Alyssa stepped into the building next, leaving him alone with Tessa for a moment.

"You think she'd notice if we bailed?"

Tessa giggled. "Not only would she notice, she would hunt us down and interrupt all that hands-on flirting you were planning. Best we get this over with."

Cordon checked his phone. "Fifty-three minutes," he said.

Tessa closed her eyes and gave a little groan. "If I get bitten by a rodent, I'm going to kill her."

Chuckling, he gestured for her to go first and she squared her shoulders before marching to the door. With a harder than necessary yank, she opened the institute and stalked inside. Cordon followed, still chuckling.

There was a stale smell to the air, like mothballs, and clothes washed without soap, and underneath that was something foul rotting. Grimacing, he flicked on his light and continued with Tessa, who had located the stairwell.

"Why haven't they torn this place down?" Tessa asked.

The stairs were concrete and solid, but the brick walls around them were pitted and crumbling and he did his best not to brush them as they trekked upward.

"Historical landmark, probably," he said.

"Yes, because everyone wants to tour a dilapidated mental hospital where all manner of nastiness occurred. Did you know some of the invalids were left with maggots in their ears?" She shuddered. "I mean...maggots."

"Yeah, I knew that," Cordon said. "Points for using the word 'dilapidated' in a full sentence, though."

Tessa snickered as they reached the top of the stairwell.

"I'll take a half a point for that one," she said. "I did also use 'nastiness' in that same sentence. Surely I could have been more creative than that."

"Sometimes the simpler word is the best word. I felt the two balanced each other out. Besides, nastiness helped allude to the maggots."

Tessa paused before the second-floor door, turning to shine her light up at his face. Cordon swore and squinted, shielding his eyes from the blinding light.

"I've missed you," she said. "Four years in the army and I never once found anyone who loved the written word as much as you do."

"I've missed you too, but could you maybe point that thing somewhere else?"

She turned the light away and he blinked, trying to dislodge the bright spots in his vision. A moment later her mouth brushed his, warm and gentle, and he grinned.

"Eyes adjusted?" she asked.

"If I say no will you kiss me again?"

Tessa snorted a laugh and shook her head. "Come on, let's try to find some non-existent ghosts."

****

The critical wing turned out to be more intact than the administration building. Its walls were still discolored, paint chipping in several areas and long, trailing smears of water damage where roof leaks had gone unattended, but there wasn't as much debris crowding the corners of the floor. Tessa imagined the rodents here were fewer and posher than those of the lower levels, as though the physical elevation somehow leant them more manners.

She smirked, her creative mind conjuring a rodent hierarchy similar to a novel she'd read and scanned the floor with her light. For a heartbeat she was comforted by the comparison, but then remembered that the novel featured rabbits, not rats, and the spell was broken.

Marisol owed her big time for this.

They stepped into the middle of the hallway and she played her light over the nurse's station. It sat in a semicircle with its back to a corner, its curved counter empty save for a few crumbling pebbles that she didn't care to speculate about. If they weren't bits of the ceiling then they were likely rodent droppings, so she turned her light to the nearest room.

"What now?" Cordon asked.

"I don't know. I suppose we turn everything on and

try talking to…whatever?"

"Right," Cordon said and began fiddling with the voice recorder.

Tessa powered on her camcorder, switching it to low-light night vision mode, and squinted at the square screen as it illuminated. The picture was grainy, but she could make out the nurse's station and doorways. Feeling altogether ridiculous, she turned in a circle so that the video caught the basics of where they were standing.

"This is Tessa and Cordon on the second-floor critical wing," she said, and Cordon huffed a laugh. "Hey, they have to be able to identify which videos are which."

"Makes total sense," he said, still sounding amused.

"If you keep laughing at me, I'm going to hit you."

"Always so violent," he said. "I thought the army would have cured you of that."

"Because the military is so gentle? If anything, they enhanced it."

Cordon laughed. "Good point."

They made a slow progression to the nearest door and Tessa scanned the room with the camcorder, taking in rows of flat cots lined against the walls. Several cots were torn at the corners, their fabric dangling onto the dusty floor. There were no privacy divides, which Tessa found odd, but this place had not been known for decency.

"So, are we just supposed to talk?" Cordon asked.

"I guess?" Tessa frowned at the image of the empty room and wondered how she'd gotten here. Cabby would have laughed to hear she'd gone on a paranormal investigation. Murphy too. "So…er…Here, ghostie-ghostie-ghostie?" Cordon's snort of amusement brought her up short and she lowered the camera. "Well if you can do any better…"

"I don't care enough to even try," he said.

"You're impossible."

"Hey now, I think I've been more than supportive about this weirdness. And really, so have you. I'm surprised you didn't put down a boundary sooner."

Tessa lifted the camcorder again and started into the room. "I gave my word that I would help." *And boundaries were always your problem, not mine.*

"What we did was a hell of a lot more than help."

"What can I say? I'm an overachiever."

"I know you are, and that's normally fine. But this isn't your project, Tess. It's hers."

"Yeah? So?"

"I'm just trying to understand what we're doing here."

Keeping her gaze on the image, she walked through the room, Cordon's question echoing through her. He was right, of course. This wasn't her job and yet she'd done almost everything for Marisol's project. Tessa wasn't even in that class, she had her own projects to worry about, so why had she dumped all of this into her schedule?

"I'm sorry, Tess. I know she's your friend. I just hate seeing you tear yourself apart for something that isn't your responsibility."

Tessa stopped and looked at him. Shadows hid most of his form, the flashlight in his hand the only indicator he was there, but she could sense where his face was. The chill of the room clawed through her coat and the tip of her nose was starting to numb. That was odd, it hadn't been this cold earlier, but she shrugged it off to focus on Cordon.

Did he realize how similar his argument was to the

one she'd given him years ago? She couldn't read his face, but she suspected he did.

On the night before she left, she'd said almost those exact same words to him, only her concern was over his family. Sara's husband at the time had lost his job and by all accounts wasn't looking for a new one. Amanda Morant, Cordon's mother, had strung herself out on prescription medicine after knee surgery and both women had clung to him for support.

At first Tessa had tried to help, to be the supportive wife while his family spun out of control, but the weeks spread into months and the months into a year. Amanda bounced in and out of rehab. Cordon chose to wait for college so that he could help support them. But the last straw was the day Sara announced she was going to business school and the look on Cordon's face as she explained hours and costs and financial aid.

The aid was not enough to cover living expenses and she didn't stop to ask if Cordon had any objections. Worse yet, Cordon wouldn't discuss work-study or some other program the school might have offered.

Tessa gripped the camcorder harder, its sleek body creaked under her fingers until she relaxed again.

"Tessa?"

"I hear you, Cord. And you're right. I don't know how I didn't see it before but, you're right."

He moved to her side, sliding an arm around her waist until she fit against him and she sighed. His lips brushed her temple, and his beard tickled her cheek. Relaxing into him, she gazed at the camcorder image, not really seeing it. Her mind tripped backward, reviewing the last few weeks as she hunted for the trigger that had brought her here.

Maybe if she could understand this, she would understand Cordon better. Granted, everything in Cordon's life had worked out. Sara owned the bookstore, Amanda was clean, and Lyndon had a male role model who wasn't going anywhere. If she'd been patient, she might have been a part of all that.

But was it fair to ask her to wait four years to start living their lives together? That seemed a stretch.

Cordon stiffened beside her, bending down to peer at the camcorder image. "What was that?"

"What?" She asked, blinking at the image, too. "What was what?"

"Can you rewind it?" He asked, but his attention had switched to the doorway.

Tessa flipped through functions until she could play back the last two minutes. They both watched the screen, which had a view of the open doorway and several cots. At one minute and ten seconds, a form crossed in front of the doorway and every little hair Tessa had stood on end. Roughly 5'8" and with the general form of a person, it stepped from left to right, barely illuminated by the camcorder's light.

She lowered the camera and glanced at Cordon, who released her waist and straightened.

"Who's there?" he asked, shining his light at the door. "Marisol?"

"That was too tall to be Marisol, don't you think?"

"Tyler?" Cordon tried again.

When there was no answer Tessa eyed the doorway, willing whoever it was to come back.

"It's probably one of the others trying to freak us out," she said.

"Yeah, or a transient."

"You think a homeless person would want to come here?"

"Homeless is homeless, Tess. And there's a storm coming on."

"Awesome," Tessa said. "Remind me to punch Marisol in the face."

"Whoever it was seems to have moved off," he said. "And I'm tired of being here already. Let's head back."

"God, yes," she said, more relieved than she wanted to let on.

She didn't have to believe in ghosts to admit that seeing the video had been creepy, and now it felt like they were being watched or something. The spot between her shoulder blades tingled and gooseflesh kept racing up her arms and neck.

Shoving the camcorder into her pocket, she walked behind Cordon, who led the way out of the room. He checked both ends of the hallway with his light, but as far as they could see no one was there. Which was good because Tessa might have hit whoever it was on sight, transient or not.

Trying to relax, she fell into step with Cordon as they made their way out of the critical wing and back to the stairs.

Chapter Sixteen

All the way to the administration building Cordon was on high alert. The sky teased them with flecks of rain and as they hurried across the yard there was a sense that it would unleash more soon.

Great. Just great. Rain would make it harder to see out in the open.

He knew they'd caught someone in that doorway, and it bothered him a great deal that whoever it was had run off. If it had been one of the other teams, they should have heard something, giggling or whispering, so his money was on a transient hunting for shelter. And while not all homeless people were dangerous or mentally unstable, he'd heard enough stories to be cautious.

Tessa reached the door first and swung it open, sending him a flirtatious wink as he shook his head at her.

"You make it hard to be a gentleman," he said as she stepped behind him.

"Nonsense. If I'm in a dress, you can hold the door for me. Otherwise, it's fair game. I'm diverse like that."

He snorted a laugh, turning toward the computer room. The tarp-laden computer station was, much to his surprise, full. Marisol, Lundy, and Alyssa crowded the computer table, but only Marisol was looking at the screen. Jackson noticed them enter first and glared from across the room. Cordon met the man's gaze, reading hostility and something not quite hinged in Jackson's face. For a second Cordon considered taking Tessa and leaving.

"What? No warning? You guys just left us over there alone?" Tessa asked.

Nobody answered, not even glaring Jackson in the corner, and Cordon's stomach did an uneasy turn. At the computer table, Alyssa placed a hand on Lundy's elbow, leaning her body into his with a suggestive smile. She whispered something low in Lundy's ear, but the intent was clear.

What the hell?

Cordon hunted for Tyler, but he wasn't in the room. Taking a step back, Cordon checked the main foyer, swinging his light around. Tyler wasn't there either. Frowning, Cordon moved to Tessa's side, who gave the room a scowl of her own.

"There's something rotten in Denmark," Tessa said, keeping her voice low so that only he could hear.

"You mean apart from you quoting Shakespeare right now?" Cordon asked, and then relented at the glare she gave him. "But you're right, something's off."

Jackson stepped into their line of sight, scratching at his forehead and looking more intense than usual. His face pinched into a scowl and he eyed Tessa in a way that had Cordon prepared to use his flashlight as a weapon. Tessa stiffened and canted her head like she was in the sparring ring, chin slightly to the right, feet shoulder-width apart. Cordon shifted too, ready to stop whichever of them threw the first punch because as much as he wanted to break Jackson's nose, the bastard had saved her life once. He knew Tessa, she wouldn't forgive herself for coming to blows with the man…

141

"So," Jackson said, completely ignoring Cordon. "I don't suppose there's any way I can swap partners?"

"No," Cordon said.

"Not a chance in hell," Tessa added.

Jackson's face twisted into something that might have been a frown, but mostly made him look like he was in pain. "You know, you weren't always such a—"

Cordon stepped in front of Tessa, forcing Jackson to look him in the eye instead. "Be very careful what you say next."

"This is between me and her," Jackson said, straightening his shoulders and puffing out his chest.

Cordon might have taken that moment to hit the man, but Tessa slid around him and prodded Jackson in the chest with her finger. The move brought her too close to the man for Cordon's comfort, but this was Tessa and fighting her own battles seemed to be the theme of her life.

"I think maybe the trauma of seeing friends get blown up has given you a rosy view of who I used to be, Jackson. Now you signed up with Marisol, so you should really—"

A strangled, squeaky sound cut Tessa off and they both turned to locate the distress. Marisol stood at the table, clutching several batteries and a flashlight to her chest, her expression shocked and hurt. Tessa followed the girl's gaze to where Lundy, the dweeb, was leaning in close to Alyssa, murmuring in her ear.

"Shit," Tessa said just as Marisol dropped her things on the table and started for the door. "Marisol, wait..."

"I take it back, I think your *Hamlet* quote fits tonight fine," Cordon said.

Marisol ignored Tessa, disappearing into the gloom

of the administration building without a flashlight to guide her.

"I'd better get her," Tessa said. "She can't go far in the dark but it's still not safe."

"Given this new development, maybe she'll call the whole thing off," Cordon said, eyeing Lundy and Alyssa again.

"One can only hope."

Tessa stretched onto her toes to kiss him once, firm on the mouth. His arm went around her waist and for a blissful moment he forgot where they were standing. But then she broke off, murmuring against his mouth.

"Try not to break any faces while I'm gone."

"No promises," he said. *Especially if Jackson continues to glare like that.*

Tessa winked up at him, then headed for the door, snagging two flashlights from the table on her way. She passed Lundy and Alyssa, who were still so absorbed with each other that they didn't notice anyone else in the room. Alyssa unzipped her bright pink jacket, revealing an impractical low-cut blouse. Lundy's gaze followed the zipper to mid-breast and then lingered there as he leered.

Unbelievable. Marisol can do so much better than this jackass.

Lundy pinched a strand of Alyssa's platinum blonde hair, lightly tugging on it as Alyssa batted her over-done eyelashes. For the zillionth time, Cordon wondered what the hell was going on. Alyssa was a flirtatious, conceited twit but he'd always assumed she stuck to one man at a time. She only moved on if the other prospect had a lot of money or a lot of prestige, neither of which she would find with Lundy the first-year psychology student.

And where was Tyler while his girl was getting the

moves from such a weird little man?

Cordon scanned the room with his flashlight, checking the corners not illuminated by blue computer light.

"So," Jackson said from just beside him, sounding tense enough that Cordon gave up his search to focus.

Of everyone here, Jackson was the most likely to come to blows with someone, and since Tessa seemed intent on not letting anyone get hurt tonight, Cordon felt obligated to keep them safe.

"So?" Cordon directed his light at their feet.

It was dark now, deep shadows filling the empty spaces, hiding the floor from view. Jackson's feet scuffed over the chipped tile as he moved closer to Cordon's side.

"You and Pines, huh?"

"Me and Tessa, yes," Cordon said, getting a little tense himself.

Yeah, Jackson was the most likely to fight someone and that someone is me.

"Is there a problem with that?" Cordon asked, not meaning to sound as confrontational as he did.

"That depends on your intentions," Jackson said.

"She's got a daddy of her own, man. I'll answer that question to him when it's time."

"Yeah, well, her daddy wasn't with her in Afghanistan," Jackson said.

"Tessa has made it very clear that this is none of your business. Drop it."

Cordon checked the door with his light even though he knew Tessa wouldn't be there. Why did this matter so much to Jackson? Was there something Tessa hadn't told him about her time overseas? Come to think of it, they hadn't talked about Afghanistan since that moment in the car. Maybe he was reading the situation wrong. Maybe Jackson had every right to be upset here.

But it wasn't like Tessa to leave out information like that. She'd sign up and join the military but carrying on with two men at once wasn't her style.

Cordon scanned the room again.

Where *was* Tyler?

His uncle's warning played back in his mind, adamant this place was dangerous. So dangerous that the man had tried to bribe him not to be here. Frowning, Cordon tucked the elastic band of his mini camera in his pocket, letting the little camera rest at his hip as he started for the door. He'd waited at least five minutes, that was long enough. He could deal with a sobbing Marisol so long as Tessa was nearby.

Jackson's hand on his shoulder drew him up short. "Hey, man, we're talking here."

Cordon shrugged his hand off, stopping just short of sending his fist into Jackson's teeth. "We're done talking."

"Man, you don't know a thing about that girl," Jackson said.

"She was my wife once; I know her plenty." Cordon gripped his flashlight hard.

"You know she got three people killed over there?"

Cordon froze, his mind flashing to the corn maze and that awful, lost expression on Tessa's face. He'd never seen post-traumatic stress disorder up close, but it didn't take a genius to recognize it on her. She'd been far away, reliving something horrific, and Cordon would be damned if he let Jackson trigger her again.

"Yeah, that's what I thought," Jackson said, sounding victorious.

"Actually, she did tell me about the IED incident," Cordon said, checking the door to make sure she hadn't come back yet. "It was a tragic and awful thing."

If he saw so much as a flicker of light in the hall, he would pound Jackson's face until he couldn't speak.

"Tragic, right." Jackson spat. "That bitch should have been in Cabby's seat. Cabby always sat on the right and suddenly he's on the left? Nah, man. She fucked with the routine. Cabby should be the one alive today, not her."

Fucked with the routine?

Cordon forced himself to take a slow, careful breath before he did something stupid like break Jackson's teeth with his flashlight. The man was completely unhinged. Grade-A lunatic who should not be able to pass a psych exam, unhinged, and it was getting more and more difficult to cut this man slack.

Maybe this was why he was here instead of with the rest of his unit. Maybe this was required leave because the stress of being at war had nudged something loose in his brain. That didn't excuse him for talking shit about Tessa, but he had lost friends. Cordon tried to hold onto that thought as he formed his response.

"Look, I'm sorry your friend is dead," he said, as calmly as he was able. "I can't possibly understand what that feels like."

"Damn right you can't," Jackson said.

Cordon checked on Alyssa and Lundy, not terribly surprised to find them lip-locked and pressed together.

Something is very off about this place.

"Listen," he said, cutting Jackson off before he could go on another tirade. "Can you keep an eye on these two? I'm going to look for the others."

There was a movement in the shadows that Cordon

assumed to be a shrug.

"Why the hell not?" Jackson asked, sounding peeved. "Seems you're as closed off as Pines is. You two deserve each other."

"Thanks," he said, already turning for the door.

Jackson could be as pissed off as he wanted. Cordon wanted out of the Ashwood, now.

Chapter Seventeen

Tessa jogged down the administration building's steps, nearly turning her ankle when she reached the bottom. Her sturdy boots managed to save her from what could have been a nasty sprain, but she paused anyway, cursing and shaking the limb out. The street- lights barely illuminated the parking lot and the front lawn, and the moon remained lost under thick cloud cover, making her little flashlight the only reliable light around.

A gust of wind stirred through the trees, peppering her face with rain. *Fifteen percent chance my ass.*

Any minute now Mother Nature would drench this place.

"Marisol!" she called, hoping the girl had the sense to stay close.

She spotted Marisol's retreating back several yards away, heading for one of the adjacent buildings, and Tessa hurried after her. What sort of lunatic went for an abandoned, rat-infested building over her own car? And then she remembered that Marisol did not own a car. Well, she could have at least stayed in the administration building and saved Tessa a trip.

Lundy wasn't that much of a catch, God damn it.

"Marisol, wait!" Tessa tried again but Marisol had reached the other building and stepped inside.

Someone needed to slap that girl with some common

sense before natural selection took her out. Picking up speed, Tessa ran to the door and pulled it open, fully expecting to find Marisol waiting there.

Except she wasn't.

Tessa swept her light over the dark hallway, catching the bare bones of the place; chipped and cracked walls like the administration building, an even dirtier floor, another creepy-ass wheelchair, and several doors. And, impossibly far down the hallway, the faint light of Marisol's phone bobbing around the corner.

"Oh, God damn it," Tessa muttered under her breath.

She glanced over her shoulder at the administration building and considered going back. Marisol obviously wanted some space and Tessa did not want to be wandering around this place alone. She could get Cordon and they would hunt for Marisol together.

Something crashed, metal clanking to the ground far away and Marisol screeched in alarm. The sound rocketed through the hallway and Tessa rushed inside without thinking. She called Marisol's name again but there was no response. In her mind was every worst-case scenario; Marisol with her skull cracked open; Marisol impaled by a rusted bit of metal; Marisol with a dozen rat bites and a mutated form of the Black Plague coursing through her system.

Tessa slowed as she turned the corner and then stopped, playing her light over the vacant hallway.

"What the hell?" she said, hunting for signs of Marisol.

Some rotten bit of shelving slanted toward the floor, rusted nails and long splinters bristling out of its surface. Several metal tools that might have been surgical equipment were scattered over the shelves, with one bedpan on the ground beside it. Tessa avoided the shelf and searched the hall again, but Marisol wasn't there.

"Marisol, come out here."

When there was no answer, she slowly picked her way down the hall, praying this building didn't have a basement. But then, falling into a crawl space was equally undesirable, so she prayed instead that the floor would hold up. It was old and wooden, not tiled, though she suspected heavy tile on rotten lumber was worse somehow. Physics seemed on the side of the tile, especially since half the floor she'd seen in the administration building had its tile missing. That had to do something to its integrity.

"Marisol, this isn't funny," Tessa said, checking the first room in the hall.

Empty.

Or at least it was empty of people. An old spring bed lay on its side in the middle of the room, its metal so corroded it looked brown, and a white wooden table stood beneath a cracked window.

She thought of Cordon murmuring to her about a hotel for the weekend and resentment swelled in her chest. She could be enjoying post-coital snuggling on a king-sized bed right now. But instead she was here, searching for an emotionally unstable girl in the middle of a health hazard that made her tours in Afghanistan look clean by comparison.

"Marisol," Tessa said, her patience fading, "I know Lundy sucks. And Alyssa sucks. But this is dangerous. Quit it."

She turned back into the hallway and froze, barely able to stop a scream of her own. There was someone at the far end of the hall. He stood with his back to her and she knew instinctively that it wasn't Marisol. He was too big to be Marisol, a good six feet, and the brownish jacket was too tattered, stretched over broad shoulders that almost reminded her of Cordon. But it wasn't Cordon either, Cordon's hair was long, not shaved.

An icy sensation crawled up her neck and for a heartbeat she forgot to breathe.

Transient? But this building was on the other side of the institute. Could that homeless man have come here when he found his shelter invaded?

"OK," Marisol said.

Tessa jumped, flicking her flashlight to the door across the hall.

Marisol stood there, downcast and sniffling, her little body framed in the shadowy doorway and her dark clothes swallowing the light. Tessa held back several admonitions about her behavior, then trained the light back down the hall where the man had been. But he was gone, which was a hundred times worse, so Tessa moved closer to her friend, still watching the far end.

"I'm sorry for running off," Marisol said glumly. "I just... I went to all this work and he just..."

"It's all right," Tessa said, trying to keep the worry from her voice. "How about we talk in the car?"

"You were right the whole time," Marisol continued, sniffling again and wiping her face with the sleeves of her jacket. "Lundy was never worth all this effort."

"He's a major dweeb," Tessa said, still eyeing the hall. "Let's go to the car."

"But I mean, I really thought he was something special." Marisol groaned and turned back into the little room, her feet crunching through something that alerted Tessa to the movement.

Tessa hesitated, not wanting to leave the hall with the path to the exit, but Marisol kept going and Tessa didn't want to lose her again. Swearing under her breath, she checked her pocket for the folding knife Joe had given her when she turned sixteen. It had been to Afghanistan and back and while it was little help in a defensive situation, she didn't have anything else.

She followed Marisol through the room then out into another hallway and mapped their progress in her head. Marisol didn't seem to be paying attention and Tessa had a bad feeling they would need a quick exit.

"Hey, Marisol, look," Tessa said, hurrying to catch up.

But her knee bashed into something solid and wooden, a flash of pain rocketing trough her leg for a blind second. She stopped, wincing both at the pain and the loud noise. No doubt their transient friend had heard that.

"Are you OK?" Marisol asked.

"I'm fine," Tessa said, checking the door they had just exited. "Listen, I don't think we're alone. We should head back."

"Of course, we're not alone," Marisol said with a wry laugh. "The place is haunted."

"No," Tessa said, trying to ignore the chill that ran down her spine. "No, I mean I think I saw a homeless man back there. I'd feel a hell of a lot better if we went back."

"It was just your imagination," Marisol said, continuing her trek, forcing Tessa to follow again. "That's what this whole thing was supposed to prove, you know? That it's all fake. Just your mind conjuring things that aren't really there."

Tessa shook her head, clearly remembering the hunched form, the shape of the man's ear in the light. There'd been something almost familiar about him, something about the curve of his jaw that niggled at her.

"Stupid Lundy with his stupid project," Marisol grumbled, turning them down yet another hallway.

"Marisol, where are we going?"

"You know he kissed me yesterday?" Marisol asked. "I brought him those mini cameras so he wouldn't look like such a loser to you and he kissed me and said I was great."

Tessa frowned. "Why does it matter what I think?"

"Ugh. As if that isn't obvious."

"It really isn't," Tessa said, still nervous about wherever Marisol was taking them but resigned to the conversation anyway. Maybe the girl just needed to get everything out of her system and then they could go back.

Marisol stopped and Tessa had to take a quick step back before they collided. With the light trained at hip level Tessa could see the girl's face, shadowed and contorted in an expression that looked both vulnerable and a little frightening. Tessa frowned, a cold knot forming in the pit of her stomach. She didn't know why but for a moment Marisol didn't look like Marisol anymore. The cheekbones were too angular, the little rosebud mouth a smidge too wide and full.

It's just the dark. But she couldn't shake a feeling of wrongness about the whole situation. Marisol was a tad reckless and excitable, but Tessa would never have pegged her as the sort to throw a fit, much less endanger herself like this. And as much as she might have been swooning for Lundy, it certainly hadn't been true love.

"You've been judging Lundy this whole time," Marisol said. "Constantly asking what he was doing for this party. Laughing about what a complete jerk he is with your perfect boyfriend over there, with your perfect hair and that perfect smile."

Tessa opened her mouth, but she was too shocked to respond. Marisol was jealous of her?

"And I just couldn't face the fact that you were right. I knew it a week ago when I asked Lundy to help me plan the time frames for everyone's investigations in the different buildings. I thought it would be a good chance for us to spend some time alone together, but he blew me off. And then he kept blowing me off for the whole week."

"God, Marisol, I'm so sorry…"

"I don't want you to be sorry, Tessa!" Marisol snapped, turning away from her again. "I want…Cordon."

Tessa straightened, too stunned to respond. She considered smacking the girl upside the head with her flashlight but managed to refrain.

"Cordon?" she asked and hoped the girl would say something sensible before she lost her temper.

"Well, not Cordon exactly but *a* Cordon. A man who looks at me the way he looks at you."

Tessa tried to relax; grateful she hadn't acted on her baser instincts.

"You know, like his whole world is right in front of him. He treasures you, Tessa. There isn't anything he wouldn't do for you. And you know it."

"Yeah, I do," Tessa said.

But then, she'd always known that, and she'd still run away. What was wrong with her? Sure, it would have been difficult, but she could have at least given him the chance to fix things before joining the military.

"And you are all goo-goo eyes for him. And it's so

damn unfair. Do you realize how rare it is to find that? I've been searching my whole life for someone like that and haven't been able to come close."

All nineteen years? Do not further upset the emotionally disturbed person, it will only lead to problems.

"Uh-huh," Tessa said and tried to think of a way to get her out of there.

God, she needed backup. She needed Cordon. And she really, really needed to know where that homeless man had gone.

Prioritize, Pines! Think!

She wasn't certain why, but it was Cabby's voice in her head, urging her to break it down, to strategize, and she took a slow breath, running through a list of what needed to be done. She needed to get Marisol to safety. Then she needed to find Cordon and tell him something was wrong with this place and together they could convince everyone to close shop.

Maybe she'd even punch Lundy in the face for being a dick. That would certainly be a highlight of the night, though she doubted Marisol would thank her for it.

And somehow, she needed to avoid all transients and rodents in the process.

Marisol nudged something with her foot that looked suspiciously like a dead rat and Tessa shuddered. *I could be in a hotel right now.*

****

Cordon made his way through the administration building, assuming Marisol and Tessa wouldn't have gone far. But with each empty office or lab room he came upon he began to suspect otherwise. The storm was becoming increasingly evident, cracking thunder overhead capable of shaking the entire building. The floor creaked under him, unsound wood dipping under his weight.

"Damn it, Tessa, where did you go?" he muttered, making his way to a large door in what he believed to be the northern wall. He'd been turning corners and searching rooms for so long he'd lost his mental map of the place.

The door was heavy as he opened it, old springs and hinges protesting with the movement, but he muscled it open anyway and shone his light inside. He thought someone was murmuring from the larger room beyond, so he stepped in, sweeping his light in search.

"Tess—"

The door behind him slammed with so much force that he jumped.

Heart hammering in his chest, he spun around. His light caught the sudden drift of disturbed dust as it fell from the doorframe and he stared at it for a moment, forcing himself to breathe normally.

Old rusty springs. The cursed place was falling apart.

Cordon turned back into the room, trailing his light over the large, open space in front of him. It was colder here. The wind howled through high windows that had long since lost their panes. Rain pattered against the balcony just overhead and, further in, falling from the broken ceiling to the ruined floor in the center of the room. Slowly, he began to recognize where he was.

This could only be the assembly room, cafeteria and sometime theater, given the stage at the far end. It had a frill of red curtains rimming the top half of the stage alcove and what looked to be a woodland backdrop, its paint peeling and bubbled from water damage and age. At center stage stood a scaffold of some sort, rickety looking with a flimsy ladder and a bucket on the second level.

Across the floor were scattered several seats, most of them pulled up from their moorings and tossed onto their sides, and in the corner nearest him it looked like someone had made a fire pit. Charred wood and metal piled together in a large circle and what appeared to be an old locker lay face down beside it.

Who would want to have a bonfire here?

The wood beneath him gave way, dipping down by an alarming degree and he managed to shift his weight before he went all the way through. Pointing his light at the hole he'd just created in the floor, he carefully returned to the door.

There was no way Tessa had come through here. He would have heard her by now or spotted her in the open space.

He turned back down the hallway, trying to retrace his steps. She wasn't in her jeep. He'd checked there first, which meant she had to be in one of the other buildings, which deeply disturbed him. He didn't like the idea of hunting through eight-hundred-plus acres of decomposing buildings any more than he liked the idea of her being there in the first place.

An odd sound stopped him in his tracks. It was like wood groaning under pressure, the sound of a ship at sea, creaking and shifting with the swell of the ocean. For a moment it felt like the hall itself tilted and he had to lean to the left, bracing himself against the nearest wall before he could fall over. His ears popped as though he'd gained altitude and the moaning of the building was suddenly muffled.

Cordon's stomach pitched. He clutched his flashlight

until it creaked in his grasp, but he was so busy trying not to vomit that he didn't notice.

The sensation continued, jumbled voices joining the low groaning of the walls and for a disoriented moment he thought he saw someone at the far end of the hall. When his stomach fully settled, he tried to yawn, opening his jaw wide in the effort to clear his ears. Leaning into the wall, he swallowed down bile and fought to concentrate. Vertigo swung the hallway in his view, and he flicked his light off, hoping the lack of sight would help fix the issue.

Taking several deep breaths, he sensed the spin of the room even in the dark and nausea clutched him again.

What was wrong with him?

The hair on the back of his neck stood stiff, a shiver of acknowledgement running down his spine and he straightened; he was being watched.

Turning his light on, he peered down the hallway, finding more discarded furniture and dirty wooden floors. He turned to check the other end of the hall.

Four feet away stood a man in military uniform, or what was left of a military uniform. It was burnt and tattered, rusty blood covering his chest and left arm. His face was pock-marked but mostly intact; sharp nose, rounded cheekbones, and a wide mouth twisted into a frown.

"Holy shit! You lost?"

Was this the transient they'd seen earlier? Deciding civility was the best tactic, Cordon kept his light trained on the man.

The man opened his mouth, but no sound came out. Cordon didn't see any weapons on him, and he didn't appear violent, but instinct was telling him not to reach out just yet.

There was a raspy, hallow sound, like wind through a deep crevasse and Cordon willed himself not to retreat. The man kept reaching for him, mouth gaping, and took a jerky step forward. His eyes were shadowed, empty, and Cordon could make out burn scars across the left side of his head.

The soldier was still staggering toward him and Cordon planted his feet.

"Hey, man, I don't know what's going on here, but I've got a girl lost in this place and I need to reach her. So, if you could just tell me what your deal is…"

A gust of wind raced through the hall, stirring up shredded bits of paper and debris and whisking it into the air. Cordon covered his face, cursing as pebbles and dirt hurtled at him. It was warm at first, carrying the scent of desert in the summer, but as the wind passed it turned icy, the cold clawing into Cordon's lungs until he coughed.

And then it was gone, leaving only the hallow echo of its passage as it disappeared down the hall.

"What the hell?" He realized an instant later the soldier was gone.

With a shaking hand he fumbled with his coat pocket and drew out his cell phone, which in retrospect he could have used earlier. The bright screen was hard to look at, but he found Tessa's name on speed dial and hit the call button.

"Come on, come on," he muttered, listening to it ring three times before she finally picked up.

"Hey," she said, sounding a little distracted.

But he breathed in relief. She was all right.

"Hey," he said, collecting his wits again. "Something is really off about this place. Let's get out of here."

"Hell yes!"

"Where are you?"

"I'm not sure, I followed Marisol into the big building on the left…" Marisol said something in the background and then Tessa was back. "The women's ward, apparently."

"All right," he said, trying to remember what the map had looked like. He should have nabbed one before he'd left. "I'm coming to you."

"No, don't," Tessa said and then her voice changed, going hushed. "Listen, I think that homeless guy is in here. He didn't seem right in the head and he disappeared before I could get a good look at him."

His pulse kicked up a notch, panic making a vise of his chest and he frowned. "That's a reason to have me there, Tessa, not the other way around."

"Yeah, but right now I don't know where I am, and I'd rather not see you get stabbed or cannibalized while hunting for me."

God, and now that image was in his head.

"Tessa, I am coming for you. Do not go anywhere. Call me if he comes back. Call me if you even think you see him."

"Cordon…"

"Just trust me," he said, already moving, "And don't talk to him if he shows."

He hung up and shoved the phone in his pocket, praying she'd listen long enough for him to reach her. Casting one last glance down the hallway, he decided that whoever the soldier was, he could damn well find his own way out of this place.

Then he ran.

Chapter Eighteen

"Let me guess," Marisol said as Tessa hung up the phone. "That was Cordon checking to make sure you're all right."

Tessa stared at the girl, standing with her arms crossed in the gloomy little room, shoulders hunched. For an instant, she considered knocking Marisol out and lugging her unconscious body out of this place. It seemed like an extreme measure, but Cordon was right, there was something seriously off about this place and Tessa, for one, wanted out.

But she was certain that would lead to legal hassles later. Marisol was her friend, but they weren't that close.

"More or less," Tessa said, earning a disgusted snort from Marisol. She ignored her, checking the exits again to be sure they didn't have any visitors. "He's coming to get us."

"Why?"

Tessa frowned, keeping her light trained on the door to the hallway. She could see into the adjacent room and it looked like something was moving in there. It wasn't exactly a shape, or if it was, she couldn't make it out, but there was movement in there, she was sure of it.

"Tessa, I do not want Cordon here smirking at me and my man troubles."

"He is coming because we aren't safe," Tessa

snapped, "Which you would know if you were paying any attention at all."

Marisol snorted. "Oh, what will happen? A rat biting me?"

"You know," Tessa said, desperate to hold her temper. "I'm not a vindictive person but I hope one does now, just to wake your ass up."

What was wrong with this girl? Marisol had never seemed the stupid sort before.

"Well that's a lousy thing to…" Marisol trailed off and then screamed, grabbing Tessa's shoulder so hard it knocked her off balance.

Tessa's heart seized for an aching second, thundering in her chest a second later as she fought to regain her footing. Her light shifted with the surge of movement and she lost sight of the white thing in the other room. Then it didn't matter because she swept it through the room, hunting for whatever made Marisol scream. A breath later the beam outlined a man standing two feet away.

"Shit!" Tessa shouted.

Acting on instinct, she yanked Marisol behind herself, holding the flashlight as if it were a weapon. It couldn't do much, but it could give them a chance to run. She just had to aim for his face.

"Hello Tessa," he said.

After a confused second, she realized he was familiar. Dark hair, jock's build, and an open sneer she'd seen him use on Cordon too often. Tyler Brannings. Only it didn't quite look like Tyler. He looked older somehow, his face a little longer, his nose more defined. He wore a tattered white lab technician's jacket burned on one sleeve and had so many stains on it that it could only have come from this awful place.

A sick knot clenched in her belly as she gazed at him. His eyes were dark, and if she wasn't mistaken, full of intent.

"Tyler, what the hell?" Marisol said from behind her. "You scared the shit out of me!"

Tessa didn't move. All her instincts told her that this wasn't Tyler, not really.

"Sorry, Marisol," Tyler said, his gaze slipping over Tessa. "I just saw you two and couldn't help myself."

White jacket, not brown. That meant the transient was still around somewhere.

Fantastic, the problems kept piling up.

"You're a real dick," Marisol said, startling Tessa even more.

Marisol Williams did not call people *dicks*. She didn't hinge all her identity on finding a man, either. And she certainly didn't pout when things didn't go her way. Maybe she'd hyperventilate and act like the world was ending, but she didn't pout.

"All right, we're heading back to central command," Tessa said. "We're done here."

"Aw, come on now, I just got here." Tyler said, stepping in close.

Tessa stiffened, frowning at Tyler's smarmy grin.

"What are you wearing?" Marisol asked, apparently noticing the lab coat for the first time.

Tyler ignored her, reaching to drag a cold knuckle over Tessa's cheek. "I was hoping we could get to know one another."

"I know everything I want to know about you," Tessa said, turning her face away from his hand.

He was built. He'd likely trained, though not at the dojo with Joe. She tried to guess at what kind of training he did, but in the end it wouldn't matter. Surprise was her best weapon here.

"Tyler!" Marisol gasped. "What has gotten into you?"

"Nothing's gotten into me," he said, leaning over Tessa to whisper in her ear; "But I know what I'd like to get into…"

Tessa jerked her head to the left, deliberately catching him in the face with her skull. Pain radiated out from the impact point, sending dizzy sparks through her vision. Tyler cursed, staggering back several steps.

Marisol squeaked in alarm. "Tessa!"

"Whoops. Ticklish." She took several steps back, bringing Marisol with her.

"Bitch!" Tyler covered his eye with one hand.

Damn. She'd been hoping to break his nose.

"Yeah, well, you invaded my personal bubble," Tessa said. "Now Cordon is on his way and we're meeting him. Quite frankly, I don't care what you do."

She inched closer to the door, half-listening in case Cordon was nearby. She wasn't certain if she wanted Cordon to show or not because she knew him well enough to recognize a fighting offense when she saw one.

"What, you think you're too good for me?" Tyler advanced on her.

Tessa's heart lurched.

That was possibly the most cliché thing she'd ever heard in real life, and she knew exactly what came next. Widening her stance, she let her flashlight slide a little in her grasp, gripping only the very end as he approached. In the dark of the room she could make out his hand as he reached for her and tried to guess where his head was.

His fingers grazed her shoulder and Tessa lashed out,

letting instinct and a hefty amount of fear lead her. The flashlight connected with a solid crack, rattling the batteries in their housing. The bulb popped and the room plunged into darkness.

Marisol screamed.

Tyler let out a surprised grunt, his hand slipping off Tessa's shoulder as he collapsed to the ground.

"Go, go, go," Tessa shouted, grasping at Marisol in the dark and urging the girl toward the doorway.

Marisol didn't need any further encouragement. She disappeared through the door so quickly that Tessa staggered a little. Stumbling along behind her, Tessa was almost out the door when Tyler grabbed her leg. She kicked back on instinct, and her foot sank into something soft.

"Oof!"

His hold loosened and Tessa ran. But she'd lost her bearings and crashed into the doorframe with bruising force. She grunted, grimacing as pain bloomed through her shoulder and down her arm. Her eyes adjusted quickly, giving a dim view of the hallway as she stumbled out. Her foot caught on something wooden and she tripped, reaching out to steady herself on instinct.

Something pierced deep into her left palm and she stilled. There was the rough scrape of old wood under her skin and the sense of something foreign pulsing pain through her hand. Her flashlight clattered to the floor, dead and useless.

Oh, God, was that a nail?

It took several seconds to process but, yes, it was a nail, and her mind flew to lock jaw. Worse yet, the thing was still in her, she could feel it as she tried to shift the hand in question.

She'd lost the feeling in three of her fingers, which was a bad sign, but with no light to see the damage she didn't know if she could pull her hand free or not.

Gingerly probing the top of her left hand, she located the sharp end of the nail. It punctured straight through, coming out between the middle and ring fingers.

Behind her, Tyler began groaning and she straightened. She couldn't stay here, not even to wait for Cordon and light. Taking a deep breath, she pulled her hand free, feeling every centimeter of the nail as it passed back through her palm.

Smothering several curses, she staggered back a step, dizzy from pain and what she suspected might be shock. Holding the wounded limb to her chest, she moved around whatever object had just skewered her and hurried down the hall, doing her best not to trip again.

****

Cordon opened the doors to the women's ward and stepped inside, his heart hammering from the sprint. Shining his light down the cramped hallway, he took several steadying breaths and continued his trek, trying not to imagine some homeless man attacking Tessa.

"Tessa!"

When there was no answer he swore under his breath and hurried around the first corner, casting his light into every open doorway he could find. Reaching the end of the hall he turned again, passing through a series of offices, each of them densely populated by old desks and long-since forgotten paperwork. It was a miracle so much history had survived here. He imagined looters and stupid teenagers would have taken or destroyed it all by now.

He paused in one office, frowning because he thought he should have come to another hallway by now. Shining his light in the other direction, he tried to remember all the turns he'd made. His sense of direction was normally spot on, but there was something about this place that made it difficult.

"Tessa!"

The eerie groaning from before rolled through the room, pulled over him, and it was all he could do not to retch all over the desk. His ears popped, and the room tilted, everything slanting to the left and he grasped at the splintered desk to keep his balance. His chest felt like sandbags were resting on it, making it hard to breathe.

Had he been drugged somehow?

He tried to think of the last thing he'd eaten, but his mind could only conjure his oatmeal and toast from breakfast. Surely, he'd had lunch, hadn't he?

"*Ashwood is dangerous.*" Phil's voice floated back to him.

Cordon's stomach heaved and he fought it back, digging for his phone. He punched the number in for his uncle, determined to get some answers. It rang twice before Phil's voice came through, distorted and patchy because the blasted storm was messing with reception.

"Cordon?" Phil's voice was thin, and static covered nearly everything.

"Yeah, listen. I'm at Ashwood. What the hell is up with this place?"

"Cord…" There was a long bit of static and then his uncle again. "Where are you?"

"Ashwood," Cordon repeated. "And there is something seriously wrong with this place."

"…can't. Stay away…" Static took over and then the phone beeped, alerting him that the call had been lost.

"Fucking fantastic," Cordon growled, checking to

make sure Tessa hadn't tried to call.

She hadn't, which was something positive; or at least he hoped it was. He shoved his phone in his pocket again and paused, spotting the edge of an old photograph on the desk. Something about it tugged at his mind and he took it, angling his light so he could see without the beam glaring against the shiny film.

One corner had water damage that stretched along both sides, rimming the photograph with dingy brown. But the age of it was not what stole his attention. It looked to be his own face smiling out at him in black and white. Whatever uniform he was wearing had been unbuttoned at the throat, revealing a white undershirt, and he had a very sated smile on his face. Cordon reeled.

What could only be lipstick smears led off from the side of his mouth, mingling with his beard, and beside him, looking every bit as rumpled and satisfied, was Tessa. Her hair was done up in tight curls that spiraled around her face and her lips curved in a dazed and sultry expression that hit him right in the gut. She had on a nurse's uniform, also open at the collar, showing off a good deal of her lacey brassiere.

"What the ever-loving hell?" he whispered, turning the picture over.

The back lower edge had only a date written; the ink somewhat faded but clearly legible; 1933.

A scream tore through the building, yanking him out of his confusion.

Panic gripped him. He crammed the photo in his pocket and rushed through the nearest door, trying to approximate which direction the sound came from.

"Tessa!"

He found another hallway, swept his light down both

directions and cursed whoever had built this place. Every few meters the hall was sectioned off by doors, most of them open or half open and he couldn't get a clear view.

Someone was running toward him, coming from the right, and he shone his light in that direction. The figure approaching was too small to be Tessa, but he waited anyway, giving Marisol the light she needed to safely reach him.

"Oh, thank God!" She threw herself on him, panting and shuddering.

"What happened?" He patted her back in an effort to calm her down. "Where's Tessa?"

"Oh, God, it was awful!"

Holding tight to his self-control he asked again; "Where is Tessa?"

Marisol buried her face in his chest, her voice muffled and pausing often to hiccup a breath, "Tessa and I were talking because Lundy is a jerk…and then you called…and then Tyler showed up…only he was acting strange, like he was wanting Tessa to…And she said no, basically, and then he went crazy and tried to grab her and Tessa up and hit him with her flashlight. And now she's back there somewhere in the dark with him and I'm an awful friend for leaving her behind!"

His blood froze, not fully understanding the girl but catching the important part. Tessa had struck Tyler, which he'd probably deserved, and now she was without a light and having to fend for herself.

Prying Marisol's arms off him, Cordon then held her back, "Where?"

"So, this is where everyone's got off to," Jackson's voice intruded from the left. "Cheating on Tessa already, are you? I knew you weren't right for her."

"I don't have time for this," Cordon said, clamping down on the urge to hit the man because there wasn't time for that either. He turned back to Marisol, who was still sniffling and looking terrified. "Where did you leave her?"

Her face crumpled. "Oh, I'm such an awful person! I should have stayed!"

"Yes, you are. Now tell me where to go, damn it!"

He didn't care how harsh he sounded any more than he cared for the derisive comment Jackson made. He was completely focused on locating Tessa. The rest of these people be damned.

"Five doors down, I think… Go left and…and…"

"And?" He suppressed the urge to shake her.

"And it's dark!" she snapped. "I can't remember!"

"Fine," Cordon said, releasing her. He gestured to Jackson with his own light. "You two get back to the administration building. We're getting the hell out of here as soon as I get Tessa."

"Hey! Who put you in charge?"

Cordon was already moving, not bothering to answer him. Marisol scuttled over to Jackson's side. Ignoring them both, Cordon counted doors until he found the fifth and then turned, praying he would find Tessa before anything else could go wrong.

Chapter Nineteen

Tessa used the light on her phone to navigate the debris-strewn hallway. She kept her left hand up and at an angle, clasping the hem of her jacket in a makeshift attempt at bandaging. Now that the initial shock had worn off a deep ache throbbed through the appendage. She wouldn't die unless lock jaw could set within twenty minutes, but she was sure her tetanus shots were up-to-date. The army had certainly poked her full of holes when she'd gone overseas. At least one of those had to have been for tetanus.

Her knee bashed into something metal and she swore, new pain spiking up her thigh. Pointing her phone at the object, she saw a large cabinet laying horizontal across the floor.

"This place is trying to kill me," she muttered and moved around it.

A deep groaning sound echoed through the hall and the hair on the back of her neck stood stiff. It seemed to be coming from the walls, creaking and moaning as though in warning just before the floor tilted under her feet. She teetered back, crashing into the cabinet and then to the floor, bashing her injured hand in the process.

Agony flared through her palm, pulsing in time with her rapid heartbeat and for several seconds she feared she would be sick. Cradling her hand against her chest, she concentrated on breathing. Slow breath in, slow breath out, willing herself to stop dwelling on her hand.

She'd been through worse, damn it.

Quit being such a baby. You've got bigger problems.

The light on her phone flicked out. Grumbling about how she needed to take the timer off the damn thing, she pressed the button on the side and her surroundings were washed in bluish light. It only gave off enough illumination to show her a few steps, making a little square window as her field of vision.

She started to her feet again, wobbling because the world was still in the process of righting itself. Which was crazy, now that she thought about it. Unless this was some kind of fun house with hidden hydraulics systems, there was no way that could have happened.

Drugs?

No. She'd had bottle water and a cola the whole day. And unless the folks over there at Quinn's had made her some special salad dressing, her food couldn't have been tampered with. Besides, it had been hours since she'd had either.

She froze, the light on her phone catching a pair of dusty combat boots in front of her. Swallowing a startled scream, Tessa tilted her phone to light her visitor, and then all the breath left her at once.

"Cabby?"

Sergeant Robert Cabarton, his pock-marked face frighteningly expressionless, gazed at her from four steps away. His eyes were pools of shadow, watching; just watching. An icy finger of fear slid up her spine.

"Just how much blood did I lose?" she whispered.

Cabby turned, his feet making no sound on the dirty floor, and disappeared around the corner. Tessa stared after him, debating her sanity.

"There are no such things as ghosts. I'm just having a really stressful night and my mind is trying to cope…by scaring me half to death."

That didn't sound nearly as reasonable as she'd hoped.

She took a deep breath and tried a different tactic.

If she were writing this story, would she have the heroine, namely herself, go after the spirit-hallucination-thing masquerading as her dead friend? If she did then there could be only one of two outcomes; either the spirit was malevolent and leading her to her death, or the spirit was benevolent and trying to get her to safety.

Or there was no spirit at all and it was just a hallucination due to harmful gases in the air. In which case she'd be wandering aimlessly until she found an exit.

Choice number two was to head back, but Tyler would be pissed off and as much as she might have trained to fight, the kid outweighed her by at least sixty pounds. Plus, she had a feeling he was only acting this way because of this place, in which case she would feel awful if she hurt him.

Choice number three was to stand there and do nothing, wait for Cordon to find her, and hope Tyler didn't get there first.

Well, shit. All those choices sucked.

But only one of them increased the distance between herself and the known danger; Tyler.

"Ghost it is," she muttered and started to walk.

Carefully picking her way through what must have been an office once, Tessa's ears popped, like gaining altitude on takeoff. She tugged on her earlobe, trying to dislodge the sensation. As she made her way down the hall, she repeated the mantra that there was no such thing as ghosts. Whatever was going on had nothing to do with the supernatural because there was *no such thing* as the supernatural.

Maybe she'd come unhinged. That certainly made sense. It would explain why she was seeing Cabby.

Should have gone to see the shrink like her dad wanted.

She cringed and entered an office. She didn't think PTSD was supposed to manifest itself like this. The first time she'd had an episode, it had been at the hotel in Hawaii before she'd come home. She was watching the news and a reporter was updating the war effort and she saw a convoy in the background.

Just the sight of it caught her and she was thrown back, her mind caged to that awful day. Somehow, she recognized the feel of the television remote in her hand and calmed down. Counting to ten. Breathing. Doing all the things Joe had taught them in high school to center and prepare for a match.

It seemed fitting to her that the techniques taught to prep for a sparring match were the same things she used to fight back to reality. But maybe it wasn't enough.

As she walked through the clinic room, she noticed light, real light. The tile was all intact here and voices came from the room on her right. Her heart leapt, thinking it must be Cordon, and she hurried to the door, flinging it wide. Bright light spilled from overhead where the lamps were actually working, and she had to blink several times as she stepped inside.

It was an office as she'd suspected, and it was impossibly clean. One desk sat prominent in one corner, with two chairs placed before it. Plaques hung on the walls along with various photographs. Some part of her brain said this must have been what the Ashwood looked like in its heyday, before time and neglect tore at its foundations. There in the center of the room was Cordon.

She almost took a step but stopped herself.

His beard was shaped differently, more trimmed, and he wore what looked like a janitor's uniform. In front of him was another man, clearly a doctor by the jacket and huddled to the side of them both was a woman in a nurse's uniform.

Tessa's mouth went dry.

The woman looked a whole hell of a lot like her.

"Eight months I've been wracking my brain," the doctor shouted. The revolver in his hand shook. "Eight months! Trying to get you to notice me!"

"Frank," the woman said. Her face—Tessa's face—was distraught as she tried to step toward Cordon.

Not Cordon. A Cordon hallucination, it had to be. This was all a hallucination and she was losing her mind or something.

Where had Cabby gone? She checked the room, but he was gone. There were only the strange look-alikes in the center of a room far too intact to be real.

"Frank, please, listen to me..." the Tessa doppelganger said.

Frank scoffed. "Why the hell should I?"

"Just calm down, doctor," Cordon said.

Frank aimed his revolver and Cordon lifted his hands in surrender.

"You don't speak!" Frank screamed. "You just fucking stand there!"

"All right! All right!" The fake Tessa's eyes darted to the gun. "Frank! Please!"

"Explain to me how this *janitor* is suddenly the love of your life?" Frank asked "He's a nothing! A nobody!"

Tessa couldn't breathe.

What was going on here? Maybe she'd passed out somewhere. She knew she hadn't lost that much blood and pride refused to let her say it was shock. She'd gone through real shock once, this wasn't it. And if this was PTSD, then her brain was so broken she didn't think there'd be any chance at sanity again.

Still, those were her father's words. She remembered the corn maze and Todd's angry tone the week before. But this Frank was no relation to the girl standing in the center. No, there was another type of tension between Frank and ghost-Tessa, an unrequited love that had Frank ready to commit murder.

"None of this is real," Tessa whispered. "None of this is real."

She closed her eyes and counted to ten, listening to the other Tessa as she tried reasoning with Frank.

"Please, he's everything to me…"

Frank barked an incredulous laugh and Tessa opened her eyes again. It was an ugly laugh, full of derision and anger that seemed to strike right into her gut.

"Well now he really is nothing." Frank pulled the trigger.

The shot cracked through the room, a deafening explosion that drowned out Tessa's scream. Tessa watched in horror as Cordon staggered back. Five more shots rang out, one after another. Frank advanced on Cordon with each shot, bald rage contorting his face.

Blood welled up in Cordon's chest, his body jerking under the impact. Frank kept pulling the trigger, even after the gun was empty, its hammer hitting the mechanism with a loud *click! click! click!*

"Oh my god," Tessa whispered, and sank to her knees.

Ghost Tessa knelt too, sobbing and clutching at Cordon's lifeless body. "Don't be dead," she cried. "Please, please don't be dead."

But he was dead. He was dead and gone and for a heart-stuttering moment Tessa thought she knew what the Ashwood wanted.

Cordon.

Chapter Twenty

Cordon rubbed his chest with one hand and pointed his light into the nearest room with the other. An odd pressure had taken up residence right at the center of his ribcage, an ache that would not go away. The paranoid part of his mind tried to rationalize that he was too young for a heart attack, but he'd read enough science fiction to know bizarre things sometimes happened.

But a heart attack at twenty-six? That seemed like a stretch. He was relatively healthy.

Grimacing, he hurried to the next door. Speculation wasn't helping. He needed to find Tessa and he needed to get her out of there now. This place was insane. The walls themselves seemed to be watching him, following his every step through the creaky building.

He jumped when his phone rang, then scowled as he fished it from his pocket. "Tessa?"

Static, and then his uncle's voice, sounding fainter this time. "Cordon…"

"Uncle Phil, tell me you know what the hell is going on with this place."

The next three rooms were empty of people, but increasingly littered by broken down beds and cabinets. He shook his head and tried to listen to his uncle's scrambled voice.

"Get out of there," Phil said.

"I'm trying to, believe me."

"Stop whatever you are doing and get out now."

Cordon entered a familiar series of offices, shining his light through the room. Despair ate at the back of his mind, a little voice telling him this place was too big, he would never find Tessa. And then there was Rusty Phil urgently telling him to abandon it all and run, cut his losses.

But that would mean leaving Tessa behind. It seemed his entire family was trying to break off this relationship. Maybe not Sara, but certainly his mother and now Phil.

"You know, if you don't have something helpful to say then you can just fuck right off," he told the phone and hung up.

Shoving the phone into his pocket again he paused. Phil was not against Tessa, Cordon knew that. Why had he said that?

He considered dialing the man up to apologize, but a soft, hiccupping sound drifted into his awareness and he froze. It was faint, seeming to come from the right, and if he wasn't mistaken it sounded like someone was crying. His feet crunched over the ground, glass and metal grinding into the floor, partially drowning out the sound.

Finally, he reached a doorway where he thought the noise was originating and shone his light inside. Sweeping the beam across the dark space he passed her once and then flicked it back, illuminating Tessa where she knelt in the middle of the room.

His heart leapt at the sight, mingled surprise, concern, and relief rushing through him as he hurried to her side. She didn't seem to notice as he crouched in front of her. In fact, she continued to gaze at a space between his feet, her expression dazed and far away.

"Tessa," he said.

When she didn't respond he touched her cheek. Up close, he spotted blood on her sleeve and hand and his gut clenched in reaction. "Oh, God, Tessa, you're hurt."

"He's dead," she said bleakly, her eyes glossy and still far away. "There was nothing I could do."

Oh, God, had she killed Tyler?

The clenching in his stomach seemed to increase and drop, as though he'd crested a hill too fast and all his control was gone. Marisol said they'd been attacked, but Tyler wasn't the sort of guy to pose a real threat. Surely Tessa had known that.

The Tessa Cordon knew would have known that, wouldn't she?

Dread made an icy rock in his chest and images of Tessa in the corn maze bombarded him. If she'd been having another episode like that, would she have even known what she was doing?

"It's all right." He cupped her face, willing images of Tyler from his mind. "Tessa, it's going to be all right."

God help him, he shouldn't have let her go alone. He should have been there to stop whatever nonsense had happened.

Tessa blinked at him. In an instant her expression changed from grief to understanding and she flung her arms around his neck with a strangled cry. She smelled of dust and sweat and faintly of her shampoo. He held her tight, kissing the side of her head, her neck, her cheek as she buried her face in his shoulder and sobbed.

The way she clung to him wrenched at his guts. He would need to see her safely out of this place then he could go see just how bad Tyler was. And then… God only knew what then.

"I saw you die. Right here in this room."

Confused, Cordon held tighter to her. "What?"

"There was this noise and then I walked in here. This man shot you six times in the chest... Or it was someone who looked like you," she said, drawing away and wiping at her face. "It was the most awful thing I have ever seen."

He curled a strand of hair behind her ear and tried to wrap his head around what she'd just said. "A noise?"

Cordon remembered the assembly room and the sensation of being submerged in a boat. And it had happened again here, before he'd found her.

"Did this noise happen to be accompanied by a strange sensation, like the building was moving?" he asked.

Tessa nodded. "I thought I was going to puke."

"Yeah, that's been happening to me too," he said. He touched his pocket and the photograph crinkled under his touch. He took it out slowly, shining the light onto the satisfied smiles and rumpled hair and impossibly familiar faces.

Tessa gasped; her gaze riveted on the photo. "What the hell is going on?"

Frowning, Cordon pocketed the photo and shook his head. "I don't know, but we are leaving. Right now."

She glanced over her shoulder, at the door beyond. "Tyler..."

"I'll deal with it."

She got that stubborn look on her face that said she didn't like the idea. "No," she said, climbing to her feet. "I know you. If you find him, you'll end up fighting him. We'll go together."

"Fighting?" he asked, confused, and then realized the

boy wasn't dead.

She hadn't meant Tyler was dead, she'd meant that he had died here.

"Oh, thank God." He clutched her shoulders and breathed a laugh as relief washed through him. "I thought you meant you'd killed him."

"Why would I kill Tyler?"

He shook his head. "Never mind, let me see that."

Not waiting for permission, he took her elbow and drew her bleeding hand into the light. An angry red hole pierced deep into her palm, situated just below her ring and middle fingers, and when she turned the hand over, he could see an exit point on the other side. There was a vein somewhere in there, he knew, and flexed his fist in an effort to control himself.

"My knife is in my pocket," she said, turning her hip toward him.

He slipped his fingers into her jeans pocket, and for a heartbeat thought about the hotel room they should be sharing. Damned Marisol with her stupid project pulling them away from what could have been a wonderful weekend. His fingers located the knife and he drew it out, momentarily distracted by the familiar contours.

Joe had given this knife to her when they were seventeen.

"Cut a strip from my shirt," she said.

"It's cold out here…"

"It's unsanitary out here. I'm already risking infection. Trust me, my shirt is best."

He frowned but cut the sleeve of her sweatshirt anyway. He thought he remembered a first aid class that had said something similar. It was better to use the wounded person's clothes because their body was acclimated to whatever germs and such had already accumulated on the fabric. Or something like that. He couldn't remember it all as he wrapped her hand with the cloth, tying it secure enough that she hissed.

"Sorry," he murmured, disliking the pain in her face. But bleeding needed pressure, they both knew that.

She smiled wanly at him. "Let's get Tyler and get out of here."

"Sure we can't leave him?" Cordon joked.

"Whatever is going on isn't his fault."

They turned together and he let her lead the way as they left the room.

"Yeah, about that," he said, preparing to take the plunge into all-out crazy. "I think it's obvious that shit is not right with this place."

She snorted a laugh. "That's an understatement."

"Best guess…reincarnation?" he suggested, cringing because of how insane it sounded out loud.

"Reincarnation?"

"Well, the photograph is creepy as hell," he said. "But there are so many holes in that theory I'm not even sure where to begin. Such as the fact that we grew up here and never had an issue before."

"We never visited the Ashwood either."

"Right. Because we were smarter in high school."

"This wasn't my idea."

"True. Though it isn't just us acting odd. Everyone else seems to be plunging into crazy-town with us."

Something moved in the shadows and he stiffened, shining his light down the hallway with a frown. His skin crawled like he was being watched. Whatever it was had stopped moving and he couldn't make anything out, not even with the light.

"What is it?"

"Nothing," he muttered, resuming their walk.

"So…reincarnation. And we're here to…what? Relive the most awful murder ever?" She shook her head, leading the way into another hallway. "I'm not sure that fits. Unless Marisol and Tyler are reincarnated too, and that's just too big a leap for me to take."

He thought of Lundy and Alyssa kissing back at base camp and shook his head too. "Yeah, you're right. Whatever this is, it's affecting us in different ways."

"Ghosts or something," Tessa mused. "Hell if I know how to define it, and I read this sort of thing constantly."

"And here I thought you only read the classics," Cordon said, trying for a lighter tone.

She cast him a smile, which was better than the weeping she'd been doing a few minutes ago so he counted it as a win.

"Although I'm sure Poe would have had a field day with this place."

To his surprise, she began to quote a poem, her voice soft and eerie as they continued through the cramped hallway; "And I cried: It was surely October on this very night of last year, that I journeyed—I journeyed down here—that I brought a dread burden down here—on this night of all nights in the year. Ah, what demon has tempted me here?"

Unsettled, Cordon glanced at her slender frame moving through the gloomy space. It was so dark he could only see her profile, the shape of her nose and the glint of her hair reflecting what little light they had. She seemed unbothered by his inspection, or maybe she just hadn't noticed, because she explained in the next moment.

"*Ulalume*, by Poe," she said. "It doesn't get as much attention as it should."

"Uh-huh," Cordon replied, trying to sound encouraging. "Awkwardly appropriate given what month it is. But I'd really like to avoid talk of demons."

"Oh, I doubt this is demonic," Tessa said, pausing outside a door. "Somehow I think a demon would be more singular in its efforts. Take just one of us and kill everyone else."

"Well that's cheerful," he said dryly.

"I'm standing in an abandoned and, by all appearances, haunted institute in the middle of October quoting Poe," she said. "I don't think 'cheerful' is anywhere in the vicinity."

"True," he said, flashing her a grin.

She snorted a soft laugh, then nodded at the door. "Just in there."

Cordon straightened his shoulders and pointed the light into the room. "Tyler?"

There was no answer and no movement.

"Tyler, are you in there?"

They glanced at each other. Since there wasn't a body on the floor, he imagined the man was all right. Ragingly pissed and on the move, but not dead. Although it did mean the chances of a fight had gone up exponentially.

Shining the light through the room, he spotted Tessa's discarded flashlight and what looked to be an exam table crammed into the far corner. The cabinets were mostly intact here, cracked and aged but not quite falling apart yet. There were scuffs in the dusty floor, several footprints trailing from one corner to the next, and a large spot where he assumed Tyler had fallen.

"Tyler?" Cordon tried again, stepping inside. Sweeping the light side to side he searched one last time before turning to Tessa. "He's not here."

"Fantastic," she said then groaned and rubbed her face. "Now what?"

"Well, now I suggest we head back to the others. Maybe he went there?" Cordon said, collecting her flashlight. There was a chance they could fix it when they got back. "And I'd like to grab a first aid kit for you."

She looked about to argue and then sighed, shrugging her agreement. "I'd say it was fine, but it hurts. And I really don't want to get an infection. Or gangrene. Let's go."

Cordon relaxed a little. He'd been afraid she would argue further and insist on getting everyone out of there first. And, to be frank, he didn't give a damn about the rest of this group, he just wanted to see her safe. Which meant seeing to that hand.

He took her elbow and led them through the maze of corridors and office rooms. She leaned into him, all her warmth a solid reassurance that things were going to be all right. He'd found her. She was wounded, but she was alive.

Nothing else mattered.

Chapter Twenty-One

Tessa breathed easier once they stepped out of the women's ward and headed for administration. Sleet and ice hammered down as they jogged their way across the yard. Frigid wet soaked her hair, seeping around the back of her collar to run down her spine as she dashed up the steps. Cordon was cursing beside her, but the actual words were lost in the roar of heavy rain.

He reached the door first and yanked it open, holding it as she ran inside. The door rattled closed behind them. For a long minute they stood in the foyer, hugging themselves and listening to a cacophony of voices coming from the other room.

Teeth chattering, she tried to make out whose voice was saying what, but it was all jumbled. It sounded like Marisol was trying to calm Jackson down, who Tessa had completely forgotten about in her search for Tyler. She flinched, hearing him say something about them not having enough supplies to last the night. And then there was Alyssa, her voice climbing over the rest as she complained that someone, presumably Lundy or Tyler, didn't understand her and never had.

Cordon moved closer, his warmth thawing one side of her body as he leaned in to whisper.

"We could make a break for it."

"I don't think we'd get far before guilt dragged us

back."

"Well, maybe your guilt," he said. "I am guilt free."

A little warmer now, Tessa sighed and started for the command center. He was right, she didn't owe Marisol one more minute in this place. But what if they left and something happened? Tessa had enough ghosts haunting her; she didn't need this on her head too. Turning into the room, she surveyed the situation once, trying to calculate the best course of action.

Alyssa and Lundy were arguing, Alyssa with her arms crossed as she glared at the scrawny boy. Lundy shouted that no one in their right mind could ever understand her. Which couldn't possibly be helping things. Alyssa's thunderous expression proved that much.

In the other corner, Jackson kept scratching at his forehead, making a bright red mark in the center that was visible even in the dim lighting. That wasn't healthy at all, not that Tessa was going to tell him that. She'd let Cordon handle Jackson. On a more bizarre note, Marisol hung on Jackson's arm, biting her lower lip and giving a flirty look that no one in their right mind could miss.

"What the holy hell?" Cordon said.

"This place is awful," Tessa murmured to him. "It's not quite possession, I don't think. Or maybe it is? I have no frigging clue. I just know that they are not themselves right now."

"Well, you're still you, right?" he asked quietly.

"I'm pretty sure, but I don't know if they even realize what is happening. So maybe not?"

"Maybe we could ask them if they've seen anything weird? I mean, I'm pretty sure you're still acting like you and I'm still acting like me. Maybe we're different because we've noticed other things?"

Tessa frowned at the group, noting that Tyler still wasn't accounted for. But that was a problem for them all to face. There would be no more hunting through this institute alone, not if she could help it. This damn investigation was over.

"Hey!" she shouted, but they were all so engrossed with each other that they didn't seem to hear. "Hey! Guys!"

The clamor continued, everyone ignoring her until Cordon let out a sharp, shrill whistle that pierced through the room. The attention swerved to him, all arguments stopping, and he gestured to Tessa, who murmured a bemused thanks before facing the small room. Which, now that she had their attention, she wasn't certain what to do with it.

Asking if they'd seen anything odd would get her a flat denial. No one ever came forward with something potentially comprising in a group forum. No, she would have to gather that information on a one by one basis. For now, she needed to address the more troubling aspects of the night.

"Tyler has gone missing," she announced at last. "He is out there in the dark without a light and is probably injured. We need to find him and then we need to close this shit down and go home."

"What?" Marisol gasped. "We can't leave! Nobody has done any investigating yet."

"Really?" Cordon asked. "You're still hung up on that? This isn't even your project. It's supposedly Lundy's project and he doesn't seem to care one way or another what we do."

Tessa glanced at Lundy, who shrugged and looked peeved, but not at Marisol or Tessa. No, his focus was still on Alyssa, who tapped her foot and rolled her eyes at them. Tessa frowned, wondering why it wasn't registering with the girl that Tyler was missing.

Just how much power did the Ashwood have?

"Hey," Marisol said, jutting her chin, "We worked hard on this. We have to get at least some investigating done. Do you have any idea how hard it was to get those permits?"

"Tyler's probably dead somewhere," Jackson said.

"No, he's not," Tessa said, trying to hold her temper. "He was moving last I heard, so he's alive."

"Yeah, for now," Jackson said.

The room erupted into argument again.

Marisol continued to complain about the permits and Cordon informed her that permits did not trump someone's safety. Then Lundy turned on Alyssa again, letting her know she was a whore who thought too much of herself and Tessa stood there, stunned.

There was an underlying darkness that permeated the room. It was growing, she could feel it passing over her skin with every acerbic remark. Not the physical shadows but something else, like a low growl rolling through everyone; a malicious, boiling anger fueling them all and she feared if they stayed even one minute longer it would consume them.

A chill slid down her spine. Jackson was glaring, which seemed his default expression for the night, but he was training that glare on her. Hate was in his eyes; uncontrollable hate and for a confused second, she tried to think of what she'd done to piss him off. But then she remembered blowing him off for a week, and the fact that he had saved her life once.

But she hadn't done anything to deserve hate.

Her mind flew back to Cabby, to his form standing in the women's ward and the way he'd turned from her. There hadn't been any malice in Cabby, had there? Just empty shadows in his eyes, like he was a shell and nothing more.

Or a figment of her imagination, she tried to reason with herself, but it felt wrong somehow. She'd seen Cabby. She knew it. It was crazy, like everything else was crazy, but she'd seen him. And he'd led her straight into that vision. That had to mean something, right?

Jackson's glare narrowed and for a long moment she felt like she'd been exposed behind enemy lines, nothing but danger and death surrounding her.

"Bastard!" Alyssa screamed.

A loud crack rent through the room, and Tessa jumped.

She flicked her gaze to Alyssa, who stormed away from Lundy with long, angry strides. Snatching up a light from the table, she shouldered Cordon aside and stalked out the door. Behind her, Lundy held his left cheek and scowled at her retreating back. A second later he was moving, already equipped with a light of his own, heading for the door.

"Wait, we should stick together…" Tessa said but it was too late.

Lundy had gone, shouting something about how he wasn't done with their conversation.

"That doesn't sound good," Cordon said, frowning at the door.

"I'll get them," Marisol said, sounding exasperated.

"No, wait…" Tessa tried again but, once again, it was too late. Marisol's light disappeared into the corridor beyond. "It's like I have this voice, and nobody hears it."

She thought of the vision in the women's ward, the nurse sobbing and desperate to get Frank's attention, and dread welled up in her chest. It was happening to her too. She was as insignificant to these people as the nurse had been against that gun, utterly lost in the tide of Frank's rage.

"I hear you," Cordon said, giving her a faint smile.

She tried to smile back, but she doubted it was convincing and shook her head. "We should go get them."

"Don't know why," Jackson said, scratching at his forehead again. "We're all going to die here. Just like Tyler. Just like Cabby."

"Tyler isn't dead," Tessa said, but her heart stuttered a little in her chest. "And Cabby…"

"Was never here," Cordon finished.

"Cabby was never here," she said, a little stronger this time. "Now we are going to get the others. Then we'll find Tyler. And then we're getting out of here."

"Whatever you say, boss," Jackson said, giving her an ugly grin. "I'll just stay here and pack things up."

"You do that," Cordon said. He grabbed up two more flashlights and the first aid kit.

Tessa frowned at Jackson, not liking the look on his face but unable to fully process why. He was up to something. Still, they didn't have time for this. The others were already so far down the hall she couldn't hear them anymore. So, she stepped back to the door, Cordon close beside her, and started out.

"I want to bandage that hand better."

"I know," she said, not stopping. "But I'd prefer to do it once we know which direction they've gone."

"I figured," he said, passing her a light that she powered on.

Chapter Twenty-Two

"All right, so here's what we know," Tessa said, shining her light into one room before continuing down the hall. "We know that everyone is being affected in some way and that, apart from the two of us, they don't seem to know it. Marisol is acting like a love-starved girl whose existence hinges on her relationship status…"

"Which isn't far from her normal self," Cordon said wryly.

"What? Yes, it is."

"Oh, come on. We're only here because of her attempts at luring Lundy into noticing her," he said.

Tessa frowned, pausing to check another hallway. "Well, I suppose that's fair. So maybe this isn't so much about possession as it is about amplifying and twisting what's already there? Does that sound too crazy?"

They entered the next corridor, this one tighter and crowded with doors every few feet, but there was still no sign of the others. Cordon led the way, avoiding several lockers and cabinets that had been crammed against the walls. The storm was muffled here but every so often the wind howled through crevasses and broken windows.

He mulled over her words, trying to think clearly and evade the weak spots in the floor at the same time. Alyssa was a known flirt and a dramatic personality, and Tyler was an egotistical jock, so those two fit the hypothesis.

He didn't know Lundy or Jackson to say for sure about them but three out of five was winning odds in his book.

"Not terribly crazy, no," he said. "Considering everything going on. But what could cause this and why aren't we affected the same way?"

"I'm not sure," she said. "I feel like somehow it's trying to tell us something. Maybe warn us."

"But why us and not the others? And what is with the photograph? How is that even possible?"

They stepped into one room and Cordon stopped her, deciding they'd gone far enough without seeing to her hand. He set the kit on a desk covered with what he assumed to be files and opened it before rifling for gauze and tape. He wasn't sure if he should use any antiseptic on a wound like this, so he only concentrated on the basics.

"I'm really not sure," Tessa said, wincing as he started untying the makeshift bandage. "Maybe it is a little reincarnation? I mean, that's definitely you in that picture."

"And you look pretty hot in a nurse's uniform," he said with a brief grin.

She twitched a smile at him, holding her hand still as he rolled the gauze around her palm. "And then there's the vision thing," she said, frowning again. "You haven't had one of those yet?"

"Not yet," he said, cutting the tape and securing the bandage in place. "Hopefully never, thanks."

Tessa huffed a laugh as he drew her hand up and brushed a kiss to her wrist, making sure to be careful because the injury had to hurt. She leaned into him, soft curves molding her weight against his body and he slid an arm around her waist, keeping her injured hand on his shoulder. Her face buried in his chest and he propped his chin on her head. He couldn't quite find the will to care about the others.

There was a window nearby rattling with the storm, but he couldn't see any streetlights. He imagined they were on the east side, facing the dried-up lake that stood in the center of the institute.

A crack of thunder drew them apart, lightning streaking past the window an instant later.

It illuminated the room to near daylight for a split second, flashing dirty corners and peeling walls at him. Tessa shouted, then gasped as the room plunged into darkness once more. He'd set his light on the desk to see to her hand, but he grabbed it now, his heart galloping.

He swept the back of the room twice with his light, finding nothing but old chairs and a cabinet. Tessa froze beside him, her light trained on the corner by the door. Cordon directed his light there too, stiffening as he took in the familiar shape of the soldier standing there.

Unease roiled in his gut. The man looked more solid this time, the shades of his uniform clearer. Desert shades, if Cordon wasn't mistaken. He'd seen enough news reports to recognize it. There was blood on his chest that looked fresh and Cordon took a protective step in front of Tessa.

"We don't want any trouble."

"You mean you see him too?" Tessa whispered.

"Yeah, I see him," Cordon said. "Last time he ran before I could ask him anything."

That wasn't quite right. The soldier hadn't run anywhere, he'd just disappeared.

"But Cordon…"

Not liking the way, the soldier continued to stare at

them, unmoving in his bloody uniform, Cordon said, "Are you hurt or something?"

Tessa tugged on his jacket sleeve, but he wouldn't turn away from the threat.

"Cordon, that's Cabby."

The name struck him in the chest and Cordon gripped his flashlight harder. "That's not possible, Tessa. Cabby has nothing to do with this place. There's no reason he would be here, ghost or not."

Good God, they needed to get out of this place.

The soldier stepped forward; his movements just as unsteady as before, only now Cordon could see why. It was a limp; a staggering, uneven limp as the soldier was forced to drag his left foot forward. He reached out a burned, gnarled hand and the wind began to pick up.

Only it was a wind originating at the doorway, from the soldier and not from the window. It howled at them, creating little dervishes in the corners and whipping up dirt to fling into their faces. Cursing, Cordon ducked his head, trying to shield his eyes from the worst of it. Tessa gripped his arm but through the haze of watery eyes and dust he couldn't see her face. An ache settled in his chest and for a second, he feared he was having a heart attack.

But he was only twenty-six. Twenty-six-year-old men did not have heart attacks.

There were no such things as ghosts either but when he lifted his head, intent on checking the soldier's position, he found the man a foot away and looking far more apparition-like than before. His skin was translucent gray, like all the color had been leached out of him, and Cordon could see the wall behind him. It was as if he'd been transposed in a photograph, there but not quite there, and Cordon's chest ached all the more.

The eyes were the worst; two horrible shadowed holes with no color to speak of.

"Oh, Cabby."

"There's no such thing as ghosts."

In response, the soldier took a jerky step forward, crowding into Cordon, arms wrapping around him. But instead of a solid grip, icy tendrils sank into Cordon's skin, burrowing down and coiling around his bones. The ache in his chest intensified and a sensation like frosted veins slithered up his arms and over his shoulders. Tessa was saying something, but he couldn't make it out.

An image tugged at his mind, foreign but familiar all at once; Tessa in uniform, weighed down by Kevlar and leaning against a clearly military vehicle. A blazing sun in an open sky and for the barest second, he thought he could smell the desert in summer.

And then it was gone, the image snuffing out faster than he could make sense of it. The wind stopped, dust and pebbles peppering back to the floor, and the chill in his veins abruptly disappeared. Panting, he braced himself on his knees and tried to coach his heart into a steadier pace.

"Cordon? Are you all right?"

She sounded frightened and he tried to smile for her.

"I'm fine," he said, rubbing at his chest.

"Thank God," she said, her shoulders slumping. "What the hell just happened?"

"I don't know," Cordon said. He straightened again and turned to face her. "But I think you're right. I think that was Cabby."

Chapter Twenty-Three

Tessa stared at Cordon, his words swirling through her mind over and over, making no sense. She'd known the instant she'd seen him that it was Cabby, or at least her imagination conjuring Cabby, but Cordon had seen him too. That meant it was real, didn't it? And if Cabby was here, didn't that mean she'd brought him?

She thought of Richard III and the hateful spirits cursing the man in his sleep and shivered. There was no reason for Texas-born Robert Cabarton to have his ghost haunting the Ashwood, the only explanation was that he was haunting her.

It was the only thing that made sense and her heart ached because of it. All those months in rehab, overcoming the physical damage from the explosion, she'd questioned what right she had to be whole. The doctors had saved her leg and her arm and called it a miracle, but she'd known the miracle had been Cabby.

Cabby covering her, curling around her in that split second before everything erupted. The sheer enormity of his sacrifice left her hollow and lost.

How could he do that to his family? To his little girl and wife? Didn't they deserve to have him home? Maybe that's why he was haunting her now. Maybe he'd come to remind her what had been lost that day.

As though she could ever forget.

There was shouting coming from nearby and she shook her head, desperate for some reality. Cordon scowled at the door.

"I think we found the others," he said.

Tessa held his gaze, so many questions bouncing through her mind she couldn't pick one. And none of them mattered, not right now. They could dissect the whole thing when they were safely out of this place. Still, as she stepped back and turned her light to the door, she couldn't help checking for Cabby one more time.

But he wasn't there. She could feel him, though. An icy, reproachful presence hovering nearby as they began following the voices. The shouting was more urgent this time and the pit of her stomach clenched.

Please be all right. Please let everyone be all right.

She moved faster down the corridor, stopping at a large double door in the middle of the hall. Cordon shoved it open with his shoulder and the voices became clearer. Alyssa yelled for someone to stay back and Marisol pleaded for her to come down. Tessa shared a worried look with Cordon before hurrying inside.

The room appeared to be an assembly space or a cafeteria, possibly both. The center was soaked, rain sleeting down from a high, broken ceiling, leaving a mostly rotten floor with several benches and tables turned on their sides. At the front of the room, positioned on the stage, Alyssa stood on scaffolding, with a noose around her neck. Tessa followed the line of rope up to where it was fastened around a metal bracing and swallowed.

They'd taken the plunge from crazy to dangerous and for a heartbeat Tessa hoped this was all an awful joke. Like there were hidden cameras in the corners waiting to see what she did. But no, it couldn't be. Marisol wasn't the sort for that and Lundy, sneering up at Alyssa like a ghoul, didn't have the brains to set it up.

"Jesus," Cordon breathed the word like a prayer and Tessa agreed with him.

How had things gotten so far out of control?

They started for the stage at the same time, the wood underfoot creaking and bending in places. It splintered at least once in her hurried trek to the stage, but it didn't give way, which was good because she knew there was a basement in this building. She climbed onto the stage, Cordon at her side.

"He isn't worth this!" Marisol said, taking a step toward the scaffold.

"Like you would understand!" Alyssa snapped back. "You with that perfect little body and those big, pretty eyes. You have everything so easy!"

"Me?" Marisol managed to sound surprised, pulling her hand back and staring up at Alyssa.

Marisol, it seemed, was back in her right mind. Or at least Tessa hoped the girl was. They shared a look when Tessa approached and the genuine horror on Marisol's face seemed to confirm things for her.

"What is going on?" Marisol asked.

Tessa exhaled and shook her head. "I don't know, but we need to get everyone out of here."

Marisol nodded, wide-eyed and terrified, and since the girl wasn't complaining about abandoning the investigation Tessa breathed in relief. Yes, her friend was back in her right mind. At least they had that much going for them. Then she looked up at Alyssa and the rope, spotting the unsteady sway of the scaffold under Alyssa's weight.

"Hey, Alyssa, what's going on here?" Tessa asked,

trying for calm and missing. Even she could hear the stress in her voice.

"Who the hell are you?" Alyssa demanded, teetering closer to the edge.

Well, that wasn't a good sign. Mentioning that they were in the same dorm didn't seem to have the right authority to it. And it wasn't like she and Alyssa spoke much, or at all.

"My name is Sergeant Pines, but I really don't matter right now. Can you tell me what's got you standing on the edge there?"

"Just let the whore jump," Lundy said.

Tessa eyed him, wishing he would take a flying leap out of something very high.

"Call me a whore one more time!" Alyssa shouted.

Lundy smirked, opened his mouth as though to speak, but Cordon was already there.

Tessa hadn't even seen him move, but there he was, grabbing Lundy around the neck with one arm then roughly turning him away.

Some of the strain in Tessa's shoulders released and she turned back to Alyssa.

"All right, he's gone for now," Tessa said, trying to regroup. "Why don't you tell me what's going on?"

"He's an asshole who never appreciated me," Alyssa said. Her eyes were wild and unfocused, but came to rest on Cordon, who was hissing in Lundy's ear. "He doesn't give a damn about anybody but himself!"

Keep the girl talking. Just keep the girl talking and figure out a way to get her down.

For the moment she chose to ignore the fact that Alyssa and Lundy had only begun their romance an hour or two before, tossing that up as one of the things this damn place was doing to them.

Tessa stepped closer to the scaffold. "I don't think anyone is a fan of Lundy tonight. But Marisol is right. He's not worth this. You are so much stronger than this."

"You don't know me! You have no idea what I'm capable of! You're just saying that to get me down," Alyssa shouted, leaning forward. "Get back!"

The scaffold wobbled and squeaked, and Tessa's heart stuttered in her chest as she took a hurried step back.

"Oh my God," Marisol said. "What the hell is going on here?"

"I've been asking myself that all night," Tessa said. "Do you know her very well?"

"Not really…" Marisol said.

"Stop whispering about me! I can see you gossiping! You don't think I know what you're saying?"

"We're not gossiping!" Marisol said. "I swear."

"She's right, we're just trying to find some answers here," Tessa said.

"Yeah, right," Alyssa said, packing as much venom into the words as humanly possible. "You think I don't know what you all say behind my back? Poor little Lyssa works so hard to be beautiful because that's all she has to offer. Regurgitating opinions and thoughts of other people because she's not quite bright enough to keep up on her own."

Harsh. This girl had real problems if that was all she thought of herself.

"No, not at all," Marisol said.

"To hell with it, let's try the truth," Tessa said. She held her hands up in surrender. "Can you tell me how you and Lundy first met?"

Alyssa's eyebrows pinched and she frowned. "It

was…um…"

She trailed off, looking confused and Tessa took a breath. This was better. Not by much, but at least she wasn't screaming and promising to jump.

"Oh, God, Tessa, what if she jumps?" Marisol whispered.

"No one is jumping," Tessa said, willing her words to be true.

Marisol started to ask more but Tessa shook her head and glared at the girl until she was quiet.

"Can you remember your first date with Lundy?"

Alyssa continued to frown; her gaze locked on the airy space before her as she worked through the question. Tessa held her breath and prayed. The girl just needed to think it through, to concentrate, and then maybe they could get the noose off her. Cordon had Lundy by the shoulder, holding him stationary as they waited for Alyssa.

An oppressive chill clawed past jackets and clothes and Tessa shivered. The walls creaked and moaned in a manner that had nothing to do with the storm and Tessa stiffened. She glanced around, hunting for Cabby or a vision or something, but their flashlights only did so much. If Cabby was there, he was hiding, and the pit of her stomach clenched.

"What is that?" Marisol squeaked.

Her eyes had gone round and she was staring at the shadows like any second they might reach out and snatch her.

"That," Tessa said through her teeth, "is the Ashwood trying to kill us."

"But that's insane. A building can't kill people."

"I said no gossiping!" Alyssa shouted.

Tessa's heart sank. The frown was gone, and Alyssa looked as wild-eyed and lost as ever. Raising her hands again, Tessa shook her head.

"We were just trying to figure out what is going on here."

"Like hell you are!"

"No, it's true," Marisol called up to her. "Alyssa, this isn't like you. Think! You're with Tyler, not Lundy."

Then the tension in the room snapped as Lundy wrenched himself from Cordon's grasp.

"She's been sleeping with Tyler, too? You really are a whore!"

"I'm not a whore!" Alyssa screamed.

She stomped her foot to emphasize the words and a crack resounded through the room. The scaffold wobbled.

Alyssa screamed again, a different kind of scream full of raw fear and surprise. It shot down Tessa's spine like a rod of lightning and she launched herself for the scaffold, not sure what she meant to do but unable to stand by and watch.

****

Cordon saw the look on Alyssa's face seconds before she lost her footing and knew that she was back in reality. He ran for the scaffold, abandoning a stunned Lundy just as Alyssa's feet left the platform. Her terrified shriek cut off as the noose took hold and he scrambled up the scaffold, praying so many things at once that it was hard to keep track.

Please don't let her neck be broken.

Please don't let the scaffold collapse before I can reach her.

Please, please don't let her choke to death.

The scaffold rocked under his weight, groaning and

creaking. Marisol was screaming. He reached the top platform at the same time as Tessa, who yanked the knife from her pocket and started opening it with her teeth.

Cordon leaned as far as he could, reaching for Alyssa's swinging body. But she swung away from him, his fingers grazing her belt and he would have leaned further if not for Tessa's grip on the waist of his pants.

Alyssa's legs bicycled in the air, her fingers clawing at the rope, trying to dislodge it. Cordon reached again, catching her as she came close and pulling her in. Alyssa's face smashed against his jaw and there was the wheeze of her breath against his beard. Her curvy weight felt heavier than normal as he tried to keep her up, to stop the rope from strangling her. Tessa stretched with her knife, sawing through the rope behind Alyssa's head, but it was thick and heavy.

Alyssa's wheezing became less evident.

God, she was going to die right in his arms.

"Hurry!" Cordon said, straining to lift Alyssa's body higher.

Tessa grunted her response, muscling her knife through the hefty corded rope until finally it snapped free. Alyssa's body slumped against him as he pulled her onto the scaffold.

"Get her down from here," Tessa ordered.

Cordon was already moving, hurrying to the rickety wooden steps.

He did not like the way the scaffold swayed as he made his way down and was grateful when he reached the somewhat more reliable stage floor. Marisol met him there, helping him lower Alyssa to the ground. He tugged twice on the noose's knot until it gave way, sliding up so that he could get the rope off her neck.

Deep red lines had burned into the skin around her throat and he knelt there, shocked. Wiping his face with his hand, he tried to process that Alyssa had just tried to hang herself. Somewhere close by someone was laughing about it, too.

The laughter was so misplaced and wrong it took him a moment to locate the source. Lundy. Anger pulsed through him and Cordon nearly got to his feet, but Marisol's panicked voice caught him before he could.

"She's not breathing! She's not breathing, and I can't feel her pulse!"

Cordon leaned over Alyssa's face to listen and feel for her breath. But Marisol was right, there was nothing. He'd taken a CPR class years ago and his card was years defunct, but that really didn't matter right now, and he knew it. Tilting Alyssa's head back, he cleared the airway, pinched her nose, and blew twice in her mouth.

Lundy continued to laugh.

"Somebody shut him up," Cordon growled, measuring with his hands for the approximate location of Alyssa's heart.

Out of the corner of his eye, Tessa headed for Lundy, her shoulders squared. He began the decompressions, counting to himself and praying he got this right. Alyssa was a twit, but he didn't want her dead, damn it.

"Come on, come on," he muttered to Alyssa, leaning over for two more breaths.

Marisol rocked back and forth; her gaze fixed on Alyssa's still face. He started decompressions again, fear slithering up his spine with every second that ticked by.

He'd forgotten something. What had he forgotten?

He leaned forward, breathed twice more, moved to start the decompressions one more time. *The police, I should have made someone call for the police.*

Alyssa coughed, dragging in a wheezy breath and Cordon turned her onto her side.

"Oh, thank God."

He'd never thought a woman wheezing could be such a beautiful sound.

Marisol wept even harder, if that were possible, and gripped Alyssa's arm, calling her name over and over until Alyssa groaned.

A loud snap resounded from stage right and Cordon turned, his chest aching so much that he had to rub at it again. In the dimness he made out Lundy, who wasn't laughing anymore. Instead, Lundy was doubled over, clutching his nose with both hands. Tessa had her flashlight out, its bulb flickering.

Chapter Twenty-Four

"All right, Lundy," Tessa said, "I don't know what the hell is going on, but you need to wake up."

"You bitch! You broke my nose!"

"And I'll break more if you push."

Near the scaffold Marisol kept saying; "Oh, thank God. Thank God."

Somebody was coughing, and Tessa prayed that was Alyssa breathing again.

Thank God indeed. Maybe they could all get out of here now. But Lundy was still cursing, holding his bloody nose in one hand. She'd sparred enough men in her lifetime to recognize the way he coiled over himself and the bunched fist he made with his free hand. He was a scrawny, gangly kid but he was tall and outweighed her. She wasn't certain her knee would hold up in a real fight and even if it did, this wasn't the real Lundy eyeing her.

"Get control of your woman!" Lundy said to Cordon.

Tessa considered hitting him again for feminists everywhere, but she had nothing to prove here.

"Why would I do that?" Cordon asked, moving to stand beside her. "I think she's got perfect control. Don't you, Tess?"

"Regrettably," she said and smirked at Lundy's glare.

"We need to get Alyssa to a hospital," Marisol called from behind them.

Tessa glanced back at where Marisol was helping Alyssa sit up. The girl had the glassy-eyed look of fever, which was better than the suicidal look from earlier but only by a little. The knot in Tessa's stomach clenched, and for a heartbeat she swore the shadows moved.

What if they were looking at this wrong? What if it wasn't ghosts or reincarnation but rather a matter of the institute itself?

The building felt restless, almost angry, and she suppressed a shiver. Whatever was happening had intended at least one casualty in Alyssa, but they'd stopped it. Did that mean it would try again?

"We need to get them out of here," Tessa said.

"So, we just leave these goons behind?" Cordon asked, nodding at Lundy. "Come back for them later? Hopefully they won't kill each other while we're gone."

Tessa frowned, thinking of Tyler, Jackson, and Lundy in a showdown. Under normal circumstances she would have bet money on Jackson winning, but he wasn't acting like himself either. And really, she couldn't stomach leaving any of them behind. She knew Cordon wouldn't leave without her, so that left only one choice.

"We'll send Marisol and Alyssa out. And then we will try to round up the others."

"Somehow, I knew you'd say that," Cordon said and heaved a sigh. He turned back toward Alyssa and Marisol. "Well, let's get this started."

His words cut off as a blur of white rushed from the shadows backstage. Something knocked into her, sent her careening straight into Lundy, who collapsed under their combined weight. They hit the ground in a jumble of limbs, his elbow knocking her temple, sending a spike of pain through her head.

Sparks burst into her vision an instant before his knee rammed into her side, knocking the breath from her lungs. Dazed, she lay there trying to breathe again.

Out of the corner of her eye, Tyler was pounding Cordon with his fist. Tyler was still in the nasty lab coat, only there was something in the front pocket this time. As if sensing that she'd noticed the object, Tyler yanked it from his pocket, revealing an old, horrifyingly thick syringe. In the next instant, he arched it high overhead as though he meant to stab Cordon in the chest.

"No!" The word tore from her throat.

Scrambling back to her feet, she moved to run for them, but her shoulder snagged, held fast in Lundy's grip. He yanked her back, giving an ugly, bloody grin.

"We ain't done yet," Lundy said, his other fist slamming into her gut.

She doubled over, a sick knot balling up in her belly. Clutching his arm, she tried to breathe around it, but she'd been unprepared, and the ball was solid now, nausea roiling through her.

"Not so tough now, are you?" He sneered.

His fist swung for her face this time. Realizing she had a heartbeat before her nose would be broken, Tessa barreled forward. Ducking her head, she rammed her shoulder into his chest. His swing missed, breezing over her head and he lost his grip.

They staggered back several steps and nearly fell over before Lundy caught his footing. Catching her balance again, Tessa shoved him back and shouted.

Lundy fell to a knee and looked like he was about to get up again, his face contorted with rage. Tessa thrust her elbow at him, smashing it into his face. Her fingers went numb as the impact shot through her arm. There was another crunch, his nose fracturing, compounding the injury, and he fell back, unconscious.

"My God, you suck," she told his limp form and turned for the fight center stage.

****

Cordon hit the ground with Tyler, registering the man's face as his fist struck him in the side of the head. Pain speared through his temple, dazing him for a breathless second. He spotted Tyler's descending arm an instant later, catching it before the syringe could make impact.

Cordon's arm strained under Tyler's weight and the rusty point dipped lower.

"Stop it! Just stop it!" Marisol shouted from somewhere.

With a shout of his own, Cordon shoved upward, knocking Tyler off and redirecting the syringe to the floor. Tyler's hand crashed into the stage, rattling the floorboards. Cordon stole the advantage and struck at Tyler's exposed side. It became a blur of movement after that, both swiping blows at each other, pounding hard and fast, desperate to get an edge on the other.

Cordon caught Tyler in the jaw with his elbow and the man's grip loosened.

Sensing the weakness, he moved to shove the man off when his chest squeezed tight, like someone had pinched him with a vice and was slowly, methodically turning the handle. The room spun, shadows darkening, and Cordon forgot to breathe.

Or maybe he couldn't breathe. He wasn't sure which.

Tyler gained control again, his fist connecting with Cordon's face this time, splitting the skin over his left eye. Agony pulsed through his head. The syringe was coming down for his face and he tried to block it. Tyler's forearm skidded over his own, bone rubbing on bone. Then the needle bit into his shoulder, slamming into the joint with a thud.

Cordon roared, pain blooming through his left arm. He held Tyler off as best he could, dizzy lights spinning in his vision. Tyler leaned into him, bringing their faces within inches of each other, and let out a primal, hateful scream of his own.

With a savage yank, Tyler pulled the syringe out and straightened, lifting the thing with murderous intent.

"Hey!"

Tessa's voice was very close, and a second later a foot shot out, crashing into Tyler's chest.

The force of the kick sent him toppling off Cordon, and then over the edge of the stage. There was a crash somewhere below. An instant later a deep groan rent through the floorboards. There was the distinct sound of splintering wood, and Tyler screamed again as the floor gave way and he fell.

Cordon pressed a hand to his chest, battling for breath still. His arm throbbed but it was minute compared to the lack of air. The ache that ran through him was like an icy hand gripping at his lungs and heart, and he thought of Cabby's ghost.

Tessa knelt beside him, her face alight with fear. He tried to smile up at her, wanted to ease that look off her face, to reassure her somehow.

"H-hey look," he wheezed up at her. "Not shot."

She didn't seem to find the humor in that. Her fingers probed around tender skin as she inspected the wound and he hissed. The ache in his chest eased incrementally and he tried concentrating on the puncture wound in his arm.

The syringe had gone straight into the meaty part of his shoulder, punching a gnarly looking hole that he suspected went to the bone.

"Stabbed with a rusty needle isn't a great option either." Tessa frowned.

"Well, if I start the zombie apocalypse, make sure you run fast," he said.

Tessa eyed him, still not amused, so he gathered her hand and pressed a kiss to her palm, seeing some of the tension release from her shoulders.

"Are you all right?" she asked. "Really, all right?"

"I'll be fine," he said, and hoped it was true. "But Tyler needs some help."

They looked to the edge of the stage, listening for any signs of movement below, but there was only the hollow whistle of the wind and rain pattering against the high roof. Several flashlights cut through the dark, most discarded on the ground, giving a bright triangle across the dusty floor. Back where he'd left them, Marisol held Alyssa, who looked lost, and off to the right he spotted Lundy's hand, limp and unmoving.

"Tell me you didn't kill Lundy."

"I didn't kill Lundy," Tessa murmured. She glanced over at Marisol and Alyssa and frowned. "We have to get them out of here."

"We all need to get out of here," he agreed, rubbing at his chest.

It didn't hurt anymore but that didn't mean it couldn't act up again.

"Yes, we do," Tessa said.

He recognized the look on her face. It was the look she gave him whenever she had something to say and she knew he wasn't going to like it.

"I need you to carry Lundy out to the car. Marisol and Alyssa will go with you. I'll find Jackson and head down to get Tyler and meet you out there."

"No," he said, imagining her wandering through this place with Jackson. "Hell no."

"Something just happened. I saw it on your face. You couldn't breathe and that's not normal. And you got stabbed with a syringe…"

"You've got a hole in your hand too," he said.

"And whatever is going on here, I don't think it's out to get me," she said, glancing at Marisol again. "The vision wasn't about me getting shot, after all. It was you. Logically speaking, I'm the best bet here."

"Nobody is going to shoot me, Tessa."

"You don't know that for sure," she said. "And you're avoiding the larger issue of whatever is going on with your chest. So, take Lundy and everyone else out of here and I'll meet you back at the car."

Cordon shook his head. "Tessa, I can't leave you here."

She glanced at Lundy's unconscious form and frowned. "You don't have to be the hero all the time, Cordon," she said. "I know your family leans on you for everything, or they did a long time ago, but I'm not them. I've got this."

"I am the furthest thing from a hero…"

But she was already climbing to her feet, cutting off his argument. Her attention had switched to Alyssa. "How's she doing?"

Marisol had Alyssa around the waist and was supporting most of her weight. "I don't know."

Alyssa looked pale and shaken, her gaze fixed on the wooden stage. Damn it, Tessa was right. These two needed to get out of here, and someone had to carry Lundy. The last thing he wanted was for Tessa to be alone with Lundy if the man woke. He did not like this plan, but he didn't have an alternative.

He squeezed Tessa's hand until she looked at him. As much as he wanted to continue this argument, this was not the place. So, he leaned forward to kiss her temple.

"I will give you ten minutes," he said. "If you're not out there in ten minutes, I'm coming back in for you."

"That seems fair enough," she said with a rueful smile.

Her lips brushed his cheek and then she stepped back, winking at him in the dim light before heading for the edge of the stage.

With an uneasy stomach, Cordon watched her go, then turned and headed to Lundy. He was tempted to kick the man. Technically, all of this was his fault. But Tessa wouldn't like that, so he refrained and leaned down, grunting as he lifted the lanky kid. His shoulder throbbed in time with his pulse and there was a pounding in his head that told him he needed aspirin, but he was still functional and that would have to do.

"Time to go," he told Marisol and Alyssa, who were both on their feet, clearly ready to be gone.

Yeah, I'm glad to be out of here too.

He just wished Tessa wasn't heading in the opposite direction.

Chapter Twenty-Five

Tessa checked the command room first, hoping to find Jackson but the man was gone. She had a sliver of hope that he'd gotten fed up with her avoidance tactics and gone home, but even she knew that couldn't be true. The way he'd been acting, he wasn't leaving until he'd given her a piece of his mind.

Sweeping her light over the tarp-draped room, she cursed Ashwood Institute to the lowest depths of hell and turned back into the hall. She'd seen a stairwell during their search earlier, so she knew where she needed to go, she just hoped there was only two levels to this thing.

Find Tyler. Find Jackson. Get out.

She repeated the mantra over and over as she made her way through the dark, cramped hallway. Her left hand throbbed, and she held it close to her chest, praying she hadn't already caught some disease. It would be her luck to survive an IED and wind up dead from some horrible illness a year or so later.

God, she was morbid.

She needed to spend a month watching Christmas movies and reading romance novels. Maybe then she'd stop obsessing over every bad thing that could happen.

Moving into the stairwell, she had to maneuver around something big and blocky as she descended the stairs. Dust fell from the floorboards above, filtering through the beam of her light, and she chastised herself for not grabbing an extra flashlight. It was possible that her batteries would fail, leaving her alone in the dark.

Tessa paused at the bottom step, playing her light down a concrete hallway that managed to be even creepier than the ones upstairs. There were no broken tables or cabinets littering the walkway, just an empty hall with closed doors set into one wall. It looked like something from a horror movie, the sort of place a monster would be hiding.

"Awesome," she muttered. "I needed this nightmare."

There would be a boiler room somewhere. All these old places had boiler rooms; she was sure of it. And it was always in the boiler room where the evil man or creature was lurking, waiting for their prey.

Ugh. Two months of Christmas movies.

Minus "A Christmas Carol" because that one had ghosts and after tonight, she had no intentions of investigating anything supernatural ever again.

"Tyler?" she called and stopped to listen.

If he was still under the influence of this place, she would have to hurt him, but she had a feeling the fall may have cured him of that. Nearly strangling to death seemed to have fixed Alyssa after all.

Tessa tried to shake the image of Alyssa's plunge from her mind and shuddered. The girl had looked so terrified before she fell, so lost and hopeless, and for a long moment Tessa wondered if that was how she'd looked while pinned under vehicle wreckage; big-eyed and horrified, staring at her own death without hope of rescue.

Swallowing her fear, she moved to the first door and gripped the handle, then turned the cold metal until the door swung open. It was the laundry room. There were shelves built into the walls and the remnants of wash bins crowding the space.

"Tyler?"

She swept her light over the floor but there were no signs of the man. No signs of the cave-in either.

Exhaling through her teeth, she turned back into the hall, her light falling on the unmistakable features of Robert Cabarton standing not two feet from her. Tessa screamed, jumping back.

She held her flashlight out, brandishing it as a clear threat. Her hand shook and the light trembled on his face but as far as she could tell he was solid.

Solid and expressionless and gazing straight at her.

"What do you want?" He didn't seem to want to hurt her, but he didn't appear friendly either.

"You shouldn't be here," she said, trying to work through the situation and praying Cordon would ignore the ten-minute rule and come for her. "Why are you here?" she murmured, squinting at his shadowed eyes. He looked hallow, empty, a mere echo of the man she'd known. "Did I bring you? Are you here for me?"

She glanced at the cement walls, sensing the unrest that had trailed her all night as it intensified around her. Gooseflesh pricked up her arms and neck. There was something in the walls here, something moving against the cement. She could make out the shape of a man there, like a profile had been drawn and come to life.

Tessa stared at them both, the man in the wall and Cabby, her mind blank. "My God, what is this place?"

As before, Cabby turned from her, moving to a door three spaces away. He stopped there, his back to her, and she recognized the shape of his ear in her light as he bent his head. A shiver slid up her spine and the shadows went darker, the cement walls colder, and she thought of Jackson roaming this place on his own.

If she'd brought Cabby, there was no telling what Jackson might have brought with him.

It was as though the foundations wanted to reach up and take her, drag her down and bury her under the Ashwood forever.

Something was here, incorporeal, seeping into her mind, looming around her.

Cabby faded through the doorway, leaving a sick knot in her gut. It was an unnatural sight, the way he stepped through wood. Tessa exhaled and started for the door. Her ears popped, that disorienting tilt of the hall forcing her to steady herself for a moment. Somehow, she kept upright with her right arm, still angling the light at the door Cabby had gone through and waited for the vision to come.

She noticed the progression this time as she made her way to the door, the way light brought life back to the empty place with every step she took. First the floors were swept, then the little yellow lights came alive, dangling overhead in their fixtures, and then the people faded into view. All were in uniforms, janitors and maids and nurses making their way in and out of different doors, completely oblivious to Tessa's presence.

Cordon was easy to spot, tall and bearded and frowning down at a slight woman in a nurse's uniform. Even from the back Tessa could recognize the bouncing chocolate locks of Marisol's perfect hair. When the girl turned, looking devastatingly beautiful in her uniform, Tessa's mouth went dry.

There was no way they could all be reincarnated or

descended from the people who used to work here. Something else was happening, but what? And why?

"Look, I'm just saying the girl has potential," Not-Quite Marisol said. "And if you loved her like you say you do; you'd want what was best for her."

"What's best for her according to you, anyway," Not-Quite Cordon said.

"According to a lot of people, actually. And if you weren't so damn stubborn, you'd see it too."

"How about we let her decide what she wants…"

There was a low groan and the vision snapped out, leaving Tessa blinking in the dark. Beside her, the wall was roiling with movement, shadows churning against each other and Tessa swallowed back the urge to scream.

She was right, something was here, and it was getting more insistent. It took her several seconds to realize she was back in the present, but the groan came again, originating from behind the door. She stood there, staring at the wall as impossible shadows swirled across it.

This wasn't just in her mind. This was real. And whatever this was, it was out for blood.

"Tessa." The voice was quiet and came from everywhere at once.

The knot in her stomach coiled tighter. Someone was shuffling in the room beyond and she forced herself to concentrate.

"Tyler?" she called, reaching for the knob.

The door swung open and her light caught on the boiler because of course it was the boiler room.

"Help, please," Tyler said from the floor.

She dipped her light to train on him, breathing in relief because he looked mostly whole. He was sitting up and while he looked a little dazed, he seemed to be in control of his faculties.

Taking a deep breath, she hurried in to help.

Chapter Twenty-Six

Cordon kicked the administration building doors open and stepped into the rain. Lundy's weight bore into his shoulder and the man's gangly arms swung to-and-fro as they moved. Behind him Marisol aided a weak and ill Alyssa as they crossed the lot to the cars. The storm had abated, the rain mostly flecks of ice now, but the wind continued to rage through the trees, pushing against him as he walked.

Stopping at his vehicle, he opened the passenger door and shoved Lundy inside, not caring whether he hurt the man.

"Put Alyssa in the back," he said, but Marisol was already ahead of him, ushering Alyssa into the backseat.

Cordon moved around the car, fishing in his pocket for his keys. He pulled them out and, even though it pained him to allow a practical stranger to drive his car, passed them to Marisol. She took them without argument, looking pale and frightened in the gloomy light. Her smaller body shivered under the storm, and for a moment he felt sorry for her.

This was obviously not what she'd had in mind for tonight.

"What the hell is wrong with this place?" she asked, her teeth chattering.

"I have no clue," he said, trying to take the edge out

of his voice. But his mind was on Tessa and the two men still inside and he knew he sounded curt. "Just get Lundy and Alyssa to the hospital. We'll be right behind you."

"What if you can't find them? This place is huge."

"I will find Tessa," he said. "You can count on that."

Marisol's expression softened, and she gave him a shaky smile. "Try not to get hurt." Her gaze slipped to his arm and the stab wound still aching through his shoulder. "Well don't get any more hurt if you can manage it."

"Trust me, I have no desire to risk Hepatitis," he said with a smirk. "Now get out of here."

She nodded and climbed into the driver's seat. Her hands were steady when she snapped her belt on and Cordon tried to assure himself that they would make it to the hospital just fine. He was banking on the idea that Lundy would be back to normal if the man woke during the trip but given the night's events even Cordon wasn't sure that was true.

The car pulled out of the lot and a minute later was rushing down the road. He swallowed back the fear that Marisol might get pulled over because at least then the authorities would know something was amiss. Marisol would fill them in. And if she wasn't pulled over, she would certainly have a tale to tell at the hospital.

Though he couldn't quite figure out what she would say; what any of them should say after such a night.

Cordon started back for the administration building.

"Ten minutes my ass," he said. He wasn't leaving Tessa alone in there.

He checked the tarp room first, not surprised to find it empty, and snagged another light before hurrying out. He remembered passing the stairwell while they'd been searching before so he headed that direction, avoiding several shelves that blocked the path. It was almost commonplace to watch his footing now, shining his light so that he could move around the larger obstacles or avoid the weak spots in the floor.

Turning the corner, he shone his light in the first room and paused.

Jackson stood there, no light, shoulders hunched, scowling at the floor. In his hand was the unmistakable shape of a gun and Cordon's stomach dropped. Where had the man been hiding a gun? Better yet, why did he have a gun?

Jackson looked up and thoughts of the gun became secondary. The man had scratched a bleeding hole in the center of his forehead. Blood trailed down his face, snaking its way around his eyebrow to drip off his chin. His eyes were dark and fixed and the smile he gave looked downright chilling.

"Cordon," he said, sounding almost normal. "We never got to finish our conversation."

"Conversation?" Cordon asked, his mind scrambling for options.

Alyssa had nearly hung herself; it was entirely possible that this man would shoot him. And if this place had its way, it would be six times in the chest, or so said Tessa's vision.

There was no getting up from that kind of thing, no rope to be cut to save him. He should have listened to his uncle and stayed out of the Ashwood.

"You and that murdering bitch of yours," Jackson said.

Cordon's rage began to build. Delusions or not, nobody talked about Tessa like that. But the man had a gun and all he had were flashlights. He'd have to time this just right.

"It's not Tessa's fault the IED went off," he said, trying to see if there was anything in the room he could use.

But of course, this room had to be empty. There was one lonely lab table fixed in the center of the room, right beside Jackson.

"She screwed with the routine," Jackson said, glaring at him.

"Right, the routine," Cordon said. Hadn't Jackson mentioned that earlier? "Because somehow a routine can save lives?"

"You're damn right they do!"

The vehemence in Jackson's voice made Cordon's blood run cold. This man was completely unhinged.

"Is that why you're here?" Cordon asked, edging closer to the door frame.

If things went badly, and he had a feeling they would, he wanted to have some cover. Out of the corner of his eye he could see a clear shot from this door to one of the junctures in the hallway. If he was fast enough, he should be able to find real cover in one of the rooms.

And be cornered at the same time.

God, where was Tessa?

"No," Jackson said, sounding even more bitter. "I wrongly assumed the girl would be feeling some kind of remorse for that day. I came here to make sure she was all right. To tell her Cabby only did what he was trained to do and not blame herself for it."

Cordon frowned, confused. "But you're blaming her for it…"

"Because she doesn't care! She never cared! If she'd shown even the smallest trace of an apology it would be different, but her ass can't be bothered to return my goddamn phone calls." Jackson paced through the room, beating his gun against his thigh as he continued to rant. "And why not? I'm only the one who held her together while the medivac was inbound. I'm the one she clung to that day, barely breathing and only able to say one thing over and over…"

"What did she say?" Cordon asked.

He figured it was best to keep the man talking. If he was talking, then he wasn't shooting anyone.

Jackson blinked at him, almost as though he'd forgotten Cordon was standing there. Then he smirked, glancing down at the floor again, some of the tension leaving his body.

"She said; Sorry, Dad. Over and over. I'm sorry, Dad." He looked thoughtful and shook his head. "Saddest thing I've ever seen. You know…most soldiers call for their mom at the end. They say it's something to do with the nurturing and the comfort mothers give their kids. Like we're desperate for it at the end, hunting for something to take away the pain."

Cordon swallowed, trying not to think of Tessa calling for anyone like that, desperate to be rid of pain. He was suddenly and selfishly grateful that chapter of her life was over.

"It sounds like you really care about her," Cordon said.

"Yeah, stupid me," Jackson snapped. "She's too busy getting it on with you to give a rat's ass."

Cordon raised his hands, placating; "We haven't actually gotten it on," he said. "We've been taking care of some issues."

What those issues were seemed silly in light of the

gun being waved at his face. They'd both been wrong and they'd both been right, and they could either cling to the past or fight for a future together.

If he survived this, he might even get a chance to tell her that.

"Yeah, right," Jackson said and sneered. "I see the way you two touch each other. I've seen the way she looks at you. I may as well be invisible standing next to you."

"Are you…" Cordon started to ask, holding tighter to his flashlight. "Are you in love with her or something?"

"No," Jackson said, turning away from him a little. "God, I don't know, man. I thought maybe…but then I told myself it was just the trauma from that day, you know? It's like…grafted into my brain now, holding onto her that day. So…no. But then…maybe?"

Cordon nodded, not entirely understanding what the man was saying. He tried to imagine what it would be like if Tessa ignored his calls and avoided him the way she had done with Jackson. It would ruin him, down in his core, in the quiet places he never showed anybody, and he would never recover. But Jackson was different. Jackson was only holding onto Tessa out of grief and pain, not real love. And Tessa had no feelings for Jackson like that, he was sure of it.

That didn't precisely help him in the moment, but it was good to know anyway.

"Look, I'm—"

"I swear to God, if you say you're sorry I will shoot you."

"No, actually…" Cordon tried again, very glad he hadn't gotten those words out. "I was going to say that if you care about her, I'm not so sure running around with a gun and calling her a bitch will win you any points."

Jackson's face screwed up into a pinched ball. He rubbed his bleeding forehead with the barrel of his gun, muttering something to himself that Cordon couldn't hear. The walls let out another deep groan and for a hazy second Cordon swore he could hear whispering coming from the shadowed corners of the room.

That couldn't be good.

An instant later Jackson's face cleared, and he pointed the gun at Cordon. "No," he said. "You stole her from me."

Cordon caught his breath in his chest. For a minute he'd thought the real danger had always been Tyler, and with Tyler out of the picture he was relatively safe. But this place had an agenda of its own and it was willing to use any one of them to see it done.

"Well, shit," Cordon muttered and ran. The gun went off behind him. With each shot Cordon ducked lower, tearing through the hall, heedless of the floor. He didn't think he'd been hit but he had no intentions of stopping to find out. He just kept running, adrenaline surging through his system, making the cramped space blur in his vision as he went.

Jackson screamed something unintelligible and there was the not so distant sound of wood splintering, breaking, but Cordon didn't turn around.

He found the stairwell and tore down the stairs at breakneck speed.

Chapter Twenty-Seven

Tessa probed Tyler's leg with her fingers. He gasped in pain around the knee area, and she held back a groan of her own. There was significant swelling around the site, and she doubted the man would do well on the stairs. And there was the unsteady floor above to contend with too. She couldn't imagine taking less than ten minutes just getting Tyler up the stairwell. Cordon would be hunting for her soon, if he wasn't already, and the idea of him wandering around the Ashwood alone made the knot in her gut tighten.

"God, what am I wearing?" Tyler asked, eyeing the ratty lab coat with disgust.

She wrinkled her nose at the coat, spying several questionable stains around the chest and crouched at his side.

"How much do you remember?"

Tyler frowned, and rubbed his forehead with the heel of his palm. He looked strained, and not only from the knee injury.

"Honestly, not much," he said. "I remember walking in and checking out your ass. It's gotten better since high school."

Her cheeks burned and she kept her attention on his knee.

"You make a habit of checking out other women

while standing next to Alyssa?" she asked, her estimation of his character plummeting.

Halfway up Tyler cursed, leaning more of his weight into her.

"Oh, God, that hurts."

"I'm sure it does," she said, not feeling an iota of sympathy.

The man had stabbed Cordon. He was due a little pain.

They hobbled toward the door, Tyler keeping most of his weight on her. Her flashlight bobbed with the unsteady movement, giving them a disoriented view of the room. She kicked broken boards and debris from their path as they went, internally praising her sturdy boots.

"I don't normally check out other women. That was weird. I noticed because it was weird for me. It's not something I do. Gotta have boundaries, you know?"

"Mmm."

She must have sounded dubious because he went on.

"No, really. I give Cordon shit and all that, but I don't like when guys look at Lyssa, so I don't know why I did it with you." He paused to breathe, gripping his thigh because he was in pain. "So, I left the room. I wanted to figure out what the hell was wrong with me. And that's the last thing I remember."

"So, you have no recollection of going to the women's ward?" Tessa asked, pausing beside the door with him.

This was taking forever.

"Women's ward?"

"Yeah, you attacked Marisol and me there," she said. "I clobbered you with a flashlight and we ran."

"Well that explains the headache," he muttered.

"If it makes you feel any better, your head broke my flashlight."

"No, it really doesn't," he said. "So, was I like…possessed?"

"I honestly have no idea, but that's as good an explanation as any so let's go with that."

The muffled report of gunfire echoed through the room and Tessa froze, every nerve she had thrust into overdrive in an instant. Her mind flashed to Frank and the fake-Cordon, seeing every round as it slammed into Cordon's chest and for a second, she couldn't breathe.

"Holy shit," Tyler said. "Is that what I think it is?"

Tessa directed him to a wobbly chair, helping him sit as she ran through a list of supplies and possible weaponry in her mind. A flashlight wouldn't do, not this time, and her little pocketknife was useless. Holding her wounded hand aloft, she reached into her back pocket and pulled out her phone.

"What happened to you?" Tyler asked. "I didn't do that, did I?"

"No," she said, handing the phone over. "Call the police."

A part of her wondered why she hadn't thought to do that from the fore, but it didn't matter now. Above them, someone screamed and heavy footsteps pounded against the unsteady floor. More shots rang out, the sound jolting up her spine and making her skin tingle.

Who was shooting?

Lundy had been out cold when she left, and Cordon was meant to carry the man out of the institute with Marisol and Alyssa. That left Jackson. But where had he gotten a gun?

Tessa swallowed, fear prickling her neck as she

turned for the door. She shut off her light, plunging the room into darkness and stood there for several seconds, willing her eyes to adjust.

Tyler stopped her, his hand making a vice of her wrist. "Wait, you can't go out there."

She could see the shape of him in the dark, but not much else. "Cordon is out here," she said. *Oh my God, Cordon is out there.*

"And I'm pretty sure he would want you to stay out of it."

She snorted an incredulous laugh and pulled her wrist free of Tyler's grasp. "It's not about what he wants," she said, whispering now because she didn't want whoever was coming down the stairs to find them. There was a good chance it was Jackson, after all. And Jackson with a loaded gun and sitting targets was a recipe for homicide.

"Wait…" Tyler tried again. "What the hell am I supposed to do?"

Tessa moved to the door and pressed her back against the wall before peeking into the hallway. There was a light turning the corner at the far end and she pulled back into the room.

Lowering her voice even further she whispered; "Call the police. Keep quiet if you can. The walls are cement, so you should have some cover. Just pray he doesn't come into this room."

"But…"

She didn't wait to hear him out. As quietly as she could, Tessa slunk out of the room, keeping one hand against the wall as she moved through the dark. It was her injured hand, but it was still good for something. Even with the ache and odd numbness she could sense the coarse cement under her fingertips.

Her heart thundered in her ears. The sound of her feet crunching through debris became so pronounced she swore someone could hear her on the other side of the Institute. This hall was bare of major obstacles at least, leaving only the darkness to contend with as she made her way inexorably forward.

Several feet in front of her was the shape of a man, but she couldn't make out who it was. She could hear them breathing hard, and then came the familiar cadence of Jackson's voice as he cursed. Her heart squeezed tight.

Where was Cordon?

Had he already been shot?

Was he dead or dying on the floor above her?

Hesitating, she glanced up but could only make out the barest imprint of a bracing above. If Cordon was up there, she should be with him. She should be staunching his wounds and willing him to survive, not hunting Jackson. But if Jackson had gone off the deep end like everyone else, she couldn't let him do more damage. Especially with Tyler sitting unarmed and wounded in the boiler room.

Maybe she could draw Jackson off. She bit her lip, trying to remember where the stairwell was. She couldn't risk using the light, not out in the open. Jackson would see, and she would have no defense, which was problematic for her entire plan.

Or lack of a plan.

Just what the hell *was* she going to do?

"I never did catch your name," Jackson said, his voice chilly. He was probably sneering. Jackson did the sneering thing quite a bit. "Cord? Something like that, right?"

Hope flared in her chest.

If Jackson was hunting Cordon, that meant Cordon was still alive, didn't it?

Tessa tried to dredge up memories of how Jackson fought, the way he preferred quick jabs in the sparring ring and his complete lack of footwork. She'd learned early on that with some men it was better to keep them moving, dodge around their attacks, force them to tire before coming in to strike. But how was she to do that while the man was armed?

Well, she was going to have to disarm him.

Light blinded her, snapping to life and aimed at her face. She cursed and tried to shade her eyes, shock and fear pounding through her as she recognized Jackson's delighted chuckle.

"Nice of you to join us, Pines."

His words slithered down her spine, coiling at her lower back in a tense knot as he came into view. A dark smear of blood painted one side of his face and his teeth shone bright, reflecting the beam of his light.

He had a gun and he was eyeing her like she was the enemy.

"Jackson," she said cautiously. "What's going on?"

"Tell me, Pines, why did you screw with the routine?"

She blinked at him. "The routine?"

"Yes! The routine!" Jackson's voice rose to a shout. "Cabby always sat on the right. Always! Why wasn't he that day, huh?"

She opened her mouth in shock, her mind thrust backward. She remembered the oppressive heat and the inescapable smell of oil in the motor pool. There was the feel of her M-16 in hand, blocky and solid. She leaned against the vehicle with Cabby, joking about who got the most care packages that week. There'd been easy smiles and the confidence of being on base.

"One of these days you're going to open a package and it'll be your own book," Cabby said to her.

"I would have to actually submit a manuscript to someone for that to happen."

"You will," he'd said, his voice fading.

For a disoriented moment she stood in two places; one foot in the Ashwood with Jackson snarling at her and the other in Afghanistan with Cabby winking, encouraging her to give up the goods and submit a book somewhere. She'd never had the heart to explain her book wasn't finished.

"What?" It was hard to breathe, like the air itself had grown thin, and her lungs strained with effort.

"He should be here, not you. His blood is on you! It's all on you!" Jackson said.

She was still in the desert with Captain Zeigler ordering them to mount up. Murphy, their driver, swatted Cabby's helmet and suggested he would have more leg room if he sat behind her this time. Zeigler didn't care. Tessa didn't care either. And Cabby grinned that boyish grin, winking as he hurried to the driver's side to get in.

She'd played that day over and over in her head for a year and a half, imagining all the ways it could have turned out different. Maybe she would have spotted the IED in time. Maybe Murphy would have gone to the opposite side of the road. Maybe Tessa would have had the courage and the wherewithal to shield Cabby from the blast instead.

Her heart ached, capturing that smile of his again.

"It was Murphy," she whispered.

"What?"

"Murphy," she said again, stronger this time. "Murphy thought Cabby would have more room over there. Zeigler was tall, kept his seat back as far as it would go."

"You'd blame a dead woman for this?" Jackson barked, stepping closer to her. "How dare you!"

"Hey!" Cordon's voice cut through and another light flicked on behind Jackson. "Come on, man! Remember why you're here. You came to make sure she was all right, remember?"

Jackson whirled around, sweeping his gun in Cordon's direction. Tessa's heart seized, remembering the vision with Frank and the gun going off six goddamn times, and cursed Cordon for not staying in relative safety.

But then, she knew he could never have stood by for this.

She kept her hands out, doing her best to placate Jackson as she fought for the right move. She thought of Cabby leading her to that vision, to Tyler, showing her the way.

And there he was again, Robert Cabarton, standing beside Jackson and watching her with those empty eyes. Her mind swirled with past and present, long forgotten conversations breezing through her so fast she almost couldn't catch them.

Cabby used to steal her writing, snagging it off her lap whenever he saw her working and he always had a comment to make. Most of the time it was good but every once in a while, he would cluck his tongue at her.

"Take charge of the story," he would say. "You're letting the characters run rampant."

Take charge of the story.

Was the Ashwood retelling a story?

She gazed at Cabby, who was as expressionless as ever.

"You heard her," Jackson was saying to Cordon. "She'd rather blame the dead than accept responsibility."

"It was war," Tessa said, praying she was right and wasn't about to get herself killed.

Or get Cordon killed.

The only way to disarm a story was to take away its ending. Force it down another path, an unknown path. That's why Alyssa was back to normal. And Marisol had gotten free of its hold. Marisol's story had derailed with the sight of Alyssa's near death. All Tessa had to do, was derail Jackson's story somehow.

She stepped closer to him. "It was war and it sucks. It's brutal and senseless and unpredictable. And it hurts." Tessa was in arm's reach now. "Sometimes it hurts so much you can't breathe. All the names and faces of friends…of brothers…people who had every right to live long, healthy lives…all of them come back to you when you don't expect it. And you hurt deep down in places that will never heal."

The gun wavered.

"Jackson," she said, positioning herself between the two men. Cordon was further away, on the other side of something blocky. "Jackson, I spent a year and a half trying to make sense of that day, trying to come to terms with it."

"Yeah, well, it looks like you did a damn good job of it."

"Are you kidding? One phone call from you and I was having nightmares again."

Cordon hissed something behind her but couldn't

make out what it was. Probably nothing happy. And that was fine. She wouldn't be happy either if the roles were reversed.

To be fair, she wasn't happy as it was.

"No, you're just saying that to save your own skin," Jackson said. "You're a goddamn coward, Pines. Always have been."

"She's standing here now," Cordon said. He'd come closer, was directly behind her now. His hand gripped her shoulder, pulling her back a step.

"She could have run off, but she didn't. That doesn't sound like a coward to me."

Jackson's face contorted, his gaze snapping to Cordon with such furious intent that Tessa knew their time was up. The gun twitched to the left, more toward Cordon, and she launched herself to follow. The shot cracked through the hallway, drowning out Cordon's shout of protest and her cry of warning.

She slammed into Cordon, the hot bite of impact searing into her collarbone. They crashed into something solid and metal, but Tessa couldn't see it. All her mind centered on the pulse of agony in her chest and she clutched at the wound.

Around them the Ashwood groaned, like the walls themselves were shifting under pressure, and she prayed she'd made the right call.

Chapter Twenty-Eight

Cordon dragged Tessa around the metal cabinet he'd intended to use for cover. Jackson shouted something unintelligible and the walls let out a deeper, more prominent groan than ever before. The sound crawled over his skin, amplified by the thunder of his heart.

He shot her, oh God, he shot her.

Cordon hadn't seen where the bullet hit but he knew it had made its mark. Grunting, he pulled Tessa down the hallway. He slammed open the first door he could find with his shoulder and dragged Tessa through.

Behind them, Jackson fired three more times. Every shot jolted through Cordon, making his spine tingle. A bullet ricocheted, zinging off the metal cabinet to chip into a nearby wall. He tasted cement and copper, registering an instant later that he'd bitten his tongue.

Kicking the door closed behind them, he was a little surprised when Tessa's light flicked on. The light shook in her hand, but he caught the basics of the room. There was another heavy locker to his right, which he grabbed and tilted, demanding his upper body strength to cooperate.

The wound in his shoulder screamed to life but he ignored it, letting out a guttural shout and leaning all his weight into the task. The locker screeched, heavy metal scraping against cement wall as it shifted. A second later it crashed to the ground in front of the door, sufficiently barricading them inside.

Tessa's weight became more substantial and he glanced at her, his heart stuttering in his chest. She had one hand clasped to the bullet wound, blood seeping through her fingers, and her face had gone an alarming gray. He went cold at the sight.

Her chest. She'd been shot near her chest. Upper collarbone.

This was bad.

Reaching down, he swept her up and carried her to the door at the other end of the room. He had no idea where it would lead but they had to keep moving, had to get away from crazy-ass Jackson and his damn gun.

Cordon ran through a series of offices, swiveling around doorways and avoiding lab tables in his retreat. Tessa's light stayed in front, bobbing with movement and granting him the barest impressions of the rooms they passed.

Stairwell. He needed to find a stairwell, needed to get Tessa to a hospital.

They came around a corner and he stumbled to a halt. Turning first left and then right, he let Tessa's light shine down the hallway and cursed.

"This place makes no sense," he said.

He strained to see if there were any signs above the doors, any indication of where the exit might be. But there was nothing, only doors half off their hinges and shadows reaching deeper into the basement. He tried to map out where they'd been, to trace his footsteps, but in the blur of Jackson's gunfire he hadn't paid attention.

Tessa made a soft sound, a mix between a hum and a groan, and Cordon held her tighter. He didn't look at her, couldn't look at her. As if looking at her would make the bullet in her chest more real.

"It's all right, Tess. We're almost out of here," he said.

Wind swirled around his feet and he smelled desert sand. He pivoted, already knowing what he would see behind him. Tessa's light tilted down, cutting a diagonal light across Cabby's chest, highlighting the scorch marks in his uniform. Cordon bit back a shout of alarm and took a step away.

But Cabby followed, stepping forward and *into* him.

Tessa shuddered; Cordon registered that much before an onslaught of cold washed over him. Ice frosted his veins, pumping out from his heart in a slow—too slow—rhythm. He lost his grip on Tessa for a split second, felt her weight slip down his arms.

With conscious effort he caught her, coaching every finger to curl, to grip, to hold fast. But there was a delay between commanding his body and the correct response, a hiccup that cost him several inches.

Her feet brushed the floor, but it was an echo, a distant recalling of sound.

He staggered backward and hit the wall as a kaleidoscope of colors smeared his vision. Dazed, he became aware of a foreign voice, thin and tinny, like a radio transmission with too little signal. At first, he couldn't make out the words and then they became clear.

"Get out."

His heart thumped a sluggish beat and Cordon wheezed a breath, his chest straining.

The kaleidoscope settled, his vision focusing on the hallway, but it looked different. The walls frosted over like a lake in early winter, the surface clear and frozen while beneath there was movement. Only here the movement wasn't fish or water. Here the movement was something else entirely.

Cordon's heart thumped again.

Across from him, trapped beneath that cold surface, stood a man in a lab coat. His face was indistinguishable, but in his hand was the unmistakable shape of a gun. It was not Jackson, the hair was too long, but the intent was clear.

The Ashwood really was trying to kill him.

"Get out." The voice was more urgent this time.

"Cordon?" Tessa asked.

She sounded weak. He fought for coherency, for his heart to beat a normal rhythm, and pulled in another ragged breath. Warmth seeped into his skin and the pressure in his chest began to ease.

A series of images flew through him, images he knew were not his own. A group of people firing M-16's down range; a formation of soldiers standing at attention; the view outside a vehicular window. Cramped streets and trash in the gutters and the glimpse of something suspicious an instant too late.

Cabby's memories, they had to be.

A moment later his thoughts were confirmed as the image shifted to Tessa, sitting to the right. Cabby threw himself on top of Tessa just as the cab erupted into fire. A new smell; burning clothes and cooking skin and Cordon's stomach turned on itself.

"Hey Pines, where are you hiding?" Jackson's voice called from somewhere to the left.

Disoriented, Cordon shook his head, banishing Cabby as the last vestiges of ice evaporated from his veins. Hoisting Tessa higher, Cordon turned right and ran.

He rushed into the first open door he could find, nearly tripping on an old table.

He kicked the door shut and shoved the table against it.

That wasn't as good as the metal locker had been, but it would do for now. He lowered Tessa into the furthest corner, propping her against the wall. Blood soaked her shirt, spreading in a wide ring over her chest and stomach.

He shrugged off his jacket and balled it up as tight as he could. "God damn it, Tessa."

"I'm so sorry, Cordon," Tessa said. She looked dazed and didn't fight him when he unzipped her coat to press his wadded-up jacket against the wound. "He was going to kill you."

"So, your brilliant plan was to get yourself killed instead?"

Fear lodged in his chest and his hands shook as he zipped her coat closed, trying not to see all the blood but seeing it anyway. He took her hand and pressed it over the would-be bandage.

Her face contorted for a moment. "I was trying to break the storyline…"

"Tessa, that makes no sense."

The door rattled, and the table scraped across the floor. Cordon glared at the light as it cut through the slowly opening door.

"Oh, Pines," Jackson called in a singsong voice. "We're not finished yet."

Too hell with this place. Someone needed to burn the whole institute down.

"The Ashwood," Tessa said. She sounded weaker. Her eyes were glossy and unfocused, but she kept talking. "Ashwood is trying to tell a story…where you get shot and killed…"

"That's insane, Tessa."

Only it wasn't. Not with all the craziness they'd already gone through. Just beside the doorway, the form of that cursed doctor ghost leaned toward Jackson's light. There was a crack in the icy sheen on the wall and what looked like wisps of gray smoke poured out, snaking through the door and out to Jackson.

The table slipped across the floor, the door opening wider and Cordon scowled. Jackson had managed to wedge his arm inside and was levering himself for a more effective push. In another minute he would be inside, coming to finish the job.

They were out of time.

Cordon released Tessa and rushed for the door. With a leap, he slid onto the table and rammed his shoulder into the door, letting all his momentum and weight crash into it. Jackson lost his hold and there was a terrible crunching sound as his arm was caught between wall and door.

Jackson shouted and through the door was the sound of feet scuffing against floor as the man tried to push back. But Cordon didn't let up. He kept his weight there, pinning the man in place.

"You want to tell a story?" he growled under his breath. "Fine. But tell it to someone else because I'm fucking done with you."

"Let me go! Let me go!" Jackson wailed.

Cordon wasn't buying it.

A shot rang out, louder and different from before. Jackson grunted, suddenly going limp. The scuffing ceased altogether and something metal hit the floor outside. For a horrible second Cordon thought the man had killed himself, but then there was another voice in the hall, a familiar voice.

"Oh, thank God," he said and straightened from the door. "Uncle Phil, is that you?"

"Yeah, boy, it's me. You're safe to come out."

"Tessa's been shot," he said, getting the important information out first. "I need help moving her."

With the table moved Jackson's weight pushed the door open and the man fell to the floor. Beyond him, Uncle Phil stood in the hallway with an old shotgun and a flashlight mounted to his sleeve. He looked ridiculous, scrawny and wild-haired, but Cordon couldn't have been happier to see the man.

Phil collected Jackson's gun and tucked it into his jacket pocket before stepping over the man to enter the room.

"Is he…" Cordon asked but Phil shook his head.

"Rock salt," Phil said. "Hurts like hell but he'll be all right when he comes to."

Cordon wasn't certain if he was relieved by that or not. Still, he tossed the worry aside to lead Phil to Tessa's corner. The paleness of her face reflected Phil's light as he crouched down in front of her. Her eyes had dark circles beneath them, and the hollows of her cheeks looked more prominent. Cordon crowded beside her, pushing the flashlight out of her hand so he could squeeze her fingers. They were cold and she didn't respond and for several seconds Cordon couldn't breathe.

Phil pulled back the bloody jacket, clucking his tongue at the mess of wound and shirt. Then he returned the wadded garment and took hold of Cordon's other hand, pressing it hard against the wound.

"Keep pressure. We'll get her out of here," Phil said, shifting to lift Tessa.

Cordon kept a firm hold on her as they hurried from the room. They stepped over Jackson, who didn't so much as twitch as they passed. It was just as well. Cordon would have kicked him if he had.

"Been monitoring the police scanner all night," Phil said as they continued through the corridor. "Bet you wish you'd taken my offer now, huh?"

Cordon stared at him. "Neither of us wanted to be here in the first place."

"And yet, here you are."

Halfway down the hall a police officer met them. He took one look at Tessa and barked information into his shoulder microphone. Several more officers passed them as they made their way to the stairwell. A paramedic was at the bottom of the stairs. The young woman took Tessa's wrist, felt for a pulse, and started relaying even more information that made no sense to Cordon.

These were medical terms he'd never heard before, but he kept pace with them until they reached the gurney. Within seconds they had Tessa strapped down and prepared for the ambulance. The paramedic asked him to let go, telling him in firm but gentle terms that it was going to be all right, that he needed to let her work now, but Cordon couldn't will himself to move.

He stared at her; his hand still pressed to Tessa's wound.

"Son, you have to let go now," she said again.

"Cord," Phil said, gripping his bad shoulder.

Cordon winced and let go of Tessa. The gurney was rolled away and lifted into the ambulance. There were lights everywhere, police and fire trucks and at least one other ambulance, but his attention stayed on Tessa until the doors slammed shut. Sirens wailed and it sped off.

He spotted Tyler propped on a gurney of his own, talking to an officer who wrote in a little book. Tyler noticed him too and stopped talking, relief evident on his face. Cordon nodded back at the man but didn't move closer.

He was all over numb and not at all certain what he should be doing. Getting to Tessa was foremost on his mind, but he knew the hospital would only keep him in the waiting room.

"Whose blood is this?" Phil asked, removing his hand to gaze at Cordon's shoulder.

"Mine," Cordon said.

"Holy Christ, son. Why didn't you tell me you'd been stabbed?"

Cordon glanced at the stain at his shoulder. It was aching now that he thought about it, but he shook his head and looked back down the road. Tessa's ambulance was out of sight, its sirens so distant he could barely hear them now.

"Well, shit. Let's get you to the hospital."

Since the hospital was where Tessa was headed, Cordon didn't argue. He trailed his uncle to the car, listened to Phil inform a waiting officer that they could take his statement after the doctor had seen him, and frowned.

Of course, they would need his statement. Not that he had any idea what the hell had just happened or how he was ever going to explain it.

Chapter Twenty-Nine

Tessa woke to the familiar sensations of heavy drugs and uncomfortable hospital beds. Someone was pacing nearby and a moment later she heard the sound of her father's voice. Fighting her eyelids open, she blinked until the haziness faded and she could focus. Her father was by a large bay window, its drapes open to let in the light, and he was on a cell phone.

The sight of his tall, broad frame comforted her a little and she breathed easier.

"They say the bullet just missed the artery," her dad said. "She's very lucky."

She frowned, glancing at the empty chair at her left. *Where was Cordon? Oh, God. Had Jackson gotten through? Had he shot Cordon?*

A bottomless grief washed over her, and the heart monitor beeped. Someone squeezed the fingers of her right hand and she swiveled her head to look, relaxing because Cordon was there. Of course, he was there. They would have had to put him in jail to keep him away and she knew it. He had a bandage on his arm and his beard was frizzing but he was smiling at her, concern and care written in his features.

"I've got to go, she's awake," Todd said.

"Are you all right?" she asked, her voice thick and raspy.

"Yes," Cordon said and smirked. "Alyssa and Tyler are fine too. Lyssa will have some scarring and Tyler has a cast for a while, but they will both live."

Her father took the other chair and sat down.

"God, Tessa, what were you thinking?"

"I was only there to help my friend, Dad," she said and prayed they could fight about everything once she was out of the hospital.

"Tessa…"

She focused on Cordon again. "Jackson?"

Cordon glanced at her father and cleared his throat before answering. "The army is having to do a big review, but he's alive and safe."

"Tessa," her father said.

She sighed, carefully turning to face him. She thought she knew what he meant to say and tried to steel herself for a fight, but his next words weren't what she'd expected.

"I thought when you got out of the military that I wouldn't have to worry about people shooting at you anymore."

She exhaled. "I know, Dad."

"And nobody is able to say what happened out there," her father went on. "They're saying it may have been a gas leak? It brought about some kind of hysteria? Paranoia?"

Tessa glanced at Cordon, who shrugged.

"I can't remember much," Tessa said slowly.

She disliked lying to her father but what else could she say?

She gave her father an apologetic smile and tried for weak and forgetful.

"Gas leak sounds about right."

He gave her a look that said he wasn't buying it. "Tessa, I wasn't born yesterday."

She sighed and closed her eyes. Cordon squeezed her hand, an unspoken message that he wasn't going anywhere.

"I am pretty sure the nurse said not to upset her."

"I think I know my own daughter a little better than you do, son."

The combative tone in her father's voice made her head throb. "And while we're on the subject, I still don't understand why you're here at all."

"Dad," Tessa said, holding tighter to Cordon's hand. She opened her eyes again to gaze at her father. "He is here because I want him to be."

"Not to mention he saved her life and all," Phil said from the doorway.

She recognized him from family barbeques in high school and blushed, releasing Cordon's hand to clumsily lift her blanket. She knew she looked awful and she felt vulnerable in the hospital gown. Cordon helped her, tucking the blanket around her shoulders and giving a supportive wink before taking her hand again.

"I'm sorry, and who are you?" her father asked, clearly at his wits' end.

"I'm the other man who saved her life," Phil said. "Though she probably doesn't remember it."

Tessa glanced at Cordon, who nodded once, and she quirked an eyebrow in question. The last thing she could remember was confronting Jackson and the sound of the gun going off, everything else was a blank. But they couldn't exactly discuss it with her father in the room.

A short, tense silence took them, her father obviously not happy about things and struggling for something to say. Cordon's mouth was flat under his beard, and there was an edge to his eyes that told her he was trying to hold onto his own temper.

"I think the nurse wanted to discuss some things with you," Phil said to her father.

"I don't—"

"I'm sure Cordon could take care of it, though," Phil said, shrugging a bag from his shoulder as he entered the room. "It's for whoever is going to be taking care of her once she's been discharged."

Todd got to his feet. "I'll just go see about that," he said and walked out the door.

Phil reached back to close it and shook his head.

"I can't say I blame him for being upset, but that man needs to relax."

"Is the nurse really looking for him?" Cordon asked.

"Nope," Phil said, plopping the bag on the bed by her feet. "A change of clothes, compliments of Marisol Williams and the homework you'll miss Monday through Friday from all your classes. If it's too much or you need more time, that's what your advisor is for. They can work with you."

Tessa blinked at the bag, and then at Phil. She opened her mouth to thank him and stopped, suddenly overwhelmed. Her eyes swam and she looked away.

It's the drugs, the damn drugs.

But it was more than the drugs. It was the kindness and the hint that he'd been there last night too, and it was all she could do to breathe. Her chest and arm began to ache, pain killers wearing off, but even that felt distant to her.

"You saved my life?" she asked, her throat seeming to close around the words.

How many people did it take to keep her alive?

She thought of Cabby and had to will herself not to sob right then and there.

"When Cordon told me, you were at the Ashwood, I came," Phil said and rubbed the back of his neck. "I heard the gunshots and was able to locate you after that."

"About that," Cordon said, his voice tight. "What the hell is that place?"

"Look, I don't exactly know," Phil said, pacing over to the window to frown out at the late October sky. "Nobody really does."

"Well you know something," Cordon said. "Or you wouldn't have tried warning me off the place so hard."

Phil sighed noisily before turning to face them. He looked resigned and exhausted as he shrugged. "Near as we can tell it's some kind of supernatural freak show. It's not always like it was last night. Normally it's just specters and hauntings and shit."

"So, what was different about last night?" Tessa asked. "Because last night was a hell of a lot more than specters."

Phil smiled at her wanly. "Well…you," he said and gestured to them. "Both of you."

"What, like reincarnation or something?" Cordon asked.

Tessa thought of the photograph and frowned. She wasn't certain she believed in reincarnation, but then again, she hadn't believed in a lot of things until last night. She supposed anything was possible.

"Not exactly, no." Phil shook his head. "It's hard to explain but that place seems to feed on deep emotion. So, the average Joe can walk in there and be fine, but a Joe who is in the middle of a fight with his girl…Well, the

Ashwood hooks into all that angst and fear and sort of comes to life, if you will."

"It starts to remember," Tessa said quietly. "And then it…what? It has to complete the memory at all costs? Because it really wanted Cordon dead last night."

Phil shrugged again. "Like I said, it's hard to explain. But it seems to do that, yes."

"But what about the photograph?" Cordon asked.

"What photograph?"

Cordon released her hand to fish in his pocket, pulling out the old, half burnt picture. Only when he opened it up and laid it flat on the bed beside her Tessa could see that the image had warped. There was still a man and a woman there, but their faces were blank, completely empty of features, and a chill crawled up her spine.

"The Ashwood plays all sorts of tricks, Cordon," Phil said. "Whatever it has to do to convince you."

"Well, that's just all sorts of bullshit," Cordon said.

Tessa smiled at him; her collarbone was aching more. Her eyelids felt heavy, but there was one more thing she had to ask before sleep took her. She turned her head to Phil and bit her lower lip, hesitant to bring it up because she somehow felt it would sound crazier than everything else.

"When I was alone in there," she said, curling her fingers into the hospital blanket. "I kept seeing…Well, I kept seeing a dead man from my unit. The same one who died right next to me…Cabby. Is that normal?"

Phil's eyebrows shot up. "No, actually. I've never heard a report like that. Normally, it's all centered on the Ashwood itself and the awful things that happened there."

"He never seemed to be out to hurt me," she said.

"Generally, he just led me places. Like the room where Cordon found me in the women's ward. And then later he showed me where Tyler was."

"Interesting," Phil said. "It sounds like maybe you brought him in with you."

Tessa swallowed hard and fidgeted with the blanket some more. "Are you trying to say I'm haunted?"

And wouldn't that just be like Cabby to be watching out for her, even in death.

"Maybe," Phil said. "Or maybe you're still carrying around a lot of grief from his death so he sort of…manifested. I'm really not the person to ask."

"Right," Tessa said and tried to smile.

"Well, one thing is certain," Cordon said, "That place needs to be demolished."

His strong fingers curled around her own and she relaxed.

Chapter Thirty

Tessa restrained another wayward lock of hair with a pin, holding it in place to keep the tight bun from losing its sharpness. One thing she didn't miss from her service days was the restrictions on hair length and style. Still, the bun gave her a hard look, all the angles of her face standing prominent and unmistakable.

Her freshly pressed uniform was as uncomfortable as she remembered, the fabric scratching her legs and waist. And the shirt was too neat, her commendations and pins a heavy weight above her left breast. The sling holding her arm in place looked ridiculous against the dark green, but she knew better than to remove it. She wished she could have worn her civilian attire, but Jackson's lawyers insisted, which made sense. She didn't have to like it, but it made sense.

She would do this. Jackson needed her to do this.

She hadn't seen him since the Ashwood, which might have been cruel of her but there was only so much she could handle at once. Dealing with an angry Todd Pines and a distraught Marisol Williams was enough of a battle.

Neatening her shirt, Tessa left the mirror and walked to the door. On the other side, Cordon stood from a bench against the wall and gave her a quirky grin. She smiled back and moved to him, comforted by his nearness.

"You ready for this?"

"I kind of have to be," she said. Her gaze caught on the conference door and unease boiled in her gut. "Do you think they'll accept the gas leak story?"

Cordon slanted a look down at her, his mouth tightening at the edges. "That's what the police are saying, Tessa. Best stick with that."

"Yeah but..." She trailed off, spotting the look of warning on his face.

He was right, of course. Talking about the Ashwood was likely to get her committed. And it wouldn't help Jackson. So, she sighed and sat on the bench, thoroughly disgruntled and with no means to fix it. Not that she imagined there was a way to fix this. She didn't believe for a second that what they'd been through at the Ashwood was from a gas leak, and she knew Cordon felt the same way.

There were too many unanswered questions, too many variables, and she hated the idea that nothing was being done. The Ashwood Institute was dangerous, a dark pit in the middle of town that could claim anyone who didn't know better.

The whole thing needed to come down.

Cordon lowered himself beside her, his warmth seeping into her side. If she hadn't been in uniform, she would have leaned into him, put her head on his shoulder and let the world fade away. But dress uniforms wrinkled too fast and she would be called in for testimony any minute.

"It hurt like hell when you left," Cordon said, his voice low as several people passed by.

Tessa glanced at him, her stomach knotting. Why was he saying this now?

"It felt like you were running away from me," he

said. "As though the idea of life with me was so horrible you had to do something drastic to get away."

"God, Cordon, no. That wasn't it at all."

"I know. But at the time it felt different," he said. "I couldn't understand the need for more than what was already right in front of us. We had each other, and I thought that should have been enough. So, when you left it was as if you were saying that I was missing something you needed."

The knots in her stomach tightened and she gazed at him. "Cordon, you have always been enough…"

"No, I wasn't, Tess. But I know why now."

"But—"

"Just let me finish, please." He gave a crooked smile. "You've always been independent. It's one of the things I love most about you. Your dad couldn't stop you from joining the dojo or dating me or enlisting in the army. You go for what you want."

Sunlight slanted down from a high window, making a bright square in the polished hardwood floor. Tessa stared at it, her mind racing to anticipate what he was trying to say.

"But I was always on call for my family," he said. "My mom and my sister needed me, and I was there, always. Like a good son. The man of the house after my father left."

"That's one of the things I love about you."

"But you hated it too. Because it squeezed you straight out of my life."

She swallowed, unable to deny it.

"It took me a long time to really see and understand this," Cordon said, then huffed a laugh. "In a crazy way, I think the Ashwood showed me the truth."

"The Ashwood?"

"When we were separated, and I couldn't find you, it was the deepest terror of my life. But you kept hunting for the others, trying to get them out safe. I know you were worried about me too, but you had to take care of them," he said. "Just like I always took care of Sara and Mom. And for a second, I knew how you must have felt back then. Sort of shoved to the side because you weren't in crisis."

Stunned, Tessa blinked at him.

"What I'm trying to say, Tess, is that I'm sorry." He ran a hand through his hair. "Maybe you left me for the army, but the truth is, I abandoned you long before that."

"I never felt abandoned, Cordon," she said, thinking—*not much, anyway*— "But I did feel unimportant."

He smiled faintly, his eyes glistening blue and she tried to read them, to figure out what he was really trying to say. He had to know she had forgiven him for that, and her own betrayal when she'd joined the army had been drastically worse.

"Cordon…"

He was gentle, brushing a kiss over her bandaged hand. She still couldn't feel three of her fingers and the doctor couldn't say when or if she ever would again. Nerve damage, he'd said. Just like when bits of the IED buried into her leg. There were still splotches of her skin that couldn't register hot or cold, but she learned to live with that.

She didn't think she could live without three fingers. She needed her hands to type.

"I love you, Tessa. You're the most important person in my life. And I'm going to prove it."

"You don't need to…"

"Miss Pines?"

They both straightened, focusing on the officer by the conference room door. He had one hand on the knob and nodded as she rose. Glancing back at Cordon, she fixed her shirt and tried for a smile.

"You already proved everything in the Ashwood," she said.

Cordon grinned. "Not yet, I haven't. But if you'll let me, I'll spend the rest of my life proving just how important you are."

Tessa stared at him. If she let him? What did that mean?

"Miss Pines, they're waiting," the officer said.

Torn between the desire to hash things out with Cordon and the need to get in the conference room, she gazed at the bearded bastard. He had such terrible timing.

"Don't worry," Cordon said. "I'll be here when you're done."

She scrunched her face at him and crossed her eyes. Impossible man that he was, Cordon probably didn't realize how much that sounded like a proposal.

Her heart fluttered as she slipped into the conference room.

Or maybe he did know, and he was flirting around the subject, trying to gauge her reaction. Crossing her eyes might not have been the best response.

The door clicked shut behind her, and the sound made her focus on the room. There was a wide mahogany table with several uniforms seated around it. For an instant she debated going back outside, smacking Cordon in the shoulder and dragging a real proposal out of him. But she spotted Jackson, who wouldn't look her in the face, and sat down on an empty chair.

Sadly, Cordon would have to wait.

"Miss Pines, thank you for coming," one of Jackson's lawyers said.

The name on his uniform was Batton and his partner was Christie. Both were tall men with competent smiles and open folders in front of them. There was a recording device on the table too, reminding her what she was here to do. Her heart picked up speed, anxiety pounding the importance of this meeting into her. Jackson's future relied on these men.

"Before we get started, Sergeant Jackson wanted to say a few words to you," Batton said.

The corners of Jackson's mouth tightened. He sat rigid in his chair, staring at the polished table.

"Nothing's changed, right? There were no charges being brought since the police ruled it an accident and I know I'm not pressing charges…"

"No, no," Batton said. "We just need your formal testimony so we can release him back to active duty. You can imagine that the army takes this sort of thing seriously. We don't like when a weapon is discharged outside of a firing range or in theater."

Tessa nodded and crossed her ankles under her chair. She didn't have to wait long. Jackson cleared his throat.

"I'm sorry, Pines. Not just because of what happened…" His gaze slipped to her sling. It took him a moment to speak again. "Not just because of that, but because I kept hounding you. I should have taken the hint and left you alone weeks ago."

Jackson wasn't an awful man, but she was certain she had never heard him apologize before. At least, he hadn't apologized to her before. Then again, he had shot her.

Maybe that was fueling his newfound humility.

He slumped in his chair, shoulders sagging. "I know I butted into your life unannounced. It was just... The unit felt wrong after that damn IED went off. And I thought making sure you were OK would put some of it right again."

Tessa looked at the gauze wrapped around her palm and the obnoxious sling. Cabby's face flashed through her memory, smiling and laughing like he used to, and her heart ached. She couldn't imagine what it must have been like for Jackson out there. He'd been in the vehicle directly behind them, he'd seen it all.

One minute the unit was whole, the next it wasn't. She wasn't even sure how many others they'd lost that day, she'd been so focused on those in her vehicle she hadn't asked. And she couldn't ask now. Not here.

"Actually, Jackson, I meant to thank you for that," she said. Her fingers were cold, and the back of her neck was clammy. Some part of her knew what she meant to say, but the larger, more terrified part wasn't ready; wouldn't ever be ready. "The truth is, I'm not all right. I pretend like I am, but I'm not."

"What?"

His face went comically blank and she nearly smiled.

Maybe it wasn't a good thing to admit all this in front of lawyers but if she didn't confront this now, she would go on pretending. And if she was right about Cordon and his not-quite-proposal waiting outside, then she couldn't go on pretending. Cordon deserved better than that.

"If you hadn't barged in, I would have kept on pretending like I...Like I didn't see Cabby every day." She exhaled and looked at the table. "I stay up all night watching movies or shows because I'm terrified of

261

sleeping. Because when I sleep, I live it all over again."

"God, Pines," Jackson said.

"I know," she said, keeping her gaze on the table. Heat bloomed in her face. "I know it's bad, Jackson. But I would have kept pushing forward because that's what we do, you know? As soldiers we just keep barreling through it."

"No, Tessa, not all the time. There's no such thing as an army of one. Didn't you learn that? Sometimes, you got to let someone else barrel through while you stay behind cover. It's the only way any of us come home alive."

Tessa closed her eyes. Jackson was right. Of course, he was right. And if she kept trying to go it alone, she knew this would eat her alive. Going to a therapist was humiliating to the extreme, but if that was what she needed to move forward then she would have to swallow some pride.

"I don't mean to interrupt," Batton said.

She opened her eyes.

He leaned across the table and slid a business card toward her. "My cousin runs this place just outside of Boston. It's secluded and quiet. They work with soldiers coming home all the time."

She took the card. In clear black letters it said; Halfway Home Recuperation Center. Doctor Charles Batton.

She stared at the words, running her thumb over the smooth letters. All the anxiety that had propelled her through school and the Ashwood released at once and if she hadn't been wearing her uniform, she would have slumped against the chair.

She'd been only part of the way home for months

now, darting from class to class and doing everything she could to avoid the looming fact of Cabby and Murphy's deaths. Cordon must sense it too. That was why he was only sort of proposing.

If she wanted the real thing, she needed to come all the way.

Smiling, she nodded to Batton and tucked the card into her sling. "Thank you."

She looked at Jackson, who watched her, his hazel eyes intent. At last he smiled and nodded.

"You're going to be all right, Pines."

It was the same thing he'd said to her that day at the vehicle, holding her leg as tight as he could as they waited for the medivac to reach them.

She hadn't believed him back then, but she did now.

Epilogue

Seven weeks later

Tessa snuggled into her favorite chair in Book Land with a fresh mug of coffee and the notes for her poetry project spread around her. Cordon counted the till and sent her quick, flirty glances whenever she looked up. The closed sign had already been put up and half the lights were out. The new Christmas display twinkled in festive reds and greens and blues.

Her arm rested in a sling, keeping pressure off the still healing gunshot wound from hell. In her mind she should be fully recovered by now, but her doctor said it could take up to a year before she was back to full health. All the damaged internal tissue was slowly knitting itself back together, but she was at least making progress. For that matter, the puncture wound in her hand was taking its sweet time too. She'd thought maybe it was healed because the scars had closed but when she gripped a weight at physical therapy sharp pain stabbed through her palm. She dropped it.

And she still couldn't feel three of her fingers in that hand. That worried her quite a bit and made typing homework a pain.

Her phone trilled. She sighed and set her mug down before picking up her cell. "Hello, Marisol."

"Oh, Tessa! It's all over the news!"

"What is?" Tessa asked, glancing over as Cordon headed to the back to lock the deposit bags.

"Someone set the Ashwood on fire!"

Tessa straightened. "What?"

"It's a little late in the game if you ask me," Marisol said, sounding irritated and elated all at once. "But hey, at least nobody will have to go through that."

"I suppose."

Who had done it? Certainly not Cordon, they'd been too busy with each other for him to get away with that. They both agreed it needed doing, though. Too much blood had been spilt there already.

Tessa had taken the time to research any reported murders at the Ashwood during its heyday and found only one. It was a chilly and eerily accurate account of a janitor who'd been shot by a jealous doctor. The picture of Frank was remarkably similar to Tyler, and she'd chosen not to reveal it.

Better the man not know how close he'd come to committing homicide.

Only Cordon knew. Just like he knew that the nurse, one Christine Freemont, committed suicide in that same room five days later.

Tessa shivered, forcing images out of her mind before they could take root. She didn't need another ghost whispering at her in her sleep.

"Good riddance is what I say. Oh, hey, Josh and I are taking pictures of light displays around town. Want to come?"

Personally, Tessa was glad that Marisol had found a new crush. This Josh fellow was a photographer and seemed to actually like Marisol, which was a plus.

Though Tessa did wish the girl would stop snapping photographs of her all the time. It was getting uncomfortable.

"There will be coffee and things. You can bring Cordon. It'll be great!"

Tessa thought of driving around town with Cordon, listening to Christmas music and watching the lights and smiled. No ghosts luring them places, no crazy moaning walls, and no nasty hypodermic needles to be stabbed with; that sounded downright pleasant.

"I'll ask Cordon if he's free," she said and smiled at him because he'd come out of the office.

He lifted his eyebrows in question, sliding his hands around her hips to draw her close and she leaned into him.

"All right," Marisol said. "But we're leaving in about an hour so don't take too long."

"Got it," Tessa said and hung up.

"Got what?" Cordon brushed a kiss across her cheek.

"Marisol wants to look at Christmas lights and invited us to come along." She closed her eyes as he began trailing his mouth down her jaw, giving her light, feathery kisses. Tessa shivered.

"I have other plans for us," he murmured into her neck.

A word about the author...

A. J. Maguire is a consumer of stories. From binge-watching shows on Netflix to spending far too much money on books, Maguire will take stories in whatever form she can get them.

A transplant to New England, she lives in Massachusetts with her husband and son, but they all agree the cats rule the house.

http://ajmaguire.com